COMPARED

KORTNEY KEISEL

First edition January 2022

Cover design by Red Leaf Book Design

www.kortneykeisel.com

To my dad.

Thank you for your never ending optimism, for always making me laugh, for teaching me how to dance, for the silly songs you sing that will forever be in my heart, for your famous quotes, for your love of family, Mexican food, and tradition, and for the way you loved Mom.

I miss you every day, but I hope you and Mom are dancing in heaven.

TRIGGER WARNING

This book deals with the loss of a spouse and the loss of a parent. Strong themes of grief and mourning are written throughout.

CHAPTER 1

MEG

Pop quiz!

As a teacher, I love a good pop quiz, but as a student, they're the worst.

Unfortunately today, I guess I'm the student, and I don't know the answer to this question.

1. When the face of a beautiful redhead with the name Genessa comes up on your boyfriend's phone, what should you do?

A) Begin sobbing.
B) Overanalyze.
C) Freak out.
D) Run!

I'm going to go with a mixture of B and C.

I glance again at the vibrating phone on the coffee table. Genessa's sapphire eyes and Disney Princess smile make me run a hand through my hair self-consciously. I'm sure there's a reasonable explanation. Perhaps Zak was trying to find a Little Mermaid look-alike to be the entertainment at a work party. Or maybe Genessa commandeered Zak's phone and forced her digits into his address book while holding him hostage.

Yep. Plenty of reasonable explanations. I have nothing to worry about.

"Zak!" I yell from his living room sofa. "Zak! Someone's calling you." He must be in the shower, because he doesn't answer.

The phone buzzes again.

Genessa: I can't wait to see you tomorrow at CrossFit. Maybe after our workout we can...

I swipe up on his phone, desperate to read the rest of the text that got cut off—*After CrossFit we can WHAT?*—but the screen is locked. I quickly type one, one, one, one into the phone, but the dots dance, mocking me for assuming Zak would have such a predictable password.

I chew on my lip. Tomorrow is Saturday. I asked Zak if he wanted to go with me to Hobby Lobby to shop for fall decor. He said he couldn't go because he has to work. If *Genessa* asked him to go somewhere, would his work schedule magically change? I push his phone away in disgust and pull out my own phone, frantically forming a text to my siblings.

Meg: Zak's in the shower. Someone named Genessa just called his phone and then sent a text that said, "I can't wait to see you tomorrow at CrossFit. Maybe after our workout we can..." Then the rest of the message got cut off. Am I crazy for jumping to conclusions? I'm crazy, right?

Tessa: You're not crazy. He's totally cheating on you.

My younger sister Tessa was definitely the answer-*D* type of girl.

Brooke: Maybe this explains why he hasn't proposed or wanted to get married. He's been seeing another woman.

Matt: Just because a woman calls a man does NOT mean he's in a relationship with her.

My thumbs fly across the phone's keypad in Zak's defense.

Meg: Matt's right. There's probably a good reason for her text.

Matt: I'm always right.

Tessa: There's not a good reason. He's cheating on you. Get rid of him!

Brooke: If you think there's a perfectly good explanation, then why did you text us?

I roll my eyes. I don't know why I texted my family. They've hated Zak since…well, the beginning.

Not *hated*. That's such a strong word. They *dislike* him because they think he's stringing me along. But they don't know him like I do. He's literally the perfect guy. Handsome. Intelligent. Driven. Goal-oriented. My mom picked up on his qualities immediately. From the first day I brought Zak home, she told me I was going to marry him. If she were still here, I'd be texting her right now, not my siblings, and she'd tell me that Zak and I have been together for three years—of course he's committed to me.

Meg: You guys are wrong. He's about to propose. I'm sure I'm just being stupid about this girl's text.

Tessa: Meg, stop defending him!!!! Break it off before he breaks up with you!!!!

Tessa's use of multiple exclamation points seems excessive.

Brooke: Text us when you find out. I'm invested now.

Zak walks out of his room, and I click the side button on my phone, causing the screen to go black so he doesn't know I've been texting my family. That's one of his pet peeves. I tell my siblings *everything*.

A tight, white t-shirt stretches across his chest, paired with gray athletic shorts. He's entirely too handsome. Of course a girl like Genessa would want to call him. If I weren't already in a relationship with him, I'd want to call him too.

"Did you say something?" he asks, rubbing the palm of his hand over his buzz cut. His short hair is new, but I like it. Think Brad Pitt in the movie *Mr. and Mrs. Smith* and you'll know what I'm dealing with here.

I stand from my spot at the couch, awkwardly bumping into his metal coffee table. I hold his phone out. "You missed a call."

"Probably from the office." He reaches for the device. I have the urge to jerk my arm away and go all *Real Housewives* on him, but instead, I take a deep breath and hand him the evidence. I shift my weight, anxious for his side of the story so we can forget about the mix-up and get on with our Friday night plans. Sitting next to each other on the couch—me grading papers and him working—has never sounded so good.

"Actually..." I give a fake laugh that probably *would* land me on *Real Housewives*. "It was from some woman named Genessa. She left you a text. Something about being excited to see you tomorrow."

Genessa.

What kind of a name is that anyway? I can't like a person whose parents use the letter *G* when they should've used a *J*.

Never mind. That's rude.

Zak looks at me. If there's a good excuse, he'll tell me now, and we can turn the television on to *This Is Us* and forget about the whole thing.

I wait with bated breath.

But he just tucks the phone into his pocket and walks into the kitchen, opening one of the gray cabinets. The vibe of the kitchen —the entire apartment, really—is industrial chic. The handles on the cupboards are rustic and match the metal barstools and welded pieces of furniture scattered throughout. He pulls out a glass and sets it on the concrete countertop.

My brows make a *V* as I watch him. The fact that he doesn't feel a need to explain who Genessa is proves that we're in a committed relationship, and her call meant nothing.

But I'm not good at pop quizzes or multiple choice tests. When I took the ACT, one of my testing strategies was to guess *C* when I wasn't sure of the answer. I've never felt more unsure in my entire life, so I'm guessing *C* and freaking out.

"Who is this Genessa girl?" I swing my arms at my side as I walk into the kitchen. The swinging is supposed to help me seem casual, but I'm guessing it's making me look more like an uncoordinated monkey.

Zak pours himself a green smoothie that he had saved in the refrigerator for dinner. "Just a friend in my CrossFit group." His face is perfectly masked as he takes a drink.

"I've never heard you talk about her. I've heard of your other CrossFit friends." I tilt my head back and forth as I rattle off his other workout buddies—*buddies* being the key word. "I know Tony, Nick, Brock—"

"This is so like you, Meg." Zak shakes his head as he gulps another swig of the kale and spinach monstrosity.

"*What's* so like me?"

"You have an overactive imagination. You always jump to the worst-case scenario."

I do my best to ignore the fact that he used the word *always*. Absolutes like *always* and *never* aren't healthy for relationships, but hey, I'm not a therapist, nor am I trying to pick a fight. I'm just trying to stop myself from bursting into tears.

"I don't *always* jump to the worst-case scenario."

His light-brown eyes stare into mine. "Yes, you do. Last week you thought the guy you see by your building all the time was following you."

"What was I supposed to think? Every time I left my apartment or came home, the guy was standing outside."

"Because he lives there and was taking a smoke break."

"The whole thing was an honest mistake. I thought he was very forgiving, considering the pepper spray and my yellow belt karate moves. We're practically building BFFs now."

Zak shakes his head at me as he finishes off his drink. Then he rinses his cup before putting it into the dishwasher.

See? Such a great catch.

Although him doing his own dishes in his own house isn't *that* impressive.

I shake the thought away, because he *is* great.

He breezes by me, making his way to the couch, and turns the TV on to CNN. I follow after him and sit on the arm of the black leather chair so that I can face him.

"Just for fun," I say, "what *would* be the worst-case scenario with Genessa?"

Zak lets out a dramatic breath. "I'm not cheating on you, Meg. She's just a friend."

Yay!

...I guess. That's the answer I've been looking for, but something about the conversation unsettles me.

"Okay. I believe you."

"Gee, thanks," he mutters under his breath.

Unfortunately, I've never been good at quitting while I'm ahead, so I press on. "It's fine that you have women that are friends, but..."

Zak stares at me with so much annoyance, I hesitate before finishing.

"…It seems like you guys are really tight, and I'm not sure I'm comfortable with that."

"Really tight? You made that assumption based off of…what? A single phone call?"

"No, a text. She said she's excited to see you and wants to make plans with you. And her picture came up when she called. I don't have pictures of my guy friends on my phone." I actually don't have any guy friends, but I don't think now is the time to mention that.

Zak turns the TV off and drops the remote onto the couch next to him, like he can't believe he has to suffer through this conversation. "The picture isn't a big deal. I snapped it one day while we were working out."

Yes, her hot pink sports bra was a good indicator of that.

"But, yeah," he says. "I guess we're tight. We work out together, and sometimes after CrossFit we grab breakfast at the protein place by our gym."

"You go out to breakfast with her? Alone?"

"Sometimes."

"Why would you want to go out alone with another woman? There isn't another man that I'd want to spend time with besides you."

I realize I sound completely clingy, but I can't help it.

He rests his arm over the back cushion, raising his fingers up as he talks. "I don't know. Things are easy with her. There's no pressure like there is with you."

Bam!

His words are a Rocky Balboa knockout punch. I'm essentially lying on the ground with the referee leaning over me, counting to ten.

Seven.

Eight.

Nine.

"Wait," I say, refusing to let the fight be called. "Why do you feel pressure with me?"

Zak leans his head against his hand. "You're always asking about marriage and when we're getting engaged."

There's the word *always* again.

And he's not wrong. It *is* our biggest argument. I want to get married, settle down, have a family, and Zak isn't ready. It's not like I have unrealistic expectations. It's been three years. That's a normal amount of time in a relationship to start thinking about the next step. I mean, there's even a song about it. *First comes love, then comes marriage, then comes the baby in the baby carriage.* I've been conditioned since I was three years old for this kind of outcome.

Except the man I love doesn't agree.

Zak reaches out to the coffee table in front of him and grabs one of my student's assignments from the top of the stack. He flips the paper over and takes my pen.

"What are you doing?" I walk over to the couch and sit beside him.

"I'm going to show you what our problem is," he says as he begins drawing.

"You're showing me with a diagram?"

He pauses, looking up at me. "I use diagrams with my team at work. The visual helps you see where you're at and where you need to go so you can move forward to success."

Zak is in sales, and unfortunately, his motivational manager speech comes out whenever we have a disagreement. It's his "sales" voice.

I lean forward and examine the sixty-degree angle line that he's drawn. His finger traces the line upward. "This is you and me."

An upward line. That's good, right? It means we're growing together.

Zak shrugs. "Actually, it used to be you and me."

Oh.

"You want our relationship to keep going on this same trajectory," he says.

Do I want to see our relationship go up from here? Yeah, I do. Is that a crime? I give him a sideways glance. "And you don't?"

He draws a straight line out from the top of the first. "I feel like our relationship has done this."

It's a plateau.

He drew a freaking plateau.

I shift my body, turning my knees into him. "Maybe we've stalled a few times, but I see no reason why we can't continue on our original trajectory." I don't usually use words like "trajectory," but this is Zak I'm talking to, and he's all about sales, graphs, and good *trajectories*, so I'm using the stupid word.

"We're not even on the same plane anymore." He draws two more lines on the relationship diagram from Hell.

"We're like this," he says, pointing to the parallel lines. "Our lives don't intersect."

His words strangle my heart. "Of course they do."

"They did at first, Meg, but now…" Zak rubs his hand over his prickly hair. "We don't even like to do the same things."

"Like what?" I'm going to need some examples, because right now, this entire conversation feels like it's coming out of nowhere.

"My life is really all about the ABCs."

"So is mine." I raise my shoulders. "I teach second grade."

"I'm talking about the ABCs of exercise. Abs, biceps, cardio."

"Is that what this is about? You want me to go to CrossFit with you? Fine. I'll probably complain the entire time, but I can do that so you feel like our lives intersect more." I fold my arms across my chest. It's all about compromise, right? I'm a second grade teacher. I can do compromise in my sleep.

"It's not just the exercise thing. I want to stay out late and party, while you want to stay in and watch every season of *Survivor*."

It's true. I do like to watch *Survivor*, and right now Zak is voting me off the relationship island of security and happily ever afters. I swallow back the hurt pooling in my stomach, threatening to rise up my throat and cause a panic attack. The last thing I want is to have to ask for a brown paper bag so I can get my breathing under control.

Nothing's more unattractive than hyperventilation.

"Does Genessa like to party?" My voice sounds small.

"She does."

We've already established that she likes the ABCs of exercise.

"Meg…" He lets out a deep breath. "If I'm being honest, I think I just…I don't love you anymore."

There it is. The big kahuna. The five words that punch into my chest and rip out my heart.

I drop my chin. "So what are you saying?"

I know what he's saying. He's saying he doesn't love me anymore, but what does that *mean*?

"I think we should break up."

Tears drip down my face, and I hate it. Normally, I would be strong enough to sit next to my boyfriend and pretend like his hurtful words aren't crushing me, but it's been a hard year, and I'm so freaking fragile there might as well be a *handle with care* sign plastered across my forehead.

"Meg, I'm sorry to do this to you right now. I wanted to wait a few more months before I said anything so you could grieve your mother's death."

Is that supposed to be comforting? Because it's not.

"How long have you been planning to break up with me?" I ask, fully aware that I don't want to know the answer.

Zak's shoulders drop. "Since right around when your mom got sick. I thought I would give it a few months, but then she died three months later, and I couldn't tell you things were over right after her death."

I close my eyes. My mom got sick seven months ago.

Wow.

Zak hasn't loved me for *seven* months?

It's another knockout blow. And this time, I'm not sure I'll get up off the ground.

To top it all off, I'm an ugly crier. So here I am, sitting on Zak's couch, doing my best Kim Kardashian ugly cry. I just wish Tessa wasn't always so dang right about men and relationships.

CHAPTER 2
TYLER

I can go anywhere I want.

Krew's at a birthday party, and the Friday night possibilities are endless, but where do I end up? The cemetery, staring at Kristen's headstone. It's been eighteen months, three days, and—I look down at my watch—fourteen hours since the car accident. That should be enough time to find something better to do than torture myself by visiting her grave every free second. I guess I like pouring salt on the wound. Feeling the sting is better than feeling nothing at all.

I look around. The place is empty. I'm sure talking to dead people is normal and no one will think twice about it if they see me, but I whisper just in case.

"We beat the Hitmen six to four." I keep my voice low. "Krew pitched and did great. He had nine strikeouts total. After he struck out the third kid in a row, he turned to me in the dugout and said, 'Wow. I'm throwing heat.'" I laugh as I think back to the moment earlier that day. "I don't think the first base coach appreciated Krew's cockiness. I can't stand that coach, so I'm glad Krew said it. It reminded me of you. Besides, he's only seven years old, so I think his confidence is okay."

I sigh. "Right? Or should I have told Krew to stop being so

cocky?" I shake my head. "I don't know what the heck I'm doing. It's tough parenting without you. I'm doing everything all wrong."

My eyes drop to Kristen's picture on the right side of the stone. It's not my favorite of her—she has on a little too much makeup for my taste—but it was her favorite of herself. The last thing I wanted to do was pick the wrong picture to put on her headstone. Can you imagine? As soon as I pass through those pearly white gates above, she would absolutely chew me out. I can't remember when or where the picture was taken. I wish I could remember details like that.

Even though it's not my favorite, she still looks beautiful. Her brown hair waves around her face perfectly, her brown eyes sparkle, and her crooked smile invites you to come closer, like she has a secret she wants to tell you.

Man, I miss her.

I bend down and pull at the grass around her headstone where the cemetery gardeners didn't cut it. Next time I visit, I'll bring my own trimmer and cut the long ones myself. I throw the grass aside and scratch the side of my neck. I've been stalling long enough.

"So," I say, letting out an overdrawn breath. "I have a date." The words feel like poison as they come up my throat, but I still manage to get them out. "It's a blind date, and I don't want to go. Logan set it up—some twenty-something woman at his office. He says it's time that I get back out there, start trying to move on." I grit my teeth. "How did we get here, Kristen? How am I going on a blind date as a thirty-three-year-old single dad?"

I can picture Kristen laughing at me. She was never the jealous type, so I'm sure she's finding it hilarious that I'm going on a blind date after thirteen years of her being the only one in my life.

A gray Lexus pulls down the lane of the cemetery and parks by the curb.

"There goes our intimate date." No more whisper conversations for me. In fact, I'll probably leave. I don't like visiting Kristen's grave when other people are there visiting their loved ones. It's awkward.

An older gentleman with a beige bucket hat and a beige fishing vest steps out of the car. I've seen him here a few times before. Apparently he likes to spend his free nights the same way I do. The man grabs a blue camping chair from the back of his car. He has a bag full of takeout and a newspaper tucked under his arm.

"Nice night," he says, nodding his head in my direction.

"Yeah." I raise my brows halfheartedly. Now what am I going to do with the rest of my evening? Krew's birthday party doesn't end for another hour and a half.

The man stops at a grave fifteen feet away from Kristen's and opens his camp chair, placing it in front of the headstone. He looks over at me. "You hungry? I ordered an entire box of tacos."

I am hungry, but I'm not about to sit down and mooch off some old widower at the cemetery, no matter how lonely I am.

"No, thanks." The smell of cilantro and lime wafts over to me as he opens the food container, and my stomach rumbles.

"Is it your wife?" he says.

"What?"

He points to Kristen's grave. "Is it your wife that you come visit?"

"Oh." I clear my throat. It never gets easier to talk about it. "Yeah."

"Me too. She died four months ago."

"Eighteen months for me."

"Her name was Marilyn. She died of lupus."

I stick my hands in my pockets. "Kristen. She was in a car accident." I don't add any additional details. The man can fill the rest in with his imagination.

"We were married for forty-five years. What about you?"

"We weren't as impressive as forty-five years." I smile. "Kristen and I were only married for ten."

The man shakes his head. "Don't discredit those ten years. It's hard work being married."

I look down at Kristen's picture, fitted perfectly into the stone. It wasn't hard to be married to her.

"You got kids?"

I shift my body toward him. "One boy. Krew. He's almost eight. What about you?"

"One boy, three girls."

"Four. Wow. Are you close with them?" I'm trying to be polite before I leave.

"Too close, but they're a nice distraction from the loneliness. My oldest, Matt, doesn't live here anymore. He's in Houston, but my three daughters all live near Tampa." He waves the box of food out in front of him. "Come have a taco with me, and we can keep talking."

I look at my watch, even though I have nowhere else to be. Eating a taco with him is better than the alternative of driving around town, killing time until Krew is done.

I shrug. "Okay."

"I have an extra chair in my car." The man jumps up before I can protest and heads to his car. I watch as he opens his trunk and pulls out another camp chair. He brings it back to his wife's grave and sets it up for me. He extends his arm. "I'm Paul, by the way."

I shake his hand before sinking into the seat. "Tyler."

"Now, neither of us is alone, and I don't think I'm the type of guy that is meant to be alone." Paul smiles, and I try to convince myself I'm only staying to talk as a courtesy to him. It's not like *I* need this. "Let's talk about our wives," he says as he bends over and picks up the box of tacos.

For some reason, Paul's bluntness about being widowed is comforting. For once, it's nice to have someone to talk to that understands a little of how I feel.

CHAPTER 3
MEG

Most girls wallow in sadness when their boyfriend breaks up with them. They lie on couches with tubs of ice cream and watch the Hallmark channel until they can't handle anymore small towns and lovey-dovey stares.

Not me.

I take my breakups like a woman—a mature woman.

I suck in another deep breath, filling my lungs to capacity, and belt out the next line of "I Will Always Love You." At the same time, one fist goes to my mouth, acting as a microphone, while the other hand moves wildly to the melody of the song. I tilt my head way back, and—it's embarrassing to say it—I *close* my eyes. I'm really getting into the lyrics now.

The chorus swells, and so does my enthusiasm. I raise my voice as loud as I can to match the blasting music from my speaker. Whitney would be so proud. Then the music stops suddenly, leaving nothing but me, screeching in the silence.

I swear I sound better than that.

"Meg!"

I whip around, embarrassed about my kitchen concert, only to find my younger sisters, Brooke and Tessa, standing in the living room of my small apartment. Brooke has one hand on my Bluetooth speaker and the other on her hip.

I drop my makeshift microphone. "What are you guys doing here?" The words come out in short, quick breaths, like I've just run a mile. Who knew singing was such a workout?

"We came to see how you're doing." Tessa glances up and down my body, no doubt taking in my pajamas, disheveled hair, and makeup-less face. "It looks like you're struggling."

"I'm fine." I tug at my ratty gray sweatshirt and look down. Where did that brown stain come from?

Then I remember. It was from one of the chocolate chip cookies I ate Friday night after Zak's plateau picture. A warm morsel pulled apart from my bite and dripped down to my shirt like a piece of string. I scratch at the crusty chocolate with my fingernail, keenly aware that both of my sisters are watching me.

"You're not fine," Brooke says, picking up my phone. She tilts the screen toward Tessa as her finger scrolls upward. "Look at this playlist. Barbara Streisand. ABBA. Phil Collins. Whitney Houston. Olivia Newton-John. *Barry Manilow.*"

"Barry Manilow?" Tessa cuts in, giving me a disappointed look. "Not again."

"What?" I tuck a piece of hair behind my ear. "I love 'Can't Smile Without You.'"

"What's with the geriatrics playlist?" she asks. "You're not seventy years old."

I walk over to the kitchen sink. Now is a good time to act like I care about the dishes that have been piling up for the last three days. I fiddle with a bowl that has dried cereal stuck to the rim. "Your concern about my choice of music is noted. Now you both can leave."

Brooke pulls out a kitchen stool and sits down, leaning against the counter. Her brown hair is darker than my light blonde, but she's added enough golden highlights to it that I'm not sure what color her hair is supposed to be anymore.

"It's not your music we're concerned about. It's you. You've been hiding out in your apartment all weekend, listening to old breakup songs. You haven't showered, and I'm guessing you've eaten an entire roll of store-bought cookie dough."

She is *so* wrong. I haven't eaten an entire roll of store-bought cookie dough. I would never do something like that. I *made* my own cookie dough and ate the whole thing. It tastes way better, and if I'm going to get salmonella poisoning, I'm going to do it the right way.

But Brooke is correct about everything else. Labor Day weekend came at the perfect time. I haven't showered in days or changed my clothes, and my breakup playlist is on repeat. I'm the epitome of frumpish.

Fine. I'm *not* handling the break up like a mature woman. I'm a complete wreck.

But everything's still so fresh. It's only been three days since Zak shattered my entire world.

I set down the cereal bowl and turn to face my sisters as new tears fill my eyes. "Mom told me to marry Zak."

"When?" Tessa pulls out the other stool and takes a seat. She coils her long blonde hair over one shoulder.

"The day she died."

"The woman was dying. She said everything she thought we wanted to hear so that we wouldn't be sad, including that you and Zak should get married."

Brooke sighs. "Meg, if she were here now, she'd tell you to forget about him."

I refuse to believe that about my mother. She wouldn't say I should marry someone unless she really meant it. I lean forward, pressing my forehead against the countertop. "I can't just forget about him." My lips smudge against the cold granite as I speak. "He was my ticket to happily ever after. What if I never get married? I'm twenty-eight-years old." I turn my head so my cheek lays flat against the counter and peer up at my sisters. "What if I'm alone for the rest of my life like some crazy cat lady?"

"You've already got the right playlist to support that kind of lifestyle," Tessa says.

"You're just lacking the cats," Brooke adds. "But those are easy to come by."

I lift my head to glare at my sisters.

"What?" Tessa shrugs. "We're not going to sugarcoat it. Pull yourself together. Suck it up. You got dumped. It's not the end of the world. Your behavior is so cliché. You're a strong, successful, beautiful woman. You deserve someone better than a guy like *Zak*."

"I agree," Brooke chimes in. "He's been stringing you along for years."

"No, he hasn't. He's been putting his ducks in a row, climbing the corporate ladder." I look at Tessa, because I know she can appreciate trying to move up in your career. "He was getting everything ready so we could build a life together."

"More like getting everything ready so he could build a life with the girl from CrossFit," Tessa mutters.

I give each of my sisters a long, hard stare. "I told you guys he wasn't cheating on me."

Tessa flips her fingers out in front of her to examine her perfectly manicured nails. "Eh, I don't believe it."

My shoulders slump. "Whether you believe it or not, I'm still in love with him. I can't just snap my fingers and forget about three years of feelings. And what about Mom?"

"What about her?"

"She's probably so disappointed right now. When she died, she thought a wedding was on the horizon."

"The only reason Mom would be disappointed right now is that you're acting pathetic. You need to move on."

Brooke's words don't make sense to me. I'm not pathetic, I'm heartbroken. And I don't *want* to move on from Zak.

I look at the clock. 5:51 on Monday, Labor Day. Did Zak work today, or did he take the holiday off?

"Maybe I should call him, just to see if he really meant to break up over a holiday weekend."

I reach for my phone, but Tessa slaps my hand away.

"Oh my gosh! Would you listen to yourself? You need to forget about him." She leans forward, and a flash of purpose flits across her face. "Let's get dressed up and go out tonight. My friend invited me to a party on a yacht."

Who has a yacht party on the Monday night of Labor Day weekend? Isn't this day reserved for obligatory family barbecues and mediocre discount deals? Besides, we live in a suburb outside of Tampa. Traffic is going to be impossible on a holiday weekend.

"I don't feel like going out," I say.

"I'm sure there will be a ton of hot guys there. We'll find you someone new."

Tessa makes meeting men sound so easy. And it probably is for her. All she has to do is wear something tight, flip her blonde hair behind her shoulder, and smile, and suddenly a flock of men comes rushing to her side.

But that's not how it works for me. I'm not the party girl. I was the roommate in college that made a chore chart. I cooked all the meals, cleaned the apartment, and picked up my friends from parties late at night when they'd had too much to drink. I'm the responsible one—the *mom* of every friend group.

"I don't care about finding someone new." I wipe my leaking nose with the sleeve of my sweatshirt.

"Too bad." Tessa spins around and hops off the stool. She heads to my bedroom, calling behind her, "Let's find you something sexy to wear."

"I don't own anything *sexy*," I yell back as I look at Brooke. "I really don't want to go."

"Oh, come on. It will be good for you to get out of your apartment. Besides, who throws a party on a yacht? Aren't you the least bit curious?"

"No, I'm not."

Tessa comes back holding a pair of my slip-on shoes. "You're right. You don't own any sexy dresses."

"Why would I? I teach second grade."

Brooke smirks. "Cleavage and parent teacher conferences don't go together?"

"No, not really." I crack a smile—a *small* smile, because I'm still wallowing in breakup grief, and I'm mad at my sisters for forcing me to leave the sanctuary of my apartment.

"Well, they should." Tessa tosses my shoes at me. "We can go to my apartment and get ready. I have plenty of sexy dresses you can borrow."

"The word 'sexy' shouldn't be in the same sentence with my name. I can't even remember the last time I shaved my legs."

Tessa takes in a deep breath as if my shaving admission is going to throw her over sanity's edge. Her eyes drift to Brooke. "How am I related to her?"

"See? Maybe I shouldn't go."

"You're going," they both say in unison, and before I can stop them, they shove me out the door.

CHAPTER 4
TYLER

"These are all good options to wear on a first date." Hillary places five button-up shirts in front of me on her king-size mattress.

I lift my gray ball cap and fit it over my hair again, nodding at my sister-in-law. Hillary looks nice, with blonde hair cut short to her chin and dark brown eyes, but she's scary. *Wife* scary—like if you don't fall in line with what she says, she won't talk to you for days. Not all wives are like that. Just a select few—a few like Hillary.

My eyes drift to the colorful shirts. Shades of pink, mint, lavender, and light blue assault me. Am I choosing items to throw in an Easter basket or picking an outfit for a date?

It's hard to tell.

My chin drops to my black t-shirt and jeans. "What's wrong with what I have on?"

Hillary scoffs like I've offended her. Maybe I have. She's serious about clothing. She has my brother, Logan, dress in a golf shirt and slacks even on Saturdays.

"Tyler, you haven't been in the dating scene for a long time." Hillary unbuttons the collar of the light-blue shirt and pulls the hanger out. "You can't show up in a t-shirt. Dating is all about first impressions."

I glance at Logan, giving him my best *I'm-going-to-kill-you* glare. It's his fault I'm even going on this date. He gave my number to a woman and didn't even warn me about it. I was completely blindsided when she called. If I had known ahead of time, I could've come up with a thousand excuses.

I can't go out with you because I need to coach a baseball game every single night of the week. I can't go out with you because I'm starting a DIY home project that I will inevitably regret. I can't go out with you because I don't own an Easter-colored button-up shirt.

But when I answered the phone call from the random number, I didn't have my excuses dialed up. I was expecting the call to be about work. I put a bid in for the landscaping job at the new city building, and I'm waiting to hear if I got the contract. Instead, I got twenty-three-year-old Candi. She's entirely too young and too forward, and before I knew what was happening, I agreed to meet her at some swanky new restaurant on the water.

Really, I didn't even need a made-up excuse to get out of the date. I could've told the truth.

I'm not ready to date anyone yet.

It's too soon.

Or maybe it only feels too soon because of *who* I'm going out with.

Either way, I didn't tell her anything like that. So the date is on, and I'm not the type of guy who's going to fake a phone call so I can leave early like they do in the movies. I'm a man, a thirty-three-year-old adult with a successful landscaping and property management business. I have a mortgage. I can suffer through a two-hour date with *Candi.*

"Hil," Logan says, eyeing my glare with caution. "I don't think it matters what Tyler wears. He doesn't want to make a good first impression."

A round of Nerf bullets shoots through the bedroom door, hitting Hillary in the arm.

"Boys!" Her voice raises as she turns to look at Krew and my nephew, Boston. "If you shoot me again, I'm throwing away all of the Nerf guns."

I bite back my smile because I don't want to get into trouble too. "Krew." I muster my best parenting voice so she thinks I'm on her side. "No hitting Aunt Hillary with Nerf bullets."

The boys turn their guns on me, and suddenly I'm assaulted with flying blue darts. One hits me in the eye, and I'm reminded once again how deadly those things are. I run to the door, but the boys scatter before I can steal their guns and use them against them.

"Tyler, no playing around." Hillary's hand goes to her hip, and I feel as though she's babysitting me tonight, too, not just Krew. "You need to get dressed, and we still have to do something with your hair."

"What's wrong with my hair?" I tug at the brown strands flipping out from under my baseball cap.

She walks to the dresser and pulls out a pair of Logan's slacks and throws them at me. "You can't wear a baseball cap on a date."

Dating.

There are so many rules and regulations.

I don't even want to date. I wish I could sit home with Kristen and Krew and watch a movie with a bowl of oversalted, overbuttered popcorn. That's the life I chose, and it seems completely unfair that it was taken from me.

CHAPTER 5

MEG

"Are you sure this is a dress? Because it seems more like a towel." I pull at the strapless black dress that is barely covering my behind. "And not even one of those pricey bath sheets at Target. I'm talking about the Great Value six-pack of hand towels."

"You look amazing!" Tessa twists a lock of her blonde hair, pleased with how my makeover went. "But don't be getting any ideas. That dress is mine, and I want it back after tonight."

I have absolutely no ideas about keeping this thing.

"Every woman should have a little black dress in their closet just like that one."

"*Little* is definitely how I would describe it." I keep my hands behind me, using them as a shield in case my butt is on display as I walk down the waterfront pier.

Brooke swats my arms away. "What are you doing?"

"I don't know!" I fidget with the dress again. "Things feel breezy and airy back there, and it's making me nervous."

"The dress isn't even that short. You're just used to wearing your nun habit to Catholic school."

Of course Tessa can't be bothered with the actual details of my life. "It's not a Catholic school," I correct. "It's a *private* school."

"Aren't those the same thing?" Tessa steers us in the direction of the dock and the waiting yacht party.

I glance around, taking in the crowd. Between the restaurants, bars, and boats, people are everywhere. The sounds of live music hang in the air from a bar down the pier, competing with the laughter and conversations of all the people milling about. The vibe is trendy, and it's literally my worst nightmare. It may be a holiday, but don't these people know it's a school night?

I don't want to be here. I want to be home with Zak, getting Chinese takeout delivered. But this is my life now. This is what single people have to suffer through.

Tessa points down to the water. "There's the yacht."

My eyes go to the sleek white boat with the words *Feelin' Nauti* painted on the front.

Clever.

Except I am definitely not *feeling naughty*. A strobe light sparkles from the top as a crowd of extremely beautiful people dance to the blaring music, but all I can hear is the bass. The steady beat thrums through my ears down to my beating heart. Have I mentioned that I loathe rap music? If the songs I listen to from 1988 didn't give it away, then I don't know what will.

If this is the life that a single woman on a break has to live, then I'm out. Target can have my mini-towel dress. I'm going home. I would run back to the car, but Tessa's stupid high-heeled death traps make running virtually impossible. I feel like I put my feet inside of a slinky. The shoes have a million straps running up my calves, not to mention the thin, four-inch heels.

I pause my steps. "I can't do this."

Tessa flashes me her flirty smile—as if that would even work on me. "Yes, you can." She spins around, tilting her head to the group of men passing by us on their way to the great and spacious yacht. One of the men curves his lips up in a sultry way as he makes eye contact with her. "See what I mean? There are so many gorgeous, single men going to this party. They'll make you forget all about Zak."

I glare at the group of guys with their perfect hair and perfect muscles. The last thing I want is to replace Zak with a "new Zak." I just want *my* Zak—well, the version of him that is ready to settle down, get married, and have kids. I've already spent three years with him. I've put in my time, and I don't want to start over again. I want a guy that's ready to commit right now. Guys like that aren't at posh yacht parties. They're volunteering at animal shelters.

At least, I think they are.

I need to hit up the local shelter scene ASAP.

"Meg, you're already here. Come in and have a drink." Brooke reaches for my arm, but I step back, shaking my head.

"I don't like the look of this situation. It doesn't *feel* safe. Even the name of the boat suggests foul play."

My sisters shake their heads, obviously irritated with my assessment, but I can't be stopped.

"Do we even know the owner of the yacht? Or what kind of party this is? There could be"—I lower my voice to a whisper—"drugs like Ecstasy. And I, for one, am not going to be drugged tonight. I've got work in the morning."

Tessa groans. "You're being ridiculous."

"Am I?" I fold my arms. "Or am I literally saving my life right now by not going into that party?"

"I can't deal with you anymore." Tessa scowls before running ahead, catching the group of men that just walked by, and loops her arm through the arm of the stranger at the end. Wow. The confidence she has is impressive.

"It's all right if you want to take your time," Brooke says, backing away from me. "Text us when you're ready to come aboard, and I'll meet you at the door."

Brooke's brown hair bounces up and down as she skips the last ten feet to Tessa's side. I watch as my sisters walk up the ramp and vanish into the yacht.

I release a heavy breath. I better get an Uber to pick me up, or else I'll be stuck here all night. I spot a metal bench behind me with a matching black lamppost next to it. My eyes dart to the man on the end of the bench. He's got a baby-blue shirt on with gray golf pants. His jaw is covered with light-brown stubble that matches his hair. He's sitting, so I can't really get a grasp on how tall he is, but I have a perfect view of how big his biceps are, and let's just say it's clear he's no stranger to the gym. He's basically Thor—the short hair version.

All the hot men in the city have gathered together to taunt women like me. It's the theme of the night, apparently.

I'm so over it. The last thing I need is another self-indulgent man who isn't ready to commit.

His light-blue eyes, the same color as mine, watch me. I give him a tense smile before sitting down on the opposite end of the bench. The cold metal planks that make up the bench sting the skin on the back of my legs. I wiggle, trying to pull Tessa's dress down so that less of my thighs are bulging through the cracks. Later, when I stand, I'm sure I'll have the exact design of the bench imprinted on my skin—reason #53 why I prefer to wear longer skirts.

I pull my phone out of my purse. It's actually Tessa's purse, because there's no way I own a small black purse that goes with a dress like this. My regular purse is more like a diaper bag—minus the diapers—but if you need sanitizer, toenail clippers, mints, gum, hairspray, Tylenol, half-graded papers, or a Band-Aid, I'm your girl.

I swipe on my phone until I find the Uber app and plug in my location. It says my ride will be at the street corner in sixteen minutes. My feet are killing me from wearing Tessa's too-small shoes, so I decide to sit on this bench as long as I can until my ride comes.

I place my phone next to me and watch as it slips through the metal cracks, falling to the cement below. I bend over, reaching for it, but if I lean over too far, my backside is going to be on full display.

So I straighten and look at the stranger next to me.

He glances at the phone on the ground between the two of us. His eyebrows slowly lift. "Do you...want me to get that for you?"

"Would you mind?" I smile guiltily. "My dress is a little short, and I can't reach it without flashing everyone on the pier."

His eyes dart to my legs. The glance is quick, but long enough for me to notice, and I feel the need to drop my hands into my lap, covering my thighs. Normally I'd be irritated about his blatant stare at my legs, but...I was the one who mentioned my short dress.

He bends over and grabs my phone. "Are you a big baseball fan?" he asks as he hands it back to me.

I shake my head. "Excuse me?"

He points to the back of my phone. "You have a Tampa Bay Rays sticker on your phone case."

I flip the device over. "Oh, yeah. I forgot. It was a gift."

He nods, glancing over me again. I don't feel like he's checking me out—more like he's assessing me.

I wave my phone out in front of me. "Well, thanks." Then I look to the side, trying to convey that the conversation is over.

"Why didn't you want to go with your friends to the boat party?"

I stop myself from smiling. It's kind of endearing that he calls it a *boat* instead of a yacht, especially when you consider how massive the vessel is. It's not endearing enough that I want to keep talking to him, but since he's opened Pandora's box, he's going to get my kind of crazy—the crazy that Zak labels as an "overactive imagination." If anything, *that* should shut him up.

"It didn't seem like a good idea. I didn't feel like being sex trafficked tonight."

His eyebrows jump up. "Sex trafficked?"

"Yeah, at the party." I look down at my phone, scrolling

through an app. "Have you ever seen the movie *Taken*? Because I have, and my father is no Liam Neeson. He doesn't have any special skills, and he will definitely not come find me."

"Okay."

I should end the conversation here, but my newfound bitterness for attractive men makes it impossible for me to keep my mouth shut. "You seem like the type of guy that would be at a yacht party. Are you going?"

"Why do I feel like that's not a compliment?"

I fake a sweet smile. "Because it's not."

"Sorry to disappoint you, but I'm not going to the party." He points behind him to the row of restaurants that line the pier. "I just escaped an awful blind date."

"Why did you need to escape?"

"Because I didn't want to be there."

"So you just left?"

"No, I told her that we weren't compatible and that I was ending the night early."

"You actually said that to her?"

"Yeah." He shrugs. "Is that bad?"

I lean back into the bench, folding my arms over my chest. "Well, it sure isn't good."

"Why not? If I already know that she and I will never work, why waste our time?"

"You could have at least given her a chance."

"I did give her a chance. I showed up to the date. Met her."

"How long did you stay?"

He bobs his head back and forth as he thinks. "I don't know. Ten minutes?"

"Ten minutes!" I can't hide my shock.

"It felt like five hours."

"How can you possibly know in a matter of ten minutes that you're not compatible with this woman?"

He runs a hand down the back of his hair to the base of his

neck. "For starters, I asked her what kind of music she likes to listen to, and she named some band I've never heard of."

"What band?"

"Froggy?" He says it like he's asking me.

"Froggy." I've never heard of them either, but then again, I'm not very cool. I straighten. "Are you sure she didn't say *Fergie*?"

His nose wrinkles, and somehow he manages to look even more handsome. It's annoying, because when I wrinkle my nose, I look like I'm about to sneeze. My pre-sneeze face is not attractive.

"She probably did say Fergie, but it was too loud in there to hear." He shakes his head. "That's a shame, because that's actually a band that I've heard of."

It's not a band, but whatever.

"So besides her taste in music, why else weren't you compatible?" I ask, not even bothering to hide my sarcasm.

"I don't know if I should answer this. Everything I say seems to irritate you."

I try to soften the expression on my face, but the truth is, I *am* a little irritated. The poor girl was probably excited for her date. If she's a romantic, like myself, she probably thought that her forever was going to start tonight. And after ten minutes, her dreams of forever were destroyed.

I angle my body toward him. "I want to know. I want a glimpse inside a man's mind."

He crosses his leg, resting his ankle on his knee. "Her name is Candi."

"So?"

"So, I don't know. It kind of sounds like a stripper name."

"How do you know? Are you a frequent visitor at Strippers R Us?"

His eyes narrow. "Hardly."

"Then please tell me you have a better reason for ditching her than the fact that you don't like her name or her taste in music."

His eyes drop and he looks away. "I guess I'm just...not ready."

I knew it.

That's every single man's problem.

They're not *ready*.

That's Zak's problem. I'm tired of these games. I definitely don't want to hang around here and learn about another man's commitment issues. I look at my phone. My ride will be here in nine minutes. I shove it back into my purse and lift my chin to say my goodbyes to the noncommittal man.

"That's all very interesting, but..." My voice drifts off as my eyes register a familiar body standing twenty feet from me.

Zak's body.

He's wearing his favorite outfit, a hot pink polo shirt and navy slacks. He's talking to a few guys I recognize as his CrossFit friends, and next to him is the fiery red hair that can only belong to Genessa.

My heart simultaneously shatters into pieces and stops beating altogether.

"Oh, no! He can't see me." I duck, but really I'm just slouching down on the bench in the most awkward way while trying to keep my legs together so the people enjoying their meal nearby don't get dinner and a show. My underwear is very plain and very white. Nothing sexy over here.

"Who can't see you?" The guy next to me follows my panicked stare to Zak.

"My ex-boyfriend."

I pull my purse up over my face, trying to hide behind it, peeking out from the side. "I can't believe he's here—and with *her*. They're not touching, are they? Wouldn't they be touching if they were here together?" I glance at the stranger beside me, hoping he'll confirm that Zak and Genessa are just pals and nothing more.

"That guy?" He points to Zak. "You're freaking out over that guy?"

"Yes." I glare back at him. "*He* doesn't break it off with a girl after only ten minutes."

"No, he seems like the type of guy that breaks up with a girl after he's led her on for a long time."

That...is a very astute observation.

Zak's hand slips behind Genessa's back, and my whole world drops. It's the smallest of gestures, and yet the action squeezes my heart so tightly.

Is this part of the breakup?

Is going out with other people and putting his hand on their lower backs part of his new trajectory?

Zak turns, gently leading Genessa with him. His head shifts, and his brown eyes lock with mine.

"He sees me!" I sit up from my slouched position and desperately look around for somewhere to hide, but there's nowhere to go. Nowhere except...

A major broken heart and the desire to make Zak feel a little bit like I'm feeling suddenly take over.

I leap toward the stranger, snuggling up to him, rubbing the side of my shoulder into his. I'm like one of those annoying cats that wants you to pet them. My nose nuzzles into his neck. And now I'm no longer a cat—I'm a bunny burrowing into this man. I'm embarrassed, but I can't even register that emotion, because I'm working myself up for the finale. I fully intend to plant the most passionate kiss on him, as if I don't even know Zak is here. As if I've been making out on this bench all night.

It's not a well-thought-out plan. It's not even a plan I'm proud of, but it's like something inside of me has snapped, triggering broken-hearted self-preservation.

My hand reaches up to the man's chin, pulling his face toward mine. His light eyes go wide, and his palms shoot up to stop me from coming in, but I'm a woman on a mission. I pucker my lips and go for the gold...

At the same time the man turns his head and swipes my hand off his face.

My lips skid across his stubbled jaw and down onto his neck —and not in a sexy way. More like how a toddler presses their mouth against a glass window and blows. The force of his karate chop to my arm sends my body off balance, and my elbow drops down connecting, with his upper thigh. He yelps and jerks his body forward, causing our heads to smack together.

The yelp suggests that wasn't his thigh after all.

"Meg?"

I lift my head up, meeting Zak's shocked gaze.

Just kill me now.

That's the most humane thing to do.

Don't make me suffer through the most embarrassing display of human interaction there ever was.

My hand goes to my head, where I probably have a goose egg from the collision. I slowly stand and face him. "Zak! Hey!" I smile, trying to pull off confidence, but there's none left. It was literally squashed along with the stranger's manhood.

Zak's eyes rove slowly over my body. In the three years we dated, I never wore a dress like Tessa's little black one, and there's no mistaking his appreciation.

A shred of confidence returns until *she* speaks, and I'm reminded of the fact that moments ago, Zak's palm was on her lower back.

"Meg?" She reaches her hand out to me. "It's so nice to meet you. I've heard so much about you."

Sure. You've heard about how Zak broke up with me and is now single.

I eye her proffered hand. Do I have to shake it? I mean, I know it's the polite thing to do, but do I really *have* to? Civility wins, and I reach for her hand. It's delicate, just like I imagined it would be. You can't look like the Little Mermaid and not have soft hands—salt water is an excellent natural exfoliator.

"What are you doing here?" Zak eyes the man my elbow just emasculated, reminding me of his presence.

"Oh." I point behind me at the stranger. "We were just talking."

"That's not what it looked like," Zak says.

"What are you doing here?" I'm hoping to change the subject away from my embarrassing display.

"Tony from CrossFit is throwing a party on his yacht."

"Oh, that's Tony's yacht? *Feelin' Nauti*?" I chuckle like a woman who's gone mad. "That's *so* Tony. If I'd known that it was his boat, I would've stayed longer."

"*You* came for the party?" The disbelief on Zak's face is insulting, as if I don't like parties. I *love* parties.

Okay, fine. I only like the kind of parties that are for kids, the ones where juice boxes are served as the drink of choice.

"Of course," I answer. "It's a real rager in there. Add a belly dancer, and it would be the best party ever."

Someone get me a muzzle.

I should never speak again.

I'm fully aware of the stranger behind me listening to my lie, but I forge ahead anyway. "I wish I could stay, but I have to get up early tomorrow for work."

I hate my excuse.

It's only eight-thirty at night—I literally just proved Zak's point about how I want to stay home when he wants to party.

"Well, okay." Zak slowly nods as his eyes pull to the man still sitting on the bench, and I swear he gives the stranger an annoyed expression. Or maybe I imagine it because that's how I want it to play out. "It's good to see you're getting out"—he hesitates before stumbling over the rest of his sentence—"and aren't too sad."

I push a ridiculous smile onto my lips. "Yep! Doing great."

Zak's hand finds its way to Genessa's back once again, and he nudges her forward. "I'll see you around."

"Have fun!" I wave back at them. Not a controlled pageant wave. No, I look like a kindergartener who just saw his mom at the back of the auditorium during his first-ever program.

So smooth.

I hold my breath until they're safely several yards away, walking down the dock to the yacht, then I release it in one long, slow motion.

The man on the bench clears his throat. "Listen, I—"

"I don't want to talk about it."

I have no desire to hear that he couldn't take one for the team and kiss me to make my ex-boyfriend a little jealous. In all honesty, I probably should be the one apologizing and explaining to him, but I'm sure he already got the gist of my pathetic life story from my conversation with Zak.

The sooner I can get home and pretend like this night never happened, the better.

I turn to go.

"Wait! I didn't mean to make you look bad."

I hear the bench creek and his footsteps following after me, but I keep walking.

"Look, my driver is meeting me at the corner, so let's just forget about it."

I hobble—because of the shoes—to where the streets intersect, but this guy can't be deterred. He stops right next to me.

"I really am sorry."

"It's fine. You aren't the one that needs to apologize." I pull out my phone, hoping that my ride is close. I step back, and suddenly my left leg drops a few inches. I stumble, but luckily I don't fall. I try lifting my foot, but the heel of Tessa's shoe is stuck in the small hole in the metal sewer lid.

The man points down. "Your shoe's caught."

My eyes snap to his. "Observation of the century."

I wiggle my leg, trying to pull the shoe out, but it won't budge.

"Do you need some help?"

My gaze turns frosty. "You better not. I'm sure my ten-minute trial is already up."

The heel is jammed so tightly that I can't move my leg up at all. Normally, I would slip my foot out of the shoe and then work on getting it unlodged, but my foot's trapped from all of the stupid straps.

I could bend down and undo the straps, but then I would be flashing the growing peanut gallery on the pier.

I suck in a deep breath, trying to find some serenity.

"Do you want some help yet?" The smugness in his expression is infuriating.

"Nope." I shake my head. "I'll find someone else to help me."

He points to a skinny, shirtless man rollerblading nearby. "Are you waiting for that guy to help you?" His hair is long and greasy, and there's a sheen of sweat on his hairy chest. "Because I can call him over if you want." His arm gestures out to the man. "Hey, buddy!"

"Stop!" I push his shoulder.

"Okay, what about that lady?" He points behind us to an old woman with a walker. "I'm sure she can bend down and help you out. No problem."

"Fine." I grit my teeth. "You can help me."

"Nah, I don't want to force you."

"Stop being a word that I don't say, and get my shoe unstuck."

His lips twitch. "If you're desperate."

"Yes, I'm desperate."

Wasn't my failed kiss from earlier proof enough of that?

―――

TYLER

I'M AN IDIOT.

When the beautiful girl came at me, I panicked. I haven't been touched by another woman besides Kristen in thirteen years.

Thirteen years.

And to strengthen my case, it's been eighteen months since I've touched a woman...period.

The defense rests its case—I'm innocent in the matter.

Okay. Not *entirely* innocent.

If someone had told me earlier that my face would be inches away from a beautiful woman's leg tonight, I wouldn't have believed them.

And yet, here I am.

The Bible width between us is uncomfortably awkward, so I decide to break the tension. "You missed a spot shaving."

She whacks me on the shoulder with her purse. "I was in a hurry!"

My finger grazes over the top of her knee. "Right here on your kneecap."

"Don't touch my leg," she hisses.

I look up. My hands have been, and currently *are,* all over her leg as I try to get enough leverage to pull her shoe out.

She shakes her head. "You know what I mean. Don't touch my leg *more* than you have to. And why are you even looking at my legs? Your eyes should be focused on the shoe only."

I smile as I drop my head. "Your thick patch of knee stubble distracted me."

She whacks me on the shoulder with her purse...*again.*

"I think we need to take your foot out of the shoe if we're going to have any chance of getting the heel loose."

"Whatever. Take the shoe off."

"I don't like your tone." Now I'm just irritating her for the fun of it.

Wait. Is this fun?

It kind of feels like it is.

"And I don't like how slow you're being," she says. "You're milking it."

"Milking it?"

"Yeah. You're purposely going slow, taking advantage of the situation."

"Why would I do that?"

"I don't know. Maybe because your head is eye level with my upper thigh, and you're sick and twisted."

I raise my chin so I can see her face. "First of all, enjoying a woman's thigh does not make me sick and twisted. Second of all, you're the one who was all over me. *Tried* to kiss me. Maybe you're the sick and twisted one."

Her jaw drops. "Trying to kiss a man doesn't make *me* sick and twisted."

"Look!" a teenage girl walking down the sidewalk says. She's pointing at us, talking to her four friends. "He's proposing." She pulls out her phone like she's going to start recording us.

"He is *not* proposing," the woman in the black dress says back to them.

My brows furrow up at her. "Shh. You don't know that."

"This is the cutest thing I've ever seen!" The girls squeal with delight, directing all their phone cameras at us.

"If I don't propose now, I'll ruin these girls' expectations of happily ever after."

"They'll be fine."

I shift my position so I'm really kneeling on one knee. My mind flashes to Kristen and the moment I proposed to her. I never would have imagined that I would be down on one knee again. This is only for fun, but in the back of my heart, there's an ache, a realization that someday I might have to propose again for real, and I hope when that day comes, I don't feel this sad, pinching feeling.

I shake my thoughts away and look up at the woman. She's glaring at me. I decide to fake propose because she doesn't want me to, and right now, playing this game with her is the most amusing thing I've done in a *long* time.

"Meg?" I think that's the name the guy called her. "I don't have much. Not even a ring to give you, but I'd be the luckiest guy in the world if you were my wife. Will you marry me?"

"Aww," the girls say in unison behind me.

And that's when Meg slaps me.

Not hard, but enough to shock me.

"No, I will not marry you. You cheated on me with my best friend, *Candi*."

"What a jerk," the girls mumble, dropping their phones in disgust. "Come on. Let's get out of here."

My hand rubs the side of my face where Meg's handprint probably lingers. "What was that for? I went from Prince Charming to a jerk."

Her mouth twitches like she might smile at me. "I told you not to propose. And how do you know my name?"

I like her almost-smile.

"The guy said it back there."

"Oh."

I look down at her shoe again. "Why are there so many straps? I can't get your foot out."

"I don't know. These are my sister's shoes."

I reach into my pocket and pull out a small pocket knife, flipping the blade open.

"Is this your way of getting back at me because I turned down your proposal? You're going to stab me?"

I glance up and see her smile.

"I thought about it." I match her playful expression with one of my own. "But I'm going to cut the straps so we can get your foot out."

"Good idea."

I slip the metal under the black leather and pull. The straps fall, and she lifts her foot upward, stepping away from me.

"My sister is going to kill me. These are her favorite shoes."

I twist and angle the shoe, finally getting the heel out of the hole. "They can still be her favorite. She just can't wear them anymore." I straighten, handing her the shoe.

A maroon sedan pulls up with the window down. "Are you Meg?"

"Yes! Thank heavens you're here." She steps toward the car, then turns back to look at me. "My Uber's here."

"I figured," I said.

"Thanks for the help with my shoes. And"—she raises her bare shoulder just slightly—"I'm sorry about forcing myself on you."

"I'm sorry I acted like a pain in the word-you-don't-say."

Her lips twist into an adorable smile. "I guess we're even."

She climbs in the car, and I stand there, watching as she drives away, surprised by the spark of life growing inside my chest.

CHAPTER 6
TYLER

I drum my fingers on the steering wheel of my truck as I drive to pick up Krew from Logan and Hillary's house. By the time I get there, it's almost nine-thirty. That should be enough time to pretend like I gave the blind date with Candi a good effort. Tomorrow at work, Logan will find out the truth, but tonight, I can act like the date went fine.

I actually spent more time with Meg than I did with Candi.

Meg.

I'm not on social media, but I wonder if I could type her name in on Instagram or Facebook and pull up her profile. There are probably thousands of girls named Meg, but maybe if I include Tampa too, I'll be able to find her.

Why do I even *want* to find her? A girl like Meg, in a killer dress like that, isn't the type of woman who wants to date or settle down with a thirty-three-year-old, widowed, single dad.

Those aren't the best credentials.

Plus, she's not my type.

I mean, she's a knockout. Her light-blue eyes reminded me of my own...and Krew's. She had straight blonde hair styled down with a deep side part. I realize I sound like I'm a hairdresser by talking about *side parts,* but right before Kristen died, we had a lengthy conversation about whether or not she should start parting her hair down the middle because that was the style. That conversation was the week she died, so it's kind of burned into my mind, along with all of our other "last" conversations.

But, besides her good looks, Meg was fun to talk to. Granted, we didn't talk for that long or about anything deep, but the conversation felt more natural than anything I got out of Candi. Then that guy showed up, and she turned all vulnerable like he'd done a real number on her. That's not the kind of situation I want to get wrapped up in.

If I were looking seriously for a woman, which I'm not, my main goal would be to find someone who would be a good mom to Krew. I don't need her to stay home and cook meatloaf, but I would want someone who's content with little league baseball, binge watching *Lego Masters*, packing school lunches, and going out for ice cream at McDonald's—the creme-de-la-creme of desserts. It's not a glamorous life, but it's awesome. Or at least, it was awesome before Kristen died.

Don't get me wrong, Krew and I are doing great...kind of. We've managed to make it through these last eighteen months like champs. I won't say it's always been pretty, because it hasn't been. Krew wears dirty baseball pants to games because I forget to wash them. I only remember to clean the toilet when visitors comment on the yellow ring around the inside of the bowl. The local Panda Express has our names and orders memorized. We never have any milk, and I've been late to school pickup more times than I want to admit.

And let's not forget about the loneliness.

Sometimes it's so suffocating, I bury myself in work to try and trick my mind into not feeling it. So basically, I'm barely surviving, drowning in a sea of single-parenthood while also trying to run my own business. In my current state, I don't have time for dating. Maybe someday when things settle down or when I actually figure out what I'm doing, but not right now.

I'm good.

Just me and Krew.

That's all I need.

I park my car on the street and walk up to Logan and Hillary's porch. Just as I'm about to knock, the door flies open.

"Ten minutes!" Hillary glowers at me. "You gave up on the date after only ten minutes?"

I guess Candi must've texted Logan already.

I step around her into their entryway. "I wasn't feeling it, and you said dating was all about good first impressions." I crane my neck, looking for Krew so we can get the heck out of here. "Krew! Krew, it's time to go."

"Tyler, you're never going to be able to move on with your life if you don't start spending more than ten minutes with a woman."

I eye Hillary from the side and shove my hands in my pockets. "Maybe I don't want to move on with my life."

"Krew needs a mom."

"I'm pretty sure he has a mom."

Her voice softens. "You know what I mean."

Unfortunately, I do know what she means.

And I know I'm failing more than succeeding, so it makes sense that Hillary says Krew needs a mom.

Logan rounds the corner holding Krew over his shoulder like a sack of potatoes. "I think you're looking for this little guy." He spins, and I can see the back of Krew's head and his brown hair, the same color as mine. Everyone says we look exactly alike, and we do, but the rest of him—his feisty, fun personality—that's all Kristen. Sometimes I shake my head at the similarities between him and his mom—his mischievous smile, his boldness, his creativity. Everything that's good about him came from her.

"It's time to go, bud. You've got school in the morning." I ruffle the hair on his head, and his blue eyes peek up at me.

"Yes!" He punches his arms out as he cheers. I don't know any other second grader that is excited to go to school, but I'm grateful for it. Last year in first grade, it was a struggle to get him to go each morning. Some days I would spend at least an hour sitting in the parking lot of the school, trying to coax him to go to class.

My business suffered because of it, but Krew always comes first, no matter what. I didn't get that same devotion from my own dad. Growing up, he never had time for me. He missed baseball games, school programs, family dinners, and special occasions.

You name it, he missed it.

The result of his absence was his successful ladder company. Dixon Ladders, the number one ladder company in the South. I hope it was worth it. When I became a dad, I knew I didn't want to be like that, but since Kristen died, it's been hard to find a balance. If I throw too much time into Krew, my landscaping business starts to fail. If all my energy goes into working, then I'm no better than my own father. It's hard. No matter what I do, I feel like I'm doing it wrong.

But thankfully, Krew is liking school much better this year. Kristen's mom is the principal at a swanky private school, and it was important to Kristen that Krew go to school where his grandma works. I drop him off early so I can go to work. When I can't make it back in time to pick him up after school, he hangs out with Grandma Diane in her office. It's a great situation.

Krew looks up at me with a big smile. "I can't wait to tell Mrs. Johnson that I won my baseball game on Friday."

Part of his excitement over school is from his new teacher, Mrs. Johnson. Krew talks about her nonstop. I haven't met her yet, since school just started, but I will at Meet the Teacher Night, and I plan on letting Mrs. Johnson know of my eternal gratitude for her influence in Krew's life.

I pull his little body off my brother's shoulder, and he wraps his arms around my neck. "Thanks for watching him," I say to Logan and Hillary.

"We didn't even talk about how you blew off Candi." Logan's eyes fix on mine as if he's trying to intimidate me. He may be older, but only by fifteen months. I'm absolutely *not* scared of him.

"Oh, I talked to him about it." Hillary's arms fold across her chest.

His wife, on the other hand…I'm totally scared of her.

I turn the knob and open the door, trying to leave before we have to hash it out.

"If you only spent ten minutes with Candi, where were you the rest of the time?" Logan asks, following me outside.

I keep walking to my car. "Just sitting on the pier."

"Well, I'm sorry it was such a bad night."

I open the back door to my truck and set Krew inside, shutting the door once he's situated. My mind flashes to Meg.

Tonight wasn't a complete waste. Her throwing herself at me and getting her shoe stuck did have some benefits. I broke down a physical barrier. Now, I won't be so weirded out the next time a woman tries to touch me.

I'm through the awkward stage.

I can only go up from here, right?

CHAPTER 7

MEG

"Hold on, Meg," my dad says. I can hear the woman at the fast food drive thru ask my dad what he wants to order. "I'll take a number two, but without the English muffin." My dad lowers his voice so I know he's talking to me now. "I'm down five pounds."

I shift the phone into my other hand and smile, because Dad told me this exact thing on Friday, the last time we talked. I think he forgets which daughter he's already talked to. "That's great."

"I know. I fit into all my skinny shirts."

"Mom would be so proud." I laugh, thinking about my mom. "Or so upset that it took her dying for you to finally lose some weight."

"And what to drink?" the fast food worker says through the speaker.

"A large Diet Coke."

I look at the dashboard in my car. It's 8:17 in the morning. He's starting early on the Diet Coke today.

"Yeah, I'm going to wear my skinny shirt to the widows' dance this Friday night."

I grip the steering wheel tighter. "Are you sure you're ready for that kind of stuff?" My eyes sting with tears, because I know *I'm* not. "It's only been four months."

"The single dances are where all the singles are at."

Yes, that's usually how it works. Single women are at single dances.

"There's a dance every weekend," he says. "So I will have plenty of chances to meet someone new."

I blink back my tears. I know my dad is lonely, but it seems too soon for him to be looking for a woman to date. It's like his forty-five years with my mom meant nothing. Like losing her was no big deal.

I can't handle this conversation, so I change the subject.

"Zak and I broke up this last weekend."

"Yeah, Tess told me."

Leave it to Tessa to not keep her mouth shut.

"How are you holding up?" he says.

I think of my embarrassing debut into the single world last night on the pier. "I've been better."

I can hear the ruffling of paper sacks as the restaurant hands him his food.

"I'm mostly sad because I know Mom wanted me to marry Zak."

"Mom just wanted you to be happy."

"Zak does make me happy."

Did. He *did* make me happy.

"If you say so."

I don't like my dad's tone. It's like Tessa and Brooke have gotten to him and turned him against Zak. There is a very real chance that Zak could change his mind and come back. But I'm not going to say that out loud to people. I don't need to add to the reasons my sisters think I'm pathetic. It wouldn't be the first time someone made a mistake and came crawling back.

I'm glad he changes the subject this time so I don't have to. "How are your Etsy sales going?"

I sell things on Etsy—digital downloads of home decor

quotes people can print out and hang on their walls. I also have a line of digital invitations that people can edit and print. It's not a big deal—I'm literally one in a million—but it brings in a decent amount of money every month. Zak thought it was a waste of time. Apparently he didn't appreciate the fact that I can design my own wedding invitation and decorate the halls of my house, saving my future family money. With this kind of hobby, I really can't understand why every single man doesn't get down on one knee and propose to me right now.

"The sales are going well." I like how my dad is proud of my little side business. He's the only one I talk to about it. "I put up some new fall and Halloween signs that have been selling."

"I think that's great." His voice is muffled through bites of his breakfast.

"Well, I'm pulling into the school, so I guess I better go," I say, turning the steering wheel into the parking lot of American Education Academy. "What's on your agenda today?"

"I'll probably stop by Mom's grave before I head home."

My heart breaks a little. I miss my mom so much. I'm constantly sad that she's not here for me. And then there's the sadness that comes because she's not here for my dad either.

"Tell her hi for me," I say, not letting my sadness invade my voice.

"I will. Have a good day at school."

<hr />

THE MORNING RECESS BELL RINGS, and I look up from my desk at my students who are writing their *All About Me* stories. "If you're finished with your assignment, you can put it in the basket as you go out to recess."

The quiet classroom becomes a flurry of noise as kids tuck in their chairs, bring their papers to the front, and grab soccer balls and jump ropes on their way out to the playground.

"Here, Mrs. Johnson." My student, Krew, hands me his paper.

"Oh, you can put it in the basket with the rest of the class."

"I want you to read it," he says, shoving the paper into my hand.

"Now?"

He smiles his cute little smile, and I can't tell him no.

"Okay."

I look down at his paper and begin reading out loud.

My mom died.

Oh.

This was not what I was expecting.

I swallow, trying to keep it together.

We go to her grave. We bring her flowrs. The yellow are her favrite. My dad is sad. He sleeps on her side of the bed and smels her pillow. My grama works at the scool and lets me help her after scool when I wait for my dad.

I bend down so that my eyes are level with his blue ones. "This is a really great paper, Krew. Did you know that you and I have something in common?"

"No."

"My mom died too, and I go visit her grave all the time."

His eyes light up the way only a child's can. "Really?"

"Yeah."

"That's cool." Krew shrugs once then runs out to recess, leaving me heartbroken.

⊂⊐

"This is the saddest thing I've ever read," I say to my friends at lunch two hours later. I plop down into a chair in the teachers' lounge, letting my soft cooler drop on the table next to me. Jen and Charlene teach second grade too and are already sitting at the table.

"What's the saddest thing you've ever read?" Jen asks, leaning forward. She's three years younger than I am, and a first-time teacher. I like her because she's eager to learn and not afraid to ask questions.

"We did an *All About Me* writing assignment this morning where I told the kids to tell me something about them that I didn't know. This is Principal Carter's grandson's response." I slap Krew's paper on the table in front of me and start reading it aloud. "My mom died. We go to her grave. We bring her flowers. The yellow are her favorite. My dad is sad. He sleeps on her side of the bed and smells her pillow." The other two let out a collective *aww* and I stop reading for a moment, giving them my *I know* look, then I pick up where I left off. "My grandma works at the school and lets me help her after school when I wait for my dad."

"That *is* the saddest thing." Jen puts a hand over her heart like she needs it there to hold herself together.

"Mrs. Carter's daughter died over a year ago." Charlene shakes her head. She's the only one of us that isn't new to the private school this year. "It was so tragic. She was in a car accident and died on impact."

I was more than flattered when Diane Carter told me her grandson was assigned to my class. I'm new to the school, and the fact that she trusts me with her own grandson speaks volumes. This is my fourth year teaching second grade, but it's my first year at American Education Academy. I've always wanted to teach here. It's my dream job. The private school is like a Japanese airport, beautiful with an abundance of state-of-the-art technology. The class sizes are small, and the pay is higher than public schools. When I saw there was a job opening to teach second grade, I jumped at the chance.

Principal Carter personally came into my classroom and

handed me my student list the week before school started. She told me Krew was her grandson, and that he'd been having a hard time since his mother's passing. She put her hand on my arm and said she'd appreciate it if I took special care of him this year. Of course, I agreed. She's my boss. But I was glad on the first day of school to learn that Krew is an adorable kid who's easy to like.

I've been worried about him, though. School has only been in session for two weeks, but I'm already noticing a pattern that he doesn't bring back or turn in any homework sent home. I could talk to Diane about it, but I'd rather bring the subject up with Mr. Dixon at Meet the Teacher Night later this week. That's *if* he shows up. So far, I haven't seen Krew's dad at the school at all.

"I went to the funeral," Charlene says. "All the staff did. Kristen Dixon was something else. She had a PhD in Child Psychology, and she specialized in helping children diagnosed with terminal illnesses. Beyond that, she was beautiful, ran multiple marathons a year, and still made time for her family."

"Wow," Jen says. "I feel like a total failure in life after hearing what she accomplished."

I glance at her. "I know."

"She was a *very* accomplished woman—Diane Carter's only child, her pride and joy. I felt so bad for her husband she left behind." Charlene sighs. "He's a real looker. I'd ride the Dixon train if I were thirty years younger."

Jen and I exchange a look.

"What?" Charlene says. "Don't tell me you both haven't thought the same thing."

"You know nothing turns me on more than a man smelling his dead wife's pillow." Jen catches herself. "That is, if I weren't already in a committed relationship with Rob."

Charlene stirs her leftover ravioli. "Well, someone should hit that. He's this school's McSteamy."

Hit? McSteamy? It's as if Charlene swallowed Urban Dictionary.

Their heads turn to me, and I straighten under their stares.

"Why are you looking at me?"

"You should date him!" Jen says excitedly.

"No."

She waves her finger out in front of me. "I thought you said this morning that you and Zak broke up. You're single now."

"I've decided to be a spinster."

"Since when?"

"Since last night. Men are noncommittal jerks, and I'm swearing them off forever."

"Not all men are noncommittal jerks." Jen stands and walks over to the microwave to retrieve her EasyMac.

"In my experience, they are."

"No offense, but I could have told you Zak was going to break your heart just by looking at him. He's kind of a tool."

I give her a tight smile. "Information like that would have been helpful three years ago when we started dating."

"I didn't know you three years ago."

"I bet Diane Carter's son-in-law is ready to settle down," Charlene says. "He was already married."

"We don't know that *Mr. Dixon* is ready to settle down." I add his name to try to keep this insane conversation as professional as I can. "We don't know anything about him."

"We know he's McSteamy."

"That's the exact opposite of what I need. I need an average guy who isn't puffed up by his good looks. Just a nice guy. Someone who is so happy to be with me, he's willing to get down on one knee and propose after three dates."

"Maybe Mr. Dixon is a nice guy." Jen bounces her spoonful of noodles at me as she talks. "We know he's sad, that he brings flowers to his dead wife, and that he smells her pillow. That sounds like nice guy stuff."

I shake my head. "It's against school policy to date a parent of one of the students. You all know that—you signed the same contract I did. And I certainly wouldn't want to break that contract with my boss's son-in-law."

Their expressions drop because they know I'm right.

Dating a parent at our school is prohibited. And it has been for the last two years, since a mom from one of the upper grades fraternized with a male teacher, trading *favors* so that her child's grades could go from C's to all A's. The student got kicked out of the school, and the teacher got fired. American Education Academy almost lost their accreditation. It was all over the local news. Now, no dating parents is a rule if you want to work at this school. It had its very own bullet point on the contract, and it was bolded.

Bolded.

I'm not about to give up my dream job over a man, even if he does look like McSteamy and is ready to commit.

I'm not that desperate...or that stupid.

CHAPTER 8

TYLER

"Do we need butter?" I ask Krew after school as I push around my cart at the grocery store.

He looks at the shopping list, taking his sweet time reading every item.

I point to where it's written out on the paper. "There it is. *Butter*."

"Stop telling me. I can read."

The problem is it takes forever for him to find things on the list, and I'm getting impatient. Kristen was much better at stuff like this than me. I just want to get our groceries and get out of here so we can go home and go to bed.

Luckily I made the list, so I know what's on there. I reach for the yogurt and throw it in the cart.

Krew frowns. "I didn't tell you yogurt."

"I know, but I remembered we need it. It's on the list."

He stops walking and throws the paper down.

"Come on," I say, slowly walking forward. "Pick it up. We don't have time for this. It's getting late, and we still haven't eaten dinner."

"No!"

I glance around. A few women have peeked over at us from

behind their own carts, and I can feel my frustration simmering.

"Krew, I'm serious. Pick it up, and let's keep going."

"No! I don't want to shop with you." His voice is growing, and so is my embarrassment.

"Fine, then." I start pushing the cart forward again. "You can stay here while I shop. I hope one of these nice ladies watching us will give you a ride home."

Every spectator snaps their eyes back to their own shopping.

I slowly walk to the milk and grab two jugs off of the chilled shelf. I'm praying this parenting game I'm playing works out for me. I'm already going through other options in my head of what to do in case it doesn't. What would Kristen do? I wish I knew. I can take away screen time or friends if the tantrum persists, but I'm never good at following through with those consequences, and we both know it.

I look back at him before moving on. "I need some help. Are you sure you don't want to keep shopping with me?"

He shakes his head. "I want to shop with Mom."

Then he turns on his heels and runs down the aisle to the front of the store. All the other women are looking at me again with so much curiosity I want to shout out at them, "Haven't you ever seen a tantrum before?"

Instead, I leave my half-full cart, pick up the crumpled grocery list off of the ground, and chase after Krew. He's almost out the front doors of the store when I grab him and pull him into my arms. His little body wiggles.

"Let go of me! I want Mom!"

I hate this tantrum.

It happens every now and again, and I honestly don't know what to do when it does. Krew was barely six when Kristen died. He doesn't have a ton of memories of her, but he does remember a feeling of being loved. Whenever he brings her up, I can't help but wonder if I'm giving him enough love, or if somewhere deep down, he knows that me alone isn't enough.

I walk out the door with him still yelling and squirming in

my arms. I see a bench outside the building and sit down, moving his body so that I can hug him close.

"I wish Mom were here too, bud. I wish she could shop with you and see how good you're reading. She'd be so proud of you."

His little fists bang against my shoulders. "Let me go. I don't want you."

"I know," I say, rubbing his back. "But you're stuck with me. We're a team, and we both miss Mom."

I don't know what else to do, so I sit on that bench outside the grocery store, holding Krew in my arms until he finally gives up fighting and falls asleep.

It's times like these that I wish I had someone else in my life, someone who could help me navigate the hard times.

Parenting is a hard job to do on your own.

CHAPTER 9

MEG

Principal Carter's dark hair is arranged perfectly into a low bun. Mauve lipstick colors her lips, matching her painted fingernails. She's the picture of class with her black pants, black blazer, and a small pendant necklace. She's sitting with me and Krew Dixon, making small talk. We've exhausted all the regular things to talk about. We've discussed Krew's school class, if he likes his seat assignment, the new friends he's made, what his favorite subject is, and whether or not he likes having school lunch or home lunch. I glance at the clock again. Mr. Dixon is eight minutes late to his assigned spot at Meet the Teacher.

My eyes shift to Principal Carter. "Did Mr. Dixon say how late he was going to be?"

Diane flips her phone over and reads his text again. "No, it just says he's going to be a little late. Thursdays are usually his busiest day." There's a look of annoyance on her face. Maybe I'm just imagining it because she's my boss, or maybe she's just as scary a mother-in-law as she is a principal.

I smile at Krew. "We can start without your dad."

Krew's light-blue eyes grow, and a huge smile spreads across his face. Not the kind of reaction kids normally give when they're being stood up by a parent.

"Dad!" he yells, and he runs to the door behind me.

"Finally," Diane mutters under her breath.

I turn in my seat and catch the end of Krew hugging his dad. It's a cute scene. Mr. Dixon has one knee on the ground so they are fully embracing, and Krew's arms wrap around his dad's neck. I can see Krew's face as his chin rests on his father's shoulder, and I feel like an intruder watching this intimate moment, so I turn back around to Diane and offer a small smile.

"Krew loves his father," she explains.

"The relationship between a father and a son is so important," I say, as if I know something about that kind of thing, which I don't.

"Sorry to keep you waiting," Mr. Dixon says as he rounds my desk.

I glance up with my professional-teacher smile on my lips, but my expression falters when I see his face.

Oh, crap.

Mr. Dixon is the man I met on the pier three days ago?

The floor drops out from under me, and I feel like I'm spiraling through the air.

MR. DIXON IS THE MAN I MET ON THE PIER THREE DAYS AGO.

"Meg?" he asks with a hint of a surprise.

Diane looks between us. "Do you two know each other?"

He's dressed differently. Tonight he has on worn jeans, a fitted gray t-shirt, work boots, and a black baseball cap turned backward. I like this style better than his business casual. It suits him more.

"No!" my pipsqueak voice comes out. They might as well cast me as the mouse sidekick in the next Disney movie.

Diane looks at Mr. Dixon. "Then how did you know Meg's name?"

My boss cannot know I tried to make out with her son-in-law. My panicked eyes plead with him.

He leans down, giving Diane a side hug, greeting her. "I must've seen her name online or something when I was checking Krew's grades."

She pats his shoulder. "*You* were checking Krew's grades this early in the year?"

I spring from my chair, standing up before Diane can question him further. My hand shoots out in front of him. "I'm Ms. Johnson. It's nice to meet you."

He takes my hand, and I flush with embarrassment. His handshake is slow and deadly.

Deadly? Really?

I don't know why I thought that, but something about his touch is killing me, so *deadly* it is.

"Krew always calls you Mrs. Johnson," he says, with emphasis on the *Mrs.* And did he just glance at my ring finger? Oh my gosh.

I pull my hand out of his grasp, taking my seat again. "No. Just Ms." I drag out the *S* so it sounds like a Z. "Krew has told me so much about you."

So has Charlene.

The corner of his mouth rises. "You can call me Tyler."

"I'm not sure that would be professional." I look at Diane. My expression probably conveys all my dirty secrets—I tried to kiss him, he became intimate with my calves, he proposed, and I slapped him. At any moment, she's going to fire me.

"If a parent asks you to call them by their first name, then you probably should," Diane says, and suddenly I feel like I'm five and just got caught shotgunning an apple juice. Sticky and guilty.

"Everyone calls him Tyler," Krew says.

"Okay."

Mr. Dixon—Tyler, as I'm supposed to call him now—tousles

Krew's hair, but his gaze stays focused on me. "So what has Krew said about me?"

"Uh…" I'm so dang flustered. I'm fighting the urge to see if sweat has leaked through the pits of my floral dress.

His lips twitch. "You said Krew has told you so much about me."

I said that?

Maybe I did, but I didn't mean it. That's what you say when you're meeting someone. I wrack my brain trying to think of something, *anything*. I glance at Krew and his Stealers baseball shirt, which he's worn at least three times since school started.

"He said you coach his baseball team, the Stealers." I straighten, proud of myself that I actually came up with a good answer.

Tyler nods. "It's a play on words…because you *steal* the bases."

"Cute."

You know what's actually cute? The way Tyler Dixon smiles. His lips curl up perfectly, revealing the tiniest of dimples on his left cheek. I didn't see it the other night, but now, it's all I can think about.

Then a dangerous gleam shoots out from his eyes. "I also feel like I know so much about you."

I instantly hate everything he *thinks* he knows about me, including the fact that I'm terrible at shaving around my kneecaps. "Oh, really?"

"Yeah, it sounds like you're giving Krew a *leg* up on his education."

And now all I can think about is Tyler's hands on my legs.

This is awful.

"I think you might finally *slap* some sense into the kid," he says. His blue eyes sparkle like Christmas lights, and I know he's loving this little exchange.

Diane eyes us in a disapproving way. "Tyler, can we move on to Krew's academics?"

She knows he's flirting with me.

Is he flirting with me?

It kind of feels like it.

"Sure. I just wanted *Miss* Johnson"—the emphasis on the *Miss* has been noted—"to know how much I appreciate all she's doing for Krew."

The sincerity in his stare knocks me off balance. "Palpitation" is a stupid word, and yet, all I can focus on is my freaking heart *palpitations*. My heart hasn't beat like this in years.

I clear my throat and fiddle with the papers in front of me, spinning them around so everyone can see them. "Here are Krew's test scores from the beginning of the year assessment."

Tyler leans forward. "I've got to be honest, these test scores mean nothing to me."

I point to the top section. "The first test was in reading comprehension." I smile at Krew. "You did great. You scored above average on that test." I lower my finger to the next paragraph. "He also scored high on language arts and vocabulary."

"What about this one? His scores look lower." Tyler points to the next part, and his fingers brush mine accidentally as they pass, causing me to jerk my hand back into my lap.

The finger brush means nothing.

I have stone cold, statue-like fingers that feel *nothing*, and I'm definitely not thinking about his hands on my legs again.

"That one is for math." My voice sounds weird, but I continue on. "He's still on grade level for mathematics. It isn't anything to be concerned about. He's doing great in every subject."

"I would like to see all of his scores go up," Diane says. "Especially in mathematics. Kristen was excellent at math. She'd want Krew's scores much higher than this."

"If Miss Johnson isn't concerned, then I'm not either," Tyler says.

Diane rolls her eyes. "Tyler, you're never concerned about things that are important."

I feel tension from Diane, so I glance down and flip through Krew's folder to the next paper, the *All About Me* writing assignment, and suddenly images of Tyler Dixon carrying yellow flowers to his wife's grave and him smelling her pillow at night flood my mind.

I'm the worst.

Worse than the worst.

I forced myself onto a grieving man.

I tried to *kiss* a man that just lost his wife.

No wonder he pushed me away. I'm not proud of the fact that this knowledge helps my damaged ego feel a little better.

And now I'm going to see him all year long. I want to roll myself inside this manilla folder and squish it into the back of a filing cabinet...like way in the back, where no one can reach.

I'm just going to breeze past this assignment, casually mention it and move on. "We did this paper in class the other day to assess each student's writing." I keep talking at a fast pace, hoping neither one of them stops to read his words. "I was looking for whether or not Krew started each sentence with a capital letter and finished it off with a period."

Tyler picks up the corner of the paper, tilting it toward him. "*All About Me*, by Krew Dixon." He raises his eyebrows at his son before glancing back at the paper.

Oh, no.

He's going to read it out loud, and then he's going to start crying because he misses his amazing wife so much and the hole in his heart is too deep. Then Diane will start crying, and I'll start crying because I miss my mom. This will turn out to be the worst Meet the Teacher Night ever.

"My mom died." Tyler pauses after reading the first sentence, looking up quickly at me and Diane before continuing. "We go to her grave. We bring her flowers. The yellow are her favorite."

I watch as Tyler's hand goes to Krew's back and he gently squeezes his shoulder. It's so adorable I might start crying because of that single shoulder squeeze, but I keep it together, since no one else seems to be crying.

"My dad is sad. He sleeps on her side of the bed and smells her pillow." Tyler coughs out a laugh and glances at me. "I don't smell her pillow."

"Yes!" Krew protests. "I've seen you."

He pulls his son closer, laughing nervously. "You're telling Miss Johnson all of my secrets."

I press my lips into a small smile, trying to ease his embarrassment. "I thought it was cute."

"Are you sure you didn't mean to say pathetic?" he asks, matching my smile with one of his own.

"Definitely cute."

Meg!

I'm the one flirting now.

I'm the face-palm emoji personified.

I dial it back, smiling at Diane who is watching us carefully. "There's also a sentence about you in Krew's writing."

"Oh?" One dark brow lifts, but her eyes pin me to my cushioned chair.

Krew reads the last line of his story. "My grandma works at the school and lets me help her after school when I wait for my dad."

Slowly, her head turns to her grandson. "You do help me after school."

"That's a great story, buddy," Tyler says.

"Mrs. Johnson is just like me," Krew says to his dad. "Her mom died too."

His blue eyes skip to mine, and there's so much understanding and sincerity behind his gaze that I want to crawl into his lap and let him rock me gently as I cry into his shoulder.

"I'm sorry to hear about your mom. When did she die?"

I hold onto my emotions, because this is a parent-teacher meeting, not a therapy session. "Four months ago."

"That really sucks."

Yeah, it does.

It sucks *so* much.

I stare back at Tyler, grateful for a little bit of understanding. Zak told me at least a dozen times that he was sorry for my loss. It's a perfectly acceptable thing to say when you lose a loved one, but just once, it would have been nice if he'd say that losing my mom sucks. That it's not fair that I got dealt such a crappy hand when everyone else gets to go on shopping trips with their mom and plan their weddings.

Not having her here just plain sucks.

And now that Zak broke up with me, I can't even do the one thing she hoped for in marrying him. It's like I've lost another piece of her.

"I didn't know about your mother." Diane's voice knocks me out of my trance. Her expression falls. "I guess we're all dealing with loss in some way." She stands, smoothing her skirt. "We should get going. Ms. Johnson's next appointment is probably waiting in the hall."

TYLER

That's it?

Meet the Teacher is over?

Aren't there more assessments we need to look at, or a drawing of Johnny Appleseed that I need to pretend like I'm impressed with? The ones where instead of a hat, the kids draw a pot on top of Johnny's head?

"There's actually one more thing I wanted to discuss with Krew's dad," Meg says.

Krew's dad—not Tyler. "Mr. Dixon" would have been better than that. It's not like Meg doesn't already know I'm a dad, because she does.

The gig is up.

But I want her to look beyond the dad status and see a single man…not a single-*parent* man. I had written her off the other night. She was a party girl in my eyes, but school teacher Meg, in a feminine, flowered dress with splotches of red paint on her arms and a pencil resting on top of her ear, is in my league. This version of her is the exact thing I am looking for…*if* I were looking.

"Sure," I say. "I'm here to talk about whatever you want."

Diane gracefully slides back down to her seat as Meg meets my eyes.

"You'll notice, Krew's folder is pretty bare compared to the other folders sitting here."

I follow Meg's eyes to the stacks of papers beside her.

"He hasn't been turning in his homework." Her words are followed by a look of disappointment.

I immediately turn toward Krew. "Bud, you've got to turn in your homework. That stuff is important."

"You said homework is stupid and that I don't have to do it."

Busted.

Meg raises her eyebrows, but maybe I can still salvage this.

"I didn't say that."

"Yes, you did. You said I'm only in second grade and that I should tell Mrs. Johnson that I don't need homework."

So, so busted.

Apparently it's my fault there's no drawing of Johnny Appleseed.

"Really?" Meg bites back her smile, and it's the cutest thing I've seen in a long time. In fact, I'm surprised by the twisty feeling in my stomach right now.

I choke on a rough laugh, shaking my head. "Kids. Why do they always say the things that we don't want them to?"

"Tyler!" Diane chides. "Krew needs to be doing his home-work and turning it in. I don't need to remind you that the American Education Academy is a premier school. Krew can't just slide by because he's my grandson. If Kristen were here, she'd be taking his homework seriously."

If Kristen were here, I wouldn't be noticing Miss Johnson's cute smile. A pang of guilt tugs on my heart.

"Principal Carter?" A voice over the PA system chimes into Meg's classroom.

Saved by the bell. Zack Morris would be so proud.

Diane's chin turns up to the ceiling. "Yes?"

"The McBrides are here and would like to see you."

"Thanks, Ms. Dunway. I'll be right there." She stands and pushes in her chair. "I need to go. The McBrides have given a lot of money to the school." She looks back at me as she exits the room. "Come say goodbye before you head home."

I nod as I watch her leave.

Meg glances at the clock above the whiteboard. "It's time for my next appointment. It was so nice to meet you, Mr. Dixon," she says as she stands.

"Tyler," Krew reminds her as he bounces out of his chair, and I make a mental note that I'm going to buy the kid an ice cream cone on our way home. Then I remember that he told her that I smell Kristen's pillow and that I think homework is stupid. So maybe no ice cream.

She walks toward the door, and I scramble to my feet.

"Hey," I say, catching up to her. "I want to apologize again for the other night."

Her face reddens. "No, *I* need to apologize. You had every right to push me away. I didn't know..." She looks down at Krew and shakes her head. "Anyway, I was just trying to make my boyfriend jealous and—"

"What happened the other night?" Krew asks, pulling on my arm, but I'm still stuck on her use of the term "boyfriend."

"I thought you said he was your *ex*-boyfriend."

"Dad, what happened the other night?" Krew tugs on my arm again. I ignore him, because I'm waiting for her to clarify.

Meg looks at Krew instead of answering me.

"Dad!" he says, pulling me again.

She scratches her ear as she lowers her voice. "Are you going to answer him?"

"Are you going to answer me?"

"I don't think that it's any of your business."

"Normally, I would agree, but you made it my business the other night when you tried to ki—"

"Okay!" She puts her hand up to stop me. "He's my ex-boyfriend. It's a very recent thing."

"Who's Mrs. Johnson's boyfriend?" Krew asks.

When you're a parent, you can't buy a moment of privacy.

"No one." I rub my brow. "No one is her boyfriend." I look down at Krew. What am I even thinking, having a conversation like this in front of him? "Come on, bud. We better let your teacher move on to her next appointment." I walk toward the door. "So I guess I'll be seeing a lot of you this year, then?"

Would I? How many meetings are needed to discuss a seven-year-old's grades?

"I don't know that you'll be seeing *a lot* of me, but Krew will."

"I'll see you. I'll find you if I don't see you."

Meg's eyes pop, and she suppresses a smile.

I'll find you if I don't see you?

I went from being the uncool single dad to the creepy stalker. All I need is a knife to complete the look.

Crap.

I do have a knife—a *pocket knife*.

Why am I suddenly stumbling over every word? It's not like I *like* her. Miss Johnson is just like any other woman I talk to every day.

Except that I don't talk to other women every day.

"That came out wrong." I lift the tip of my hat and fit it over my head again. "I promise I'm not trying to recreate the movie *Taken*, especially since we already established that your dad wouldn't be able to find you."

She gives me a courtesy laugh.

A *courtesy* laugh.

It's time to go before I say something else equally stupid. Although, I'm not sure anything can top *I'll find you if I don't see you.* "It was nice meeting you...officially."

"You too."

"Wait!" Krew picks up a flyer off of a desk by the door and shoves it into my face. "Dad, there's a carnival!"

My head kicks back as my eyes try to focus on the paper one inch from my nose.

"Yes, the fall carnival is next week after school. It's a big fundraiser." Meg lifts her shoulder as she talks. "You should come."

Because *she* wants me there, or because my son goes to the school?

"Sounds fun." My eyes lock with hers. "I'll be there."

Krew grabs my fingers. "What about me?"

"We!" I say a little too aggressively. "*We* will be there. Next week. It's a date." Her expression drops, and I immediately correct myself. "Not a *date* date. Just an appointment." I nudge Krew forward. I can't get out of here fast enough. I'm a bumbling idiot. "See you then."

I stop by the front office on our way out of the school. Krew runs ahead and makes himself at home. He fiddles with a prize machine, trying to rig it so that a bouncy ball drops down.

"I don't think you should play with that. It's not a toy," I say, more for the other parents around us than for Krew. Yes, my parenting these days is all about just doing enough so that other parents don't judge me. I wasn't always like this. When Kristen was alive, I didn't care what anybody else thought about our parenting. We had a plan *together.* But now that I'm doing this alone, I'm constantly trying to minimize the judgmental looks coming my direction. Kristen was the one that was good with this kind of stuff. I'm completely inadequate.

"Hi, Mr. Dixon," the woman behind the desk says. She's the

secretary here at the school, but I can't remember her name, even though I've met her a dozen times. She's in her late twenties with a cute face and nice eyes, but nothing else is memorable about her, including her name. She smiles at Krew, and I steal a quick glance down at her name plate.

Melinda Dunway.

"Hey, Melinda," I say. "How's it goin'?"

"So good." Her entire face brightens, and she leans forward. For some reason, I wish Meg Johnson was this excited to talk to me.

"Tyler," Diane calls from inside her office, waving me in.

"The principal wants to see me," I say with a grimace, and just like I knew she would, Melinda erupts in laughter.

It wasn't even a funny joke.

"Krew, are you okay out here?"

"I'll watch him," Melinda chirps.

I nod politely and walk into Diane's office. She stands from her desk and shuts the door behind us.

"I must really be in trouble if you're shutting the door." I take a seat in one of the leather chairs across from hers.

"There's something I want to talk to you about." Her voice is all business, and I start to squirm in my seat a little. Diane and I have always had a good relationship. How could we not? She loved Kristen, and Kristen loved me. I might be a little rough around the edges and not as polished as she wanted for her only daughter, but I took good care of Kristen, and she knows it.

She takes her seat and looks directly at me. "I want to hire you."

"Is there some sort of teacher shortage?"

"No. The McBrides just okayed the funding for the new play area and grounds remodel. I want to hire you as my landscaper. You'd have to submit a bid, and you'd be up against other landscape contractors, but you're as good as anyone. I see no reason why the job wouldn't go to you."

I smooth my hands down my Levis and rest them just above

my knees. Landing this would be huge for my company. "This job would be perfect. I'd be right here by Krew every day."

"I'm not guaranteeing anything. Your proposal will go through the board of trustees."

"I know."

"It's a big job. You'd have to have it done before Christmas so the students can enjoy it the last half of the school year, which means you'd only have a few months."

"That's no problem." I can't hide my smile. "Thanks, Diane. I know you didn't have to tell me about the job, but it means a lot that you did. I'm sure my bid will come in under budget."

"I probably *shouldn't* have told you about the job. You'll have the female half of my entire staff in love with you before the playground is completed."

"Yeah, right."

"I see the way they all look at you."

"Who?"

She glances out to where her secretary sits. "Melinda."

"That's just one person. Not your entire staff."

She nods. "I know you're starting to date again. It's been over a year since Kristen died, so I guess that's to be expected, but I would prefer it if you didn't date anyone on my staff. It's against the rules at American Education Academy for a parent to date one of the employees."

I remembered the school scandal from a few years before. Diane called Kristen all the time for advice. It was a big deal, and Diane was concerned she would lose her job. But none of that has anything to do with me, and I can't figure out why Diane thinks it does.

"I wouldn't say I'm dating again."

"Krew told me you went out on a date the other night. Are you sure you should be telling him things like that? Kristen wouldn't want that. In fact, are you sure you should be dating again? It seems like you have your hands full with Krew. I'm not sure adding dating into the mix is a good idea."

I sit up in my chair. "I didn't tell him I went on a date. He must have overheard me talking to my brother about it. It was a blind date that didn't last long, and I'm pretty sure it won't happen again."

"I see." Why does Diane's expression look relieved? "Well, then, forget what I said about parents dating members of my staff. It wasn't a necessary reminder."

"What about a landscaper?" I joke. "Is it against the rules if your landscaper dates someone on the staff?"

"I would prefer it if the landscaper I hired kept everything professional."

"That's really a shame," I say, shaking my head. "I'm going to have to let Melinda down gently."

Diane's eyes turn serious. "Tyler, just keep to yourself and focus on Krew. That's your role right now."

"I plan to." But right as those words leave my mouth, Meg Johnson's smile crosses through my mind. Keeping to myself may be harder than I think.

CHAPTER 10

TYLER

"Hang your baseball bags on the fence, grab your gloves, and start throwing the ball with your partner," I say to Joey and Noah, the last two to show up at practice.

I watch the boys on my team attempt to throw the ball back and forth. More balls are dropped than caught, but I'm not too worried about it. This is their first year in competitive baseball, and I love the progress they've made so far.

"Looks like Noah's mom is staying for practice again," Wayne says. He's Zander's dad and my assistant coach, and once upon a time, he and his wife, Nikki, were our *couple* friends. But now I'm not a couple. I'm a single, so I only see Wayne at baseball practice. Couple friendship is another thing I lost when Kristen died.

I glance over my shoulder at Noah's mom, Beverly Ulrich. The second she sees me look at her, she smiles and gives a little wave. She has long, brown hair; a perfectly botoxed face; a medically enhanced body that she has no problem showing off; and way too much interest in me. I lift my eyebrows in acknowledgment, then turn back around.

"She's so into you. When are you going to ask her out?"

"Never." I fold my arms, watching the boys in front of me.

Wayne whistles. "Dude, I don't know how you're staying away from her. If a woman like that wanted me, I'd go for it. You have more willpower than I do."

I eye him. "Does Nikki know you think that?"

"Nikki is way better than Beverly Ulrich. Nikki's the marrying type. She's the woman you want to be the mother of your kids. The kind of woman you actually enjoy hanging out with."

"And what's Beverly?"

"She's the woman you date after your wife dies. The woman that gets you back out there. She's the Band-Aid you rip off. It will sting at first, but then you'll be glad you did it."

"I'm not dating, and even if I were, Beverly Ulrich is not my type."

I know she's already a mom, but for some reason, I can't picture her soothing Krew when he has a tantrum like the one he had at the store last week.

"Well, somebody better tell Beverly that she's not your type, or else she's going to be hanging around our practices for the next five years."

My brows rise. "Five years?"

"I'm just guessing. How long do you think it will take for you to date again?"

Five years?

That number is so depressing. Will it really take me five years to be ready to date? I'll be thirty-eight. Krew will be twelve. The thought of being a single parent and lonely for that long makes me want to give up on life right here and now.

"I don't need *five* years to be ready. I went out on a blind date last week."

"What?" Wayne slaps me on the back. "I can't believe it. How did it go?"

"It ended early."

"Was she hot?"

"I don't know."

"You don't know? How do you not know?"

"I don't know."

"So are you going to ask her out again?"

I shake my head. "Nope."

"Well, at least you went. That's a good first step." Wayne leans forward, looking in my eyes. "Kristen would be proud."

"I'm not so sure about that."

"Tyler, it's been almost two years. Stop beating yourself up about it. It's time."

I know he's right. It *is* time. Krew needs a mom. I'm slowly seeing that. And I'm making small steps. I went out with Candi. I flirted with Meg. In fact, I've thought about Meg several times this week, specifically her smile. These are all signs that my heart is shifting. I know I need to stop fighting the shift, but it's hard.

"Did you go to Meet the Teacher Night?" I ask.

"Yeah, Nikki made me go."

"So you met Zander's teacher, Miss Johnson?"

"Yeah." He looks at me, and it takes him a few seconds to realize where I'm going with this. "Dude. You liked her, didn't you?"

I'm suddenly embarrassed. "No." I scratch the side of my ear. "I was just impressed with her as a *teacher*. I think she's good for the kids."

"No." Wayne smiles. "You think she's good for *you*."

"Shut up," I mutter, holding back my smile.

"I love everything about this. I can really see you fitting with her."

"You don't even know her. Neither do I."

I should've never mentioned Meg to Wayne.

It's nothing.

But I can definitely picture Meg comforting Krew when he misses Kristen, and I can see Krew letting her.

"Okay, that's enough. Bring it in," I call out to the team, trying to end the conversation, because the visual in my head both breaks my heart and pieces it together at the same time.

CHAPTER 11
MEG

I've got exciting Friday night plans.

I hook another cheap plastic toy to the fishing pole that was thrown over the painted-blue plywood and give the line a tug so the child knows to pull up.

I don't actually mind that my *exciting Friday night plans* are me attending the school carnival alone. This is where I fit. I like volunteering at carnival games and watching the kids run around with cotton candy stuck to their lips. But this particular game isn't too exciting. When I told Mr. Hunsaker that I would fill in for him at the "fishing pond," I didn't expect to be hiding behind a board, clipping toys onto wooden dowels. But better me than him, since he currently has a migraine.

My volunteer partner, some mom I don't know, looks down at her watch. "My shift's over. I'm supposed to switch to nachos. Do you want me to wait until the next volunteer comes to relieve me?"

"No, I'm sure I can do double duty for a few minutes."

"Okay. Have fun." The mom gives a little wave and leaves.

A new string snaps over the plywood, and I pick up a plastic frog hopper and attach it to the clothes pin. Then another string comes over, and another. I'm all business. This game will not be like real fishing. These children will not wait for their catch.

I'm so focused on getting toys on the poles that I jump when someone says "Hey!" behind me.

I turn around to none other than Tyler Dixon.

He's in his jeans and tight, fitted t-shirt again, but this time he's without his hat. His brown hair has the perfect amount of waves that makes me want to scream, *"Don't you dare get a haircut!"*

"I didn't mean to scare you. I'm here to help with the fishing pond game."

My brows climb. "You signed up for the fishing pond?"

What kind of glorious and terrible coincidence is this?

"I don't know." He looks around. "Diane told me to find Mr. Hunsaker." He rubs his chin, and I can't help but notice the brown stubble that curves over the hard lines of his jaw. "Am I in the wrong spot?"

"No, this is right. Mr. Hunsaker wasn't feeling well, so I stepped in for him." I turn back to the waiting strings and try to ignore the excitement rolling through my stomach.

Is this fate's way of testing me because I said I was no longer attracted to handsome men?

Because so far, it's been testing me a lot.

I spent my entire drive home from Meet the Teacher Night thinking about Tyler Dixon. Even the dramatic songs on my 80's breakup playlist didn't derail me. His barely noticeable dimple on his left cheek, his easy smile, and the way his strong hand wrapped around Krew's shoulder played on repeat through my mind over and over all week long.

I've decided there's nothing sexier than a man snuggling his son close.

But I shouldn't be thinking about Tyler and his sexy, fatherly attributes. I've sworn off men. Or at least men that are as attractive as Zak Kershaw and Tyler Dixon.

Yep, I'm changing my type. Turning over a new leaf and dating the nice guy.

Muscles?

Pffft. Who needs them?

Gorgeous smiles?

Overrated.

Mad flirting skills?

Lame.

Give me all your pudgy, *doormat* kind of men. Yeah, that's my new type.

Tyler pulls his folding chair right next to mine and takes a seat. "Put me to work."

Did I hope I'd see Tyler Dixon at the carnival tonight?

Yes.

Did I want to be *this* close to him?

No.

Because when I'm this close to him, my heartbeat does new things.

"Where's Krew?" I ask.

"He's with Diane."

So we're alone? Well, us and the five hundred children running around—but it really, really feels like we're a*lone.* Maybe it has something to do with the giant piece of blue plywood hiding us from the rest of the world.

But this isn't a big deal.

I can resist a man like Tyler.

I straighten. "The game is easy. When a child throws their fishing line over the board, you grab a prize and attach it to the line."

"I can handle that." He smiles, and I can see the trace of his dimple. I avert my eyes. His dimple might be a weapon, but it will not destroy me.

We sit in awkward silence for several painful seconds.

"How have you been?" Tyler finally asks.

"Uh, fine." Short answers. That's the key to success in this situation.

After a few seconds of more silence he says, "It's your turn to ask how I'm doing."

Right.

That's the polite thing to do.

My focus stays on the game. "How are you?"

"It's been a long week. Work's been crazy, and Krew's had two baseball practices, a game, and then this carnival. I kind of feel like I'm drowning."

My movements slow as I glance at him. I wasn't expecting such an honest, genuine answer. Especially two seconds after he sat down. Suddenly I can picture Tyler trying to play the part of dad and mom while also trying to earn a living, and my heart breaks for him.

"I bet it's hard doing everything all by yourself."

He shrugs. "It's not ideal."

Shoot. What happened to my short answer policy?

"And what about you? You haven't snuggled up to any new men this week trying to make your ex-boyfriend jealous?"

Do not engage.

I repeat: *DO NOT ENGAGE.*

"No, that was a one-time deal that I won't repeat." I smile back at him.

I'm weak.

So very weak.

"And what about the shoes? Was your sister mad?"

"She didn't speak to me for a week."

He laughs, and the sound sends a flutter through my heart. If this is a test, I'm currently failing it.

His eyes drop to my shoes. "Are those tennis shoes?"

I glance down. "Yeah—well, they're Keds."

"You're wearing them with a dress?"

"It's the practical choice, since I'm on my feet all day."

He nods. "It is practical."

Then his eyes go back to the game, and I'm left wondering what all that was about. Does he have a shoe fetish?

"So…are you and your boyfriend going to get back together?"

I give him a look that conveys this topic is none of his business.

"It's just a question." He puts his hands up in defense, and dang it, why is that so charming?

"No, we're not going to get back together. I mean, I hope we do, but I would be an idiot to think that we will. I'm pretty sure it's over for him."

"How long were you guys together?"

"Three years." I shrug. "I thought we were going to get married. That was the next step for me, not breaking up. So basically he broke my heart and shattered my dreams." I don't know why I'm telling Tyler all of this. It has to be breaking some confidentiality agreement between teachers and parents—the HIPAA of educational relationships.

"If he broke your heart, why do you hope you get back together again?"

I give him a pointed glare. "You're very nosy, Mr. Dixon."

"Tyler," he corrects me. "And I'm not nosy. I'm just trying to get to know Krew's teacher."

"Most parents don't care about my personal life."

"I'm not most parents."

No, he's not. I catch a glimpse of his strong arms as he reaches in front of me to grab another string, and I make a mental note to keep my eyes on the prize.

Literally.

He tilts his head toward me. "How about I tell you something personal about me, and then you tell me something personal about you? Then we're even."

Oh, this game sounds dangerous.

"I'll start," he says before I even have the chance to tell him no. "I own my own landscaping business and property management company. I like being able to work outside, and I like that I can set my own hours so that I can be there for Krew whenever he needs me."

That explains the large biceps. I picture him wearing work gloves and throwing those heavy pieces of sod around like it's no big deal. Oddly enough, he's shirtless in this fantasy.

Stop picturing him shirtless, Meg!

I shake my head.

Eyes on the prize.

"Now it's your turn." Tyler nudges me with his elbow, and I freeze. I've never been nudged by a parent before.

I clear my throat. This is a normal parent-teacher conversation. Parents nudge teachers *all* the time.

"I own an Etsy shop," I say. "You probably don't even know what Etsy is."

His brows bunch together. "Etsy. Does that stand for Energetic Teachers Sell Yams? You own a shop that sells yams?"

I shake my head as I laugh. "No. Etsy is an online marketplace where you can sell handmade or vintage specialty items."

"Yams aren't a specialty item?"

"I guess they could be, but that's not what I sell."

"Then what do you sell?"

"Digital signs that people can print out and hang in their house."

He gives a big nod. "Right. Like the Gather sign."

I bite back a smile, secretly loving that he knows what the Gather sign even is. "Yes, like that. Although, I hope my signs are a little more unique."

"How did you get started in something like that?"

"Nope. It's your turn to tell me something personal."

His shoulder bumps me this time. "Oh, you're a rule follower."

I bump him right back. "To a T."

Except I'm not following the rules right now because I'm flirting with a parent—literally flirting with disaster.

"All right, then. I love baseball," he says.

"That's not personal. I could've already guessed that because I know you coach Krew's team."

"Do you know anything about baseball?"

"My brother, Matt, played a little bit, but I never paid attention so...not really."

"Then I'm going to have to teach you everything about it."

It sounds like he's setting up a second meeting—the male version of leaving his purse behind—unless he plans to tell me all about baseball at this very moment.

"Isn't baseball the most boring sport out of all of them?"

He shakes his head. "You're confusing baseball with golf, and it's only boring if you don't know how it works."

"Did you play in high school or something?"

"And in college."

Oh, brother.

He was a college baseball player. Now I'm envisioning him in those tight uniforms that make every man's butt look amazing.

"Were you any good?" Just by looking at him, I can already tell he was incredible.

"I was all right." There's enough cockiness mixed in with his modest answer that my heartbeat topples over itself. As if I needed another reason to be attracted to Tyler Dixon.

"Your turn," he says.

"Well, I can't top being a collegiate athlete, so I'm not even going to try. I'm going to come up with something so lame, you'll regret ever having this conversation with me."

His blue eyes stare right into mine. "I doubt that's possible."

My stomach lurches over the edge of a cliff. It's freefalling through the air in the most fun way.

Get a grip, Meg. It's just blue eyes. You're such a lightweight.

"Um." I swallow. This is me pulling myself back together. "I have terrible taste in music. I listen to stuff from the eighties and the early nineties." Now he'll know how incompatible we are. This is the perfect plan.

"What? Like Def Leppard?"

"No. Nothing that cool. I'm talking about the cheesiest love songs you've ever heard."

"So you're a romantic?"

"No, just a girl who likes sappy love songs." If he ditched stripper Candi after ten minutes because he didn't like the band *Froggy,* he's definitely going to be repulsed by this.

"I'd love to hear these sappy songs. Make me a playlist."

My chin drops. "Make you a playlist?" I definitely didn't see that coming. Are we in high school again, burning CDs for our crushes?

Not that Tyler Dixon has a crush on me. That is *not* what I meant.

"Yeah. I want to see what we're dealing with before I decide to write you off forever. I mean, it can't be as bad as Froggy."

Shoot.

He's on to me.

"Fine. I have a breakup playlist I can send to you in Krew's next report card."

"I don't want breakup songs. I want love songs."

"A love song playlist?"

"Is that a problem?"

"Why do you need love songs?" The last thing a widower should want to listen to is cheesy love songs.

"So that I have something to look forward to." Tyler smiles in his easy way, casually showing off his dimple.

I cannot send this man *love* songs.

"I have a *She's Dead* playlist you might like better," I blurt.

A deep rumble of laughter bursts out of him. "Is that what it's called? *She's Dead*?"

"Yes." I bite back my smile. "You know, because my mom's dead."

His features soften as his eyes sweep across my face. "Is that what you do? You sit and listen to sad songs when you're sad?"

"I guess so."

"Does it make you feel better?"

"No, it's like taking a knife and stabbing it directly in my heart and then twisting it all around."

"Then why do you do it?"

"I don't know. I guess I like…the drama of it all."

His smile morphs into something serious. "I understand."

I can see the sadness in his eyes, even though he's putting on a good face, and I instantly hate myself for making him feel bad. "Sorry. I shouldn't have brought up that subject."

"You don't have to be sorry. I talk about Kristen all the time. But I do think I'll pass on your *She's Dead* playlist. Thank you for the offer, though."

"Probably a good choice," I say.

"Who's ready to go fishing?" a tall, lanky man says as he pops his head around the board.

Tyler and I stare back at him with blank faces.

"We're here to relieve you," the man says, pointing to the woman next to him.

Is it wrong that I'm disappointed?

Yes, Meg. It's wrong.

We give our chairs up to the couple and walk across the lawn. Dozens of kids with bags of prizes and candy run past us.

I point to the right. "I'm supposed to go volunteer at Tic-Tac-Toe."

"And I should find Krew. It was nice talking to you, Miss Johnson."

"Same to you, Tyler." I give a small wave and turn to leave.

See? No harm, no foul.

Everything between Tyler Dixon and me is under control.

I DON'T LISTEN to my usual breakup music during my ride home from the carnival. Instead, I find myself scanning through my favorite songs, picking out which ones to include on a love song playlist for Tyler Dixon. Not that I will ever actually send it to him, because I won't. But I make the list anyway.

It's titled *Un-frog-ettable Love Songs*.

CHAPTER 12
TYLER

"She was the best dressed woman there," Paul says.

It's Sunday afternoon. We're sitting at the cemetery between our wives' graves. Krew runs out in front of us, and I send a football through the air. Because of my sitting position, I don't get enough force behind it, and the ball ends up short at his feet.

"What was she wearing?" I'm intrigued. What do sixty-plus-year-old men find attractive when looking for a new wife?

"She had on a nice black dress and heels with pretty jewelry. Her hair was arranged in a nice way. She looked very nice."

Nice.

An image of Meg at the carnival comes to my mind. She had on a green dress with white flowers, a white cardigan, and Keds. Kristen always said a woman should wear heels with dresses. So I'm conflicted, thinking Kristen wouldn't like Meg because of this tiny detail. For some reason, I want to think that Kristen and Meg would be friends. But Keds are practical for a teacher, and Meg looked casual and cute. Exactly what *I'm* looking for.

It's weird that I'm cataloging things that I'm looking for in a woman. Three weeks ago, when I went on the blind date with

Candi, I wasn't even entertaining the idea of dating. Now, the possibility is growing on me.

The ball comes flying back to me, and I reach my arms above my head to catch it. "But you said the woman you met at the dance last night looks like your wife."

Paul's brows lift. "Exactly like my wife." He starts fumbling with his phone. "Here, I'll show you a picture. I searched her up on The Facebook."

Paul's on Facebook? Or as he says, *The* Facebook. I don't even have a social media presence.

He hands his phone to me. "There," he says, pointing to the picture of a woman with chin-length black hair and dark features. "That's Anna Mae."

"Anna Mae? Two names?"

"Yes."

I zoom in on the picture. "She's very pretty."

Paul grabs his phone back. "Now look at a picture of my wife, Marilyn." His fingers swipe a few times before he shoves the phone back in front of my face. "Don't they look alike?"

My mouth drops. "Is this the same woman?"

"No, that's my wife, Marilyn."

I squint my eyes, staring at the picture harder. I see chin-length dark hair, dark features, and a bright smile. "*This* is your wife?" I glance at Paul and catch him nodding. "They don't just look *alike*. They look *exactly* alike."

"I know. My daughter, Tessa, made a side-by-side for me this morning. Swipe one more time so you can see their two pictures next to each other."

I can't believe what I'm looking at. Anna Mae, the new woman Paul is interested in, is the spitting image of his late wife, with only a few subtle differences. Anna Mae's lips are a little thinner than Marilyn's, and Marilyn has on more dramatic makeup, but other than that, they look like they could be twins...sisters, at least.

"Dad, throw the ball!" Krew yells. I fumble with the football in my lap, finding the laces before sending it across the cemetery to him.

"Isn't it weird to be interested in a woman that looks exactly like your dead wife?"

Paul chuckles. "A little bit at first. But when Anna Mae talks, that's when I can see the differences between her and Marilyn, and I forget that they look alike. In my mind, they are two very different people."

I shake my head as I hand his phone back. "You must really have a *type*."

"I guess so."

Is that true for everyone? Kristen and Meg don't look alike, and from what I know about Meg, I don't think their personalities are the same either. Kristen was the life of the party, and Meg seems like the type that's happy to sit in the back and let others be the center of attention.

"Anna Mae was the best dancer at the dance. She knew the cha-cha, the two-step, the waltz, the jitterbug, and the Electric Slide. She's just a wonderful person." Paul's face lights up with happiness, and I envy him.

"When are you going to see her again?"

"We're going out to lunch on Tuesday. Something casual."

"Do you feel guilty about it? Like you're moving on too soon?"

Paul shifts in his chair. "After I came home from the dance last night, I cried for about an hour. It's hard to start over. It's hard to meet someone new, especially when she reminds me of Marilyn so much. But when I woke up this morning, I didn't feel as lonely. I had something to look forward to."

"I think I know what you mean."

After I talked to Meg at the school carnival last week, I felt sad. Not because I didn't enjoy our conversation, but because I enjoyed it *too* much. In some ways, I feel like I'm cheating on Kristen. In other ways, I'm excited thinking about the prospect of something new and different. But each night when my head hits my pillow, it's Meg that's on my mind. I want to get to know her just *because*. Thinking about Meg gets me giddy. It makes me look forward to the future. I think that's a good sign that maybe I am ready to move on. It's taken me a long time to get to this point, and it's crazy that I tipped over the last little bit so quickly, but there's something about Meg that pushed me over the edge.

"Dad, let's go." Krew pulls on my leg. Usually I would leave, but I want to talk to Paul about Meg. I feel like he's the only one who would understand me. I pull my phone out from my back pocket and hand it to Krew. "Five more minutes. You can play on my phone while you wait."

"Yes!" Krew takes the phone and immediately begins doing who knows what with it. He walks away just as I hear him say, "Hey Siri, how do you spell poop?"

Good. He's distracted.

I turn back to Paul, lowering my voice a little so Krew can't hear me. "I met somebody too." I shrug, feeling a little self-conscious. "I hardly know her, and I'm sure nothing will happen, but it's the first time since Kristen died that I've noticed another woman, or even *thought* about another woman."

"Do you feel guilty?"

"Sometimes, but if I'm being honest with myself, I know Kristen would want this for me."

"I think that's natural."

"A few weeks ago, I wasn't ready to move on, but when I look at this other woman, I feel like making plans."

"Making plans?"

"Yeah, planning when I'm going to see her again or planning to ask her out. Do you think it's too soon? Or that people will judge me?"

"Too soon?" Paul scoffs. "You're asking me? It's been five months for me, and I'm already going out to lunch with a woman." He pulls on the brim of his tan bucket hat. "Your wife's been gone almost two years. If you're ready to move on with your life, don't worry about what other people will think. They aren't the ones dealing with loneliness."

"You're right."

Paul slaps me on the shoulder like a father would his son—like my father never has. "Of course I'm right. I want you to go home and call the girl up. Ask her to go to lunch with you."

I laugh. "We aren't exactly there yet. I'd have to get her number first."

"Well, find it. This relationship is going nowhere if you don't even have her number."

Technically, the relationship is *supposed* to go nowhere. Diane made that clear at Meet the Teacher Night.

But Diane also signed me up to volunteer at the fishing pond game at the carnival. She probably thought she was being wise, pairing me up with Mr. Hunsaker, a male teacher, but her plan backfired when Meg stepped in for him.

Lucky me. The twenty minutes we spent at the carnival game talking were the best twenty minutes of my week.

Now I'm planning out how I can talk to her again.

CHAPTER 13
MEG

"What did you do today?" I ask my dad as I finish the last touches on the fall field trip sign-up sheet. I'm having a hard time balancing the phone on my shoulder as I type, so I give in and let the phone fall to the bed. It takes a minute for me to find the speaker button, and when my dad's voice comes on, I realize I've missed half his answer.

"He's good to talk to, you know, because his wife is dead too."

"Yeah, I bet," I say so he knows I'm still here. I can't answer more than that because I missed the entire context of what and who he's talking about.

"We ate lunch and talked a little bit. Then I came home."

I straighten. "Wait. You went out to lunch with some guy?"

"No. I picked up some tacos, and we ate them at the cemetery between Mom's grave and his wife's."

"Ohhhh." I drag out the word now that I get the gist of what he's talking about. "That's great you've found a friend." I glance over my email one more time, making sure the link to the Google Doc is attached, and push send.

"He's not the only new friend I've made."

"Really? Who else?"

"I met a woman."

Everything freezes, and my chest feels tight.

"Meg?"

"Sorry, I was sending an email." I try to keep the shakiness that I'm feeling out of my voice. "You said you met a woman? Where?"

"At the singles' dance last night."

"I thought the dance was last week."

"I told you, there's one every weekend."

My body tenses as I listen to him. "Oh."

"Her name is Anna Mae. She's a wonderful dancer. A wonderful person, really."

I glance at the picture of my mother on the nightstand next to my bed. It's a picture of the two of us the day I graduated college. I close my eyes and tears spill out, trickling down my cheeks.

"We danced the entire night, and then I asked her if she wanted to go to lunch with me this week."

My stomach is in knots. "What did she say?"

"We're going to my favorite taco place on Tuesday."

It's just lunch, Meg. Don't overreact.

"Look at you, making so many new friends." I infuse my words with as much cheeriness as I can so that my dad doesn't know I'm dying inside.

"There's one other thing."

I hold my breath. I don't know if I can handle *one other thing*.

"She looks like your mother."

My chest falls as I release the tension I've been holding. "What do you mean?"

"Anna Mae looks exactly like your mom. They have the same hairstyle, same coloring, same kind of makeup. It's really something. I'll send you a picture of her and Mom next to each other that Tessa made."

"You already told Tessa?" Why didn't she tell me?

"Yeah, she helped me look Anna Mae up on the Facebook this morning."

I swipe at the tears on my cheek, leaning forward to my laptop. "I've got my computer right here," I say as I open Facebook. "What's her last name?"

"Anna Mae Covey."

I type the name into the search bar, and then I see her. My hand goes to my mouth as I stare at a beautiful woman who looks exactly like my mother. I can hardly believe what I'm seeing. They could be twins.

"Did you find her?"

I drop my hand. "This is weird."

My dad laughs. "I know. I did a double take when she walked into the dance last night."

I keep scrolling through her Facebook page, looking at every picture and post. It doesn't get better. She looks like my mom in every single one.

"Are you sure it's a good idea to go out with someone who looks exactly like Mom?"

"I don't see what the problem is."

The problem is I can barely breathe.

"My friend from the cemetery says that I have a *type*, and this must be it."

How reassuring.

"I'm trying not to get my hopes up, but she's a wonderful person," he says.

"Yeah, you said that already."

"I'll let you know how it goes."

I nod but don't say anything.

"Well, I better let you get back to your school stuff. I'll talk to you later."

"Okay, bye."

I hit the speaker button and grab the picture of my mom, holding it up to the computer screen.

"Is this some kind of joke?" I say to the picture. "Mom, there's no way you're happy about this."

There's only one thing worse than my dad dating again, and that's my dad dating someone who looks exactly like my dead mother.

I throw her picture down on the bed and rub both hands over my face. First my mom dies, then Zak breaks up with me, and now *this*. I'm barely hanging on to the rope of life. In fact, I don't even have hold of the actual rope. It's more like I'm grasping at the frayed thin pieces that are unwinding at the bottom.

I pick up my phone and text my siblings.

Meg: How many of you know about Dad's lunch with another woman this Tuesday?

Matt: Are you talking about his lunch with our off-brand Mom?

How does Matt know about this before me? He doesn't even live in Florida.

Brooke: Off-brand. That's funny. I think it's cute he asked someone out.

Tessa: Who knew Dad was such a player?

Meg: It's not cute. It's way too soon. He's heartbroken and not in a good place to make a rational decision.

Brooke: It's just lunch, Meg. Calm down.

Meg: Forget about the fact that he's going to lunch with another woman. Aren't any of you freaked out that she looks exactly like Mom?

Brooke: I cried when I saw the picture of her.

Tessa: Me, too.

Meg: I cried too.
Meg: I was beginning to think that I was the only one struggling with how much they look alike.

Matt: I don't cry, but I can admit that the off-brand version of our mom is a lot to take in. You're not the only one.

Meg: Okay, thank you.

It's nice to know that I'm not crazy. We're all dealing with grief and struggling in our own way.

An email alert pops up on my computer screen, and I'm more than happy to click off of Anna Mae's face. I open the response—some parent who can't figure out how to use the Google Doc to sign up for the field trip. I click on the link and the page pulls up. It's a live document, so I can see who's in it and who's not. Five out of the six spots are already filled. There's one spot left. A cursor with the name Tyler Dixon hovers over the square.

My heart skips a beat. Who knew Google Docs could be so romantic?

Tyler Dixon is signing up to come on the field trip with me.

No, not with *me*—he's signing up to go with Krew.

This is a very normal parent thing to do that has nothing to do with me.

Except somehow, it feels like it has *everything* to do with me.

CHAPTER 14

TYLER

"Krew, bring me your backpack," I yell from the kitchen table. "Do you have homework?"

You better believe that ever since Meet the Teacher Night, I've been going through Krew's homework.

It's because of education.

Not to impress his teacher.

"We don't have any homework because tomorrow's Friday, and that's when our spelling test is."

Krew slings the backpack onto the table, hitting me in the face with the straps, then he runs off.

"Thank you for that," I say as I rub my eye. I pull out his class folder, fact-checking my seven-year-old. It's empty except for the October monthly project—something about gathering different types of leaves. It's not due for two more weeks, but I read over the instructions anyway. It seems pretty self-explanatory. Collect leaves. Glue them to paper, and label what kind of tree they came from.

Maybe it's Paul and the way he's jumping head first into dating again, but I've been thinking about Meg nonstop.

I googled Etsy.

I'm not proud of it.

But you'd be surprised by the good stuff you can find there, including Meg's designs. That's right, I searched the depths of the website until I found her shop.

Made by Meg.

It's got a good ring to it, and her designs are incredible. Definitely something that Kristen would have loved.

But stalking her shop and thinking about her smile doesn't get me any closer to talking to her. On Wednesday, I tried to pick Krew up from school right when the bell rang so that I could bump into Meg while she was out doing bus duty or even afterward when she was in her room, but do you know how early kids get out of school? It was impossible for me to get there before 4:00pm when all the teachers leave for the day.

So I did something crazy.

I asked Melinda at the school for Meg's number.

I thought she would tell me that it was against school policy to give out teachers' phone numbers, but I played it off that Krew has really been struggling with his mom's death, and I needed to talk to Miss Johnson about a plan of action.

Yes, I used the death card. No judgment, please.

There have to be some perks to being a widower.

The perk in this instance is that I now have ten digits that belong to Meg Johnson.

Normally, parents don't text teachers, and I can't figure out why I'm considering doing it, especially when Meg could lose her job over something like this—not the text, but where the text could lead.

I'm being stupid.

This is just a simple text.

It's not *leading* anywhere.

But I have to have a reason for my text, or else I'll look like a stalker. I glance at Krew's open folder, lying on his backpack. The October monthly project seems like the perfect excuse. I pull out my phone and stare at it for a second.

Am I really going to do this?

I take a deep breath and type.

Tyler: Hey…sorry to bother you, but Krew is working on his October monthly project, and we're wondering if you wanted these leaves glued onto regular paper or something more like cardstock?

I'm channeling Paul's confidence, so I push send. Then I immediately drop the phone onto the table like it's a hot potato.

What did I just do?

Paper versus cardstock. I can't even believe I went with that. It's literally the stupidest excuse, but there's no turning back now. My text is out there. I sink back into my chair, waiting.

The seconds are excruciating.

Then my phone lights up. I fly forward, my fingers fumbling with the screen.

Meg: Who is this?

I forgot to say my name.

I suck at this.

Tyler: Sorry. This is Tyler Dixon. Do you have more than one Krew in your class?

Meg: No, Krew is the only one, but I was confused.

Confused.

That is not the word you want to hear when you text a woman.

Confused because I shouldn't be texting her?

Confused because she's not interested?

The dots are still jumping, letting me know she's typing something out.

Meg: When the text came in, my phone said…"From maybe: Lord of Darkness." Are you Lord of Darkness?

The lines on my forehead crease. *Lord of Darkness?* Then it hits me, and I frantically scroll to my settings.

She's confused because my name *is* Lord of Darkness.

"Krew?" I yell.

"What?"

"Did you change the name on my phone?"

"I don't know."

"You're not in trouble." Actually, I would like to kill him right now. "Just tell me what you did."

"I told Siri to call me Lord of Darkness."

I shake my head. Dating was so much easier when I didn't have a seven-year-old sabotaging me at every turn, and I'm not even dating. I'm just texting.

Tyler: Krew was playing with my phone earlier today and messed with the settings. Apparently I am Lord of Darkness now.

Meg: How did the Lord of Darkness get my personal phone number?

Tyler: I asked the school secretary for it. You know, just in case I had a question about Krew's homework.

Meg: In case you were wondering about the thickness of paper for a second grade assignment?

She's on to me.

Tyler: Call it dedication to Krew's homework.

Meg: I thought you didn't think second grade homework was important.

Tyler: I do now. His college scholarships are riding on this decision.

Meg: You can use any paper for the assignment that you want.

I can't just end things here. I went to all this trouble. The Lord of Darkness would never back down now.

Tyler: Thanks.
Tyler: What are you up to tonight?

Meg: I'm watching *Survivor*.

Another piece to the Meg Johnson puzzle.

Tyler: Don't tell me what happens. I've got it recording.

Meg: You like *Survivor?*

I lean back in my chair, settling into a groove.

Tyler: Is that so hard to believe?

Meg: I guess not. You're full of surprises.

Tyler: Like what?

Meg: You signed up for the class field trip.

Tyler: I love pumpkin farms.
Tyler: Are you going to be there too?

Meg: I am the teacher.

Excellent.
My evil plan is working.
Maybe I *am* the Lord of Darkness.

Tyler: By the way, where's my love songs playlist?

Meg: Do you plan on listening to it on the field trip?

I smile. I forgot how fun it was to flirt.

Tyler: No, I plan on blasting it when I'm laying sod with ten other manly guys.

Meg: Ha! I'm sure they'd love that.
Meg: And just so we're clear, I'm not making you a love song playlist.

Tyler: But you want to.

Meg: I never said that.

Tyler: You didn't have to.
Tyler: I found your Etsy shop.

Meg: You found my Etsy shop!?!

Tyler: I was looking for yams, but I didn't find anything. I had to settle for home décor, and then I just stumbled across your shop. Such a coincidence.

Meg: Did you find a Gather sign?

Tyler: Unfortunately, no. I might have to purchase one

from one of your competitors.

Tyler: Your designs are incredible, by the way. You should be really proud.

She doesn't send an immediate response, and I start to panic. I shouldn't have told her about Etsy. I freaked her out. I exit out of our text thread so that it doesn't look like I'm just waiting for her to respond, even though that's exactly what I'm doing.

I stand up from the kitchen table. I clear a few dishes away. Glance at the clock. It's been a few minutes. She's not going to respond.

It's time to bow out gracefully.

Tyler: Thanks for the help with the paper. We'll surprise you with our choice.

I set my phone down and lean against the counter, letting out a dramatic exhale.

Learning to date again is going to kill me.

CHAPTER 15
MEG

"I've split the children into groups of four. I don't have a group, so I'll be available to help if you need it." I hand each parent volunteering for the field trip a folder with their instructions. I pass by Tyler. He's wearing dark jeans, a light-blue v-neck shirt, and a blue baseball cap turned backward. I didn't know I was a sucker for a backward baseball hat, but I'm telling you right now, I am. I give him the folder with the name *Lord of Darkness* on it and keep walking. I see his lips move into a smile before I go.

"We'll be at the pumpkin patch for four hours. There will be a bin inside the main building that holds our class's lunch boxes. Feel free to eat lunch with your group whenever you want. We'll meet back at the bus at 2:30 p.m. The address to the pumpkin patch is in your folder, for those of you who are driving your own cars."

Tyler halfway raises his hand like he's one of my students, and I try to ignore the way his tricep protrudes. Regardless of my efforts, I can still confirm that his muscles look good from any angle.

"Do we have to drive our own car? Or can we go on the bus with the kids?"

"It's a small bus, so I can't fit every parent. Maybe one or two."

"Tyler, you can come in my car with me," Beverly Ulrich says. She's Noah's mom—divorced and single as can be. She's pretty. One of those women that will look hot no matter what age she is or how many babies she's popped out. She's working with a completely different gene pool than I am. Her gene pool is more in line with J Lo's, whereas mine more closely aligns with an Oompa Loompa.

"Dad, come on the bus with us." Krew tugs on his arm.

Tyler shrugs at Beverly. "I think I'll go with the kids." Both hands go to Krew's shoulders, and he gives him a little squeeze. I forgot how attractive Tyler is when he's in dad mode.

I need to forget that again.

I smile at him—not my flirty, *I'll-never-forget-your-triceps* smile. I'm retiring that one. Today, I'm all about professional teacher-parent relationships. And this teacher is happy he's not driving with beautiful Bev.

I force my eyes away and clear my throat. "Okay, let's line up to load the bus." The kids form a straight line behind me as the parents funnel out the door—all the parents except for Tyler. No, he's standing right by me, hands in his pockets, looking so handsome.

By the way the tension is building in my chest, you would think that I've never seen a handsome, rugged man before. It's because of my hot man ban (I just made that name up; we'll see if it sticks). The second I put my foot down and say I'm not dating brawny, manly men, that's exactly what I find.

But guess what?

Tyler Dixon and his sturdy arms aren't just against my man ban, they're against the rules of my job. And my job always wins. Period.

I lead the class out of the building and catch Jen's eye as she loads her students onto the bus behind ours. She nods toward Tyler and wags her eyebrows up and down. I give her a warning look. I want to shout, "Ms. Jen Anderson, you know as well as I do that dating a parent is prohibited." Since I can't yell that across the parking lot, I try to convey the message with my eyes, but I think it only makes me look like I have an eye twitch.

Tyler weaves into the line of children right behind Krew. "I'll save you a seat," he says in a low voice that only I can hear. Then he uses those triceps to climb inside the bus.

My heart stutters.

It's going to be a long day.

⸺

I MANAGE to ditch Tyler once we get to the pumpkin patch. Yes, I *ditch* him. I'm purposefully trying to avoid him and the effect he has on my overall well-being. I walk over to the corn maze and snap a few pictures of some of the groups. I plan to upload them on our class website for parents to see.

A hand swipes over my arms. "Tag. You're it." Krew, Zander, and Gibson run out in front of me to the entrance of the maze. Krew stops just before he's completely hidden by cornstalks and smiles back at me. "I said you're *it*, Mrs. Johnson."

Tyler walks past me, bumping me with his shoulder as he goes. "You heard the boy. You're it." He turns around so he's walking backward.

Sexy backward walking.

That's what's happening right now.

"I don't know if I dare enter the corn maze with the Lord of Darkness," I say.

I slowly head toward him, giving in way too easily. But I'm *it*, so…

His eyebrows raise in playfulness. "Are you afraid?"

I'm afraid of what's happening to my heartbeat right now. I should probably go to the nurse's station and get checked for a heart attack, but instead I'm following Tyler inside the maze.

I look around at the wall of cornstalks. "We're never going to be able to find them."

"So you're saying we have to go through this maze alone? Together? Maybe that was my plan all along."

Okay, no. I can't do this alone. I can't fight flirty Tyler all by myself. He has to take some responsibility for his illegal actions. Then again, maybe he doesn't know his actions are illegal.

"You know it's against the rules to flirt with a teacher."

"Who says?"

I give him a pointed look. "Diane Carter. And the entire board of trustees at American Education Academy."

"Eh, Diane's harmless."

"Not to me. There are rules, you know. Teachers aren't allowed to date parents. It's in our contract."

He smiles, letting his amusement show. "I wasn't aware that we were dating."

Oh my gosh.

Why do I say the stupidest things?

"We're not." I laugh, leaning into my humiliation coping mechanism. "I was just stating the school rules."

"Are there any other school rules I need to know about? Like no running in the halls, or only grabbing one carton of milk at lunch?"

I bite back my smile. "No, I think the rest are pretty self-explanatory."

We walk a few paces in silence before Tyler speaks again. "Let's say I were to ask you to dinner sometime...hypothetically." He shrugs innocently. "What would you say?"

"Hypothetically?"

"Yes."

"I would say no. I like my dates to last longer than ten minutes."

"I can assure you that ours would."

"You can't assure me of anything. You might decide when you get there that we're not compatible."

"Except I already know that we are." His smile tilts.

For someone who probably hasn't been in the dating scene very long, Tyler has entirely too much confidence. In a good way. In a way that makes me want to say yes to every hypothetical situation he throws at me.

"It doesn't matter if we're compatible or not. I would say no, because you're the dad of one of my students."

"Dads go out on dates, too." He shoves his hands in his pockets. "Or do you think that once you become a dad, you're no longer attracted to women?"

"Of course you're still attracted to women."

"Not all women." His smile widens. "Maybe just second grade teachers."

Dang it.

That was cute.

And did the sun just move a few inches closer to the earth? I suddenly feel the need to tug at my shirt a few times and let some air in.

"That's not what I meant." I'm flustered again. Tyler Dixon has that effect on me. "I meant that teachers aren't allowed to date parents. It's a school rule." I shrug with finality. "Like I said, it's in my contract."

He leans in, putting his face a few inches from mine. His voice lowers. "Good thing we're not dating then."

I swallow.

Krew and his group of friends run past us at a fork in the trail. "There they are!" They squeal in delight before running off again.

I've never been so grateful for an interruption in my life.

Tyler chases after them, picking up Zander. He raises him to the side of the corn stalks, acting like he's going to drop him down on top of them. Zander giggles, and the other boys pull on Tyler's arm until he lowers him back down onto the path.

"The boys like you," I say as we continue to walk after them.

"Well, I coach those three."

"Yeah, I've seen them wearing their Stealers jerseys to class."

"You should come to a game sometime." A playful smile tugs at his lips. "I'll let you sit in the dugout with me."

"I'm not going out with you."

"I didn't ask you out. I asked you to come support your students at a community baseball game."

As long as Tyler is the coach of the team, I won't be attending.

"You don't have to answer right now. Just think about it."

I don't need to think about it.

We walk a few more paces before he strikes up conversation again. "So how long have you been teaching?"

Finally, a topic of conversation that doesn't make me feel like an electric shock is shooting through me.

"This is my fourth year."

"But your first year at American Education Academy?"

"Yes, but I've been dying to get a job at this school. It's one of the best in the county, but there was never an opening. I'm actually surprised I even got the job when a spot did become available. This year is a trial year. If at the end of the school year the board likes what I've done, they'll offer me a five-year contract."

"Krew absolutely loves you. I don't know what you're doing in class each day, but it's definitely something special."

The weight of his stare and his kind words make it impossible to keep my breathing steady. This was supposed to be the easy part of our conversation. I glance away. "I bribe them with candy and video games."

"No you don't. Any fool can see that you care about these kids."

"Thank you. That's a really nice compliment."

His eyes don't leave my face. I feel a blush coming on like I'm thirteen years old again, so I find refuge by looking at the ground in front of me.

"I heard your company is going to be putting in the new playground at the school."

"Yeah, I won the bid. It's a big project that has to be done in a short amount of time, but I'm glad I got the job. It will be nice to be at the school every day with Krew."

Every day? Tyler Dixon will be at the school every day? Why hadn't I realized that?

"It looks like you're going to make it safely out of the maze after all." He points to the opening ahead of us. "But in all fairness, I'm the Lord of *Darkness*. I don't make my moves in broad daylight."

Really? Because I feel like he's been making moves on me this entire time.

Tyler throws a wicked smile in my direction and then jogs toward the group of boys at the end of the path.

Sheesh. Can we add jogging to the list of things I find attractive that I never knew about?

"You coming, Miss Johnson?" Tyler yells back at me.

I pick up my pace. I'm following after him, and I have no clue why.

We walk toward a small wooden stage where a bunch of kids from the class are sitting on bales of hay. Silver buckets are spaced five feet apart, and there's another huge can full of apples.

"I need teams of two to come stand in front of each bucket," an older gentleman with a cowboy hat explains.

"Dad, let's do it!" Krew pulls on Tyler's arm, dragging him up to the stage.

After a few more seconds of other students pairing off into teams, the old man explains the game. "This is called Pass the Apple. One team member will start with an apple tucked in their neck and walk it over to the middle. The other team member has to take the apple from them, tuck it in their neck, walk it over to the other bucket, and drop it inside. Here's the only rule"—the old man pauses for dramatic effect—"you can't use your hands."

The kids laugh and clap in delight, and I catch Tyler raise his eyebrows at Krew.

"You can use the rest of your body to pass the apple, but if it drops on the ground, the first person has to go back and get a new apple. Does everyone understand?"

"Yes!" the kids say in unison.

The old man looks at the teams and shakes his head. "Now, hold up." He goes over to Krew and gently moves him away from Tyler to a new bucket. "Your team won't work because your partner is too tall." He pulls Gibson from his bale of hay and pairs him with Krew. Then his eyes scan over the crowd until they land on me.

Oh, no.

I take a step back.

I've seen this game before at family reunions, and there is no way I'm playing it with Tyler.

But the man gestures for me to come to him. "You're tall. You be partners with this gentleman."

Tyler's eyes light up with amusement.

"Come on, now." The man waves me over again.

"I'm good." I shake my head. "I don't want to play."

The students start chanting, "Ms. John-son! Ms. John-son! Ms. John-son!"

No amount of seven-year-old peer pressure will get me to play this game.

"I'll do it!" Beverly raises her hand in the back. She removes her jacket, revealing a tank top underneath. My eyes scan over her toned arms and her very nice amount of cleavage. There's a lot of bare J Lo skin, and suddenly I can't stand the thought of Tyler playing this game with beautiful Bev.

I find myself walking up to the stage, motioning for Bev to sit back down. "I better do it for the kids."

I'm face to face with Tyler.

The corner of his mouth rises into a crooked smile. "For the kids?"

"Shut up," I say under my breath.

He laughs, fully aware of my motives.

"Are you ready for this, Miss Johnson?"

It's no big deal.

I'm doing this *for the kids*.

"Ready? Go!" the man yells.

Tyler scrambles to the first bucket. It takes him a second, but he manages to get an apple into his neck and walk it over to me. I hesitate before going up on my tiptoes, but that alone isn't going to be enough. I'm going to have to *lean* in.

Tyler stands there, his shoulders hunched over. "You know this is a race, right?" His words are muffled by his awkward position.

I roll my eyes and take a step forward. My chest presses against the hard planes of his. It's like I've just collided with a brick wall. I move my face slowly toward his, and my nose grazes the side of his cheek.

Wow, he smells good.

I close my eyes and breathe in.

It's some kind of woodsy scent mixed with pure manliness. The name of his cologne is probably something like *Let Me Cradle You in My Arms and Show You All the Ways I'm a Man.*

My arms are out to the side, hanging there like bird wings. We do an awkward two-step dance as we try to transfer the apple, but I can't get it. Then his arms wrap around my back, and his body hunches over me like he's giving me the biggest bear hug I've ever received. Heat spreads over my body, and my heart races as his warmth envelops me. My hands react, finding his firm shoulders.

Take the apple away, and we're at stage one of foreplay, leading up to a make out.

Necking, as my dad would say.

I dip my head back farther as he leans in closer. His chin rests on the side of my cheek as he slowly rolls the apple into the crook of my neck. I know it's supposed to be a game, but I'm going to need to fan myself after this encounter.

I have the apple now, but for some reason both of our arms

are still wrapped around each other, and our bodies are pressed against one another.

I can hear the kids laughing in the crowd, and it's not until one of them yells, "Mrs. Johnson, put the apple in the bucket!" that I realize I need to break apart from him. I rush to the bucket on the other end and drop it inside. When I turn around, Tyler is in the middle again with another apple.

For the love!

How many times do I have to do this?

I'm not sure my professional-teacher heart can handle it.

I run to him, and this time, we don't even bother with the slow stuff. He wraps his arms around me, and I curl into him. My hands find the back of his neck and I try to tilt him to the spot I need so I can retrieve the goods. It doesn't work. The apple pops out, rolling down to his chest, and now I'm using my chest to keep it pressed between our two bodies so it doesn't fall to the ground.

It's a good thing Bev didn't play. The apple would have been lodged in her cleavage.

The sensual tension from our earlier pass is gone, replaced by humiliation and awkwardness as we roll our bodies together, trying to get the apple back to my neck.

I want to kill whoever made up this game—probably some horny teenager.

"I thought I'd be better at this." Tyler laughs.

"Do you pass apples often?" The fruit is somewhere between my shoulder and his arm.

"No, but I am pretty skilled at using my body." His smile turns devilish, and my insides flip over themselves.

I step back, letting the apple drop to the ground, and a group of children groan behind me.

"At *work*." Tyler laughs. "I'm skilled at using my body at *work*."

I want to throw an apple at his smug smile.

"Okay! Okay!" The older gentleman waves his arms out.

"That's enough. Let's see which team won." He looks in our bucket first and shakes his head. "The adults only have one apple."

"Boo!" the kids shout.

Tyler walks by me, whispering in my ear as he passes. "Don't judge all of my talents based on this."

His hot breath makes me shudder.

I'm never playing Pass the Apple again.

Especially not with Tyler Dixon.

CHAPTER 16

MEG

I must be losing my mind.

That's the only plausible explanation for my behavior today.

But I've come to my senses. The problem is, I came to my senses in front of the five other parents on the field trip who will surely gossip about my date—I mean *field trip*—with Tyler Dixon. Everyone knows he's Principal Carter's son-in-law.

I stand by the bus, watching as the children load up, when Silvee's mom, Monette Peterson, comes up to me.

"Thank you so much for helping out today," I say.

She shoots me a sly smile, and her eyes dart to Tyler. "You two are really cute together."

I pretend to be confused. "Who?"

"You and Tyler Dixon. I've been watching you today."

Fabulous.

"You know what happened to his wife, right? It was so sad. Anyway, you guys are adorable."

Monette winks at me before walking away, and I feel sick. The gossip has already begun.

I hang back until all the children are on the bus and the

parents are walking to their own cars, and then I climb in. I look down the rows and rows of seats. There's only one spot left, and it's next to Tyler.

Why on earth didn't I charter a bigger bus?

He glances up at me with a smile. "Krew wanted to sit with his friends. So I guess you're stuck with me."

It's literally the last place I want to be right now.

"Oh, come on." He pats the seat beside him. "It's still daytime. Lord of Darkness won't come out until tonight."

I sit down, doing everything I can to keep my body from touching his, but we're on a freaking school bus. The seats aren't made for adults, especially men with broad shoulders like Tyler's. A shiver goes down my spine as the side of our arms, hips, and thighs touch.

MERCY!

I'm calling mercy, because I can't take this anymore. I'm in distress, and it's all because of Tyler's stupid dimple, his perfect smile, and now his very muscular hip and thigh that are pressed against mine. And let's not forget about all the cute things he does and says.

He's an excellent dad, and I'm not just getting that from the field trip. Krew talks about him nonstop. It's more than the regular stuff kids say about their parents. Krew idolizes Tyler. I knew by the third day of school that Tyler put the time in to foster a relationship with his son. Good looks come and go, but being a dependable dad is something that is attractive forever.

I also like the way Tyler asks thoughtful questions. I feel like he's really trying to get to know me. In the last year with Zak, I felt like he stopped being interested. He didn't care if he knew me or not. It was an easy thing to let slide, especially since my mom got sick and my thoughts were fixated on her, but the few conversations I've had with Tyler over the last month have reminded me how much I like feeling important enough to know.

I mean, he found my Etsy shop.

Who does that?

He's a Trojan horse. He entered my life unexpectedly, and now his little army of cuteness has opened the gates to my heart.

But I'm slamming them shut.

I'm taking back control of my heart, and I'm doing it now.

"That was fun." He turns his head, smiling at me.

Yes, fun for people who haven't been caught flirting all day.

"So there's something I have to tell you." I scratch my head, trying to find the words. "I've changed my taste in men."

"Really?"

"Yep." I wipe my hands on my dress. I have no clue why they're even sweaty in the first place. "I'm going for the exact opposite of Zak. You know, since he completely broke my heart, and we didn't work out."

"And what would you consider the exact opposite of Zak?" Tyler relaxes back into the seat.

"Just an average Joe. A little soft around the edges. Nothing too flashy."

"Give me a few months and I could be that."

My eyes scan up and down his body before glancing away. "No, you can't."

"I see."

I feel him staring at me, but I refuse to look.

"And why are you telling me this?" I can hear the playfulness in his voice.

Why am I telling him this again?

Oh, yeah. It's just another layer to why whatever this is between the two of us can't go on any longer.

I play with the seam of the seat in front of me. "I just thought you should know about my hot man ban." I can tell by the twitch at the corner of his mouth that he likes my choice of name. So do I. "So between the school rules and my newly found preference in men, I'm just trying to let you down easily."

He lets his smile free, drawing my eyes to his mouth. "Letting me down easily?"

"Yes. I just…you know…" I roll my hand out in front of me, gesturing that he can fill in the blanks himself.

"No, I don't know. Could you explain it to me?" He folds his arms across his chest, clearly amused.

I puff out an annoyed breath. He's doing this on purpose, making me spell it out for him. "You asked me out and—"

"No, I didn't." His smug smile is back. "That was all hypothetical."

My eyes turn sharp. "Well, it *seemed* like you were flirting with me."

"I was just passing the apple."

"Of course you were," I say, unable to hide my sarcasm. "Anyway, I wanted to let you know that we can be friends."

"Friends?"

"Yes."

His brows rise. "I'd love to be friends."

"Great." I finally relax, proud of the way I handled the situation.

"I just have one question about our friendship," he says.

"What's that?"

"Are we friends with benefits?"

I slap his shoulder, and he laughs.

I thought being friends with Tyler Dixon was going to be easy as apple pie, but I think I might be mistaken.

AFTER BUS DUTY, I'm walking back to the school when I hear Diane Carter's voice behind me. "Meg?"

I spin around to greet her. "Hey, Diane."

She falls in stride next to me as we make our way back inside the school. "I heard the field trip went well today."

I'm sure you did.

"Yeah, it went great."

"My friend Monette said that you and Tyler spent a lot of time together."

I'm convinced that Monette Peterson moonlights as a spy.

"I wouldn't say we spent *a lot* of time with each other. I didn't have a group, so I meandered around, taking pictures of all the groups." I'm hoping she can't hear the quiver in my voice.

"That's good. I hate to bring it up, but you know the rules here at American Education Academy. We don't tolerate any relationships between the staff and the parents. We had a bad experience a few years ago that almost led to a lawsuit, so we had to institute that rule. You understand, don't you?"

"Of course. Not only do I understand, but I fully support it."

"Excellent. Besides, Tyler shouldn't be dating right now. All of his efforts need to go to parenting Krew."

"You don't have to worry about me," I say. "I'm not interested."

"I'm glad to hear that."

I thought Diane would turn and go her separate way, but nope. She's still here.

"Have I ever told you about my daughter Kristen?"

I shake my head. "No, you haven't." I glance at the school. We're still thirty paces away from the door.

"She was something really special. Superwoman was what all of her friends called her."

Superwoman.

That's not intimidating at all.

"She could do everything and look put together while doing it. Whether it was her PhD or motherhood or her work with sick children, she gave it 110 percent. I feel bad for Tyler." Diane sighs. "He'll never be able to find another woman as perfect as Kristen. How can anyone even come close to measuring up?"

My smile is strained, but it's there. "I'm sure no one could."

"Well, it was nice talking to you, Meg. I'll see you tomorrow."

I watch Diane walk away. Five minutes ago, I was only worried about losing my job, but now I'm worried that I'll never be as perfect as Kristen Dixon.

For Tyler, or for anyone.

CHAPTER 17

TYLER

"I've been friend-zoned," I tell Paul. We're in our usual spot at the cemetery, sharing a bag of pistachios. Krew is stretched out on a blanket beside us with a coloring book and crayons.

Paul lifts his brows. "Friend-zoned?"

"Yeah, it's when the woman tells you she only wants to be friends."

"That sounds bad. What did you do?"

"I didn't *do* anything." I grab a handful of nuts and pass the bag back. "There are rules."

"What kind of rules?"

I don't really feel like going into all the details of why Meg's school won't allow her to date me—it's a lot. Besides, I don't want Krew to hear me talk about Miss Johnson. So instead, I settle for the easy answer. "It's complicated." I exhale, as if that will somehow make me feel better. "It's probably for the best. I don't have time for dating. I'm struggling as it is with this single parenting thing. I've got real problems. I somehow lost all of Krew's underwear. We had to make a stop at the store this morning to buy more. I've already got too much on my mind. I don't need to add a woman to the equation."

Paul drops a shell into the paper cup between us. "If it weren't complicated with this woman, would you still feel the same way?"

"Yeah." I'm trying to convince myself. "I'm over dating and trying to make a connection. It's not worth it. I was lucky enough to fall in love once in my life. It doesn't need to happen again."

"I have the perfect thing to make you feel better." His face lights up. "Game night."

I'm envisioning a senior center full of elderly people with bingo cards in front of them.

"Game night?"

"Yes! Next Saturday night is game night with my kids. You should come. I'm bringing Anna Mae. It's the first time my kids will meet her, and I could use some moral support."

"Won't Anna Mae be your moral support?"

"No, she'll be my date."

"I think it will be awkward if some random guy shows up to your family game night."

"My daughters bring dates all of the time. There are always random guys there."

"No. I don't want to be the only one without a date. Besides, it will mess up the numbers for the games."

"You can be one of my daughter's dates. I have three of them."

I shake my head emphatically. "I just told you that I'm done with dating."

"You didn't mean that." He takes out his phone from his pocket and lifts his reading glasses to his eyes. "Let me text my daughters and see which one wants to be your date."

"Paul, I really don't want to come."

"Nonsense."

I can't believe my life has come to this. I'm being set up by a seventy-year-old modern-day Romeo wearing Crocs. My head falls back, and I swipe a hand down my face, keeping it at my jaw. I rub my chin, feeling the gritty stubble against my fingers.

Paul's phone dings as texts come in. "Brooke's already bringing her friend, Ben," he mutters. Another ding. "Oh, Meg's already got a blind date that she's bringing, but Tessa's available." He looks up at me. "She says she's okay with it as long as you're not a psycho. Are you a psycho, Tyler?"

I shake my head, still hung up on what he said. "Sorry, what are your daughters' names? Did you say Meg?"

"Yeah, Meg. She's my oldest daughter."

Information starts to fall together in my mind. I glance at Marilyn's grave and the carved-out letters, *JOHNSON*. I've seen it before, but it didn't mean anything until this moment.

"And your last name is Johnson?"

"Yeah. Why?" His attention goes back to his texts.

I let out a surprised laugh. "No reason."

Paul is Meg's dad!

I can totally see it now. They have the same light hair and eyes. I don't tell him his daughter is the woman that's completely turned my world upside down for the last month and a half. He already knows too much, and I don't want him telling Meg anything.

Paul looks up at me. "I told Tess that you're not a psycho, so it's a date."

"You said *all* of your daughters will be there?"

He nodded. "They're meeting Anna Mae."

"Right." Originally, I didn't want to go to game night, but that was before I had all the facts. I know it's wrong, and I know nothing can come of it, but I'm dying to see Meg again—preferably away from the school and away from Diane. Game night with her family sounds like the perfect opportunity. We won't be breaking any rules. We'll both be on dates with other people, and maybe if I see her with another man, it will finally sink in that she and I are, in fact, just friends…or at least I *hope* it will sink in.

Then I can move on with my single parent life and forget about Meg Johnson.

"Sounds fun," I say. "Let's plan on it."

CHAPTER 18

MEG

pull up to my childhood home and park in front. My eyes scan across the two-story red brick house and lush green yard. The place seems empty now without my mom here.

"Are you ready for this?" I ask my date, Nigel.

Charlene really came through for me by setting me up with her sister's grandson. He's exactly what I'm looking for—a little unassuming, a little boring, lacking muscles, but nice.

"I love game night." Nigel's eyes brighten. "Do you think we'll play Settlers of Catan? Because I'm excellent at that game. I own the extension."

I feign interest. "Maybe."

We pass by Tessa and Brooke's cars as we walk to the front porch. I give a few raps on the door before opening it. "Hello?"

"We're in the kitchen," Brooke calls.

I shoot Nigel a reassuring smile, hoping that my sisters play nice. I've never brought a man like this home.

"Hey," I say as we walk into the kitchen. The room is outdated in every way, with blue Formica countertops and dark cupboards, but it's home, so I would never want it to change. "This is Nigel." Everything about how I'm acting is over the top —my smile, the high pitch of my voice. I just want everyone to know that boring Nigel is a good fit for me. I gesture to him. "Nigel, this is my sister Tessa." She's sitting at the kitchen table with her nose in a tabloid. "And my sister, Brooke, and her friend, Ben." They're behind the kitchen island putting together a vegetable tray.

"Hey," they all say back in unison, not giving us their full attention, except for Ben.

He extends one hand to Nigel. "How's it going?"

"Good. I'm ready to use my intellect to destroy you guys in some games." Nigel laughs at his own joke. "Don't worry. I'll keep things friendly."

Tessa finally glances up, giving me her *you've-got-to-be-kidding-me* look. Nigel turns to grab a celery stick from the tray, and I take that moment to mouth to Tessa behind his back. "Hot man ban. Remember?"

She rolls her eyes, shaking her head as her attention goes back to the magazine.

"Where's Dad?" I ask, looking around.

"He's still upstairs getting ready," Tessa says, flipping the page. "He wants to look his best for his date with Anna Mae."

I straighten. "This isn't a date. He's just bringing a friend. It's no big deal."

"He's actually bringing *two* friends," Tessa says.

"What do you mean?" Are there going to be two women here that I have to pretend to like?

"Haven't you heard?" Brooke throws a teasing smile Tessa's way. "Dad is setting Tess up with his friend from the cemetery."

"What? I thought he was like, seventy."

"Nah, he's thirty-something."

That's a big age gap for Tessa. "Like, lower thirties or older?"

"I'm not sure. I'm just doing this as a favor to Dad."

I lean against the kitchen counter. "Well, this is going to be an awkward night."

"I think it sounds exciting," Nigel says as he takes another celery stick, dips it in ranch dressing, and pops it in his mouth.

Brooke gives him a half smile. "That's because it's not your dad bringing a date."

"I told you, it's not a date."

"Meg, you're fooling yourself if you think this isn't a date. Dad spends all of his free time talking about Anna Mae. They hang out at least three times a week. I think it's safe to say she's more than a friend."

"Is this the one that looks like your mom?" Ben asks.

Tessa closes the magazine and pushes it away from her. "Yeah. Has Brooke shown you the pictures?"

Ben nods. "The resemblance is uncanny."

I hate this. I hate how casually my sisters are talking about my dad dating.

"Doesn't this seem..." I look behind my shoulder to make sure my dad isn't coming. "Doesn't this seem too soon?"

Tessa shrugs. "I don't know. He's lonely, and he misses Mom."

"We all miss Mom, but that doesn't mean we're going to go out and find a walking, talking replica to replace her."

Brooke puts the rest of the vegetables back in the refrigerator. "He's not replacing her."

"That's what it feels like."

"Meg, I would've thought you'd be all about this. Everyone knows you're Dad's favorite," Brooke says.

"If you don't like his new girlfriend, you're going down a notch." Tessa raises her brows toward me, adding, "Which means I can move in and take your place."

Brooke turns to me. "All I'm saying is that I thought you would be a little bit more understanding."

I'm trying to be understanding. I really am. I want my dad to be happy, but at the same time, it feels like he's betraying my mom.

"And I thought that you guys would be on Mom's side a little bit more."

"How can we be on Mom's side? She's dead."

I give Tessa a barbed look. "You know what I mean."

"I'm sure Anna Mae is a *wonderful person*," Tessa says, impersonating my dad.

"Has anyone ever thought about how Anna Mae's name sounds exactly like *anime*?" Nigel asks.

We all stare back at him with blank faces.

"Her name *is* Anna Mae," Brooke says.

"No, like Japanese animation. A-N-I-M-E." Nigel looks around. "Anime is my favorite pastime."

"That's great," I say, with a halfhearted nod.

Nigel is what I want—a nice man. I need to embrace everything that comes with it.

"Meg?" My dad says, coming around the corner. "When did you get here?"

"A few minutes ago." I lean in for a hug, and a whiff of his cologne slaps me in the face. "You look nice."

"I've got my skinny jeans on."

He doesn't mean *actual* skinny jeans. He's talking about the smaller-size jeans you leave at the top of your closet for ages, hoping that someday you'll fit into them again.

"I'm down ten pounds." He shakes Nigel's hand while he's still talking about his weight loss. "I haven't worn this shirt in five years." He tugs at the hem of a plaid button-up with long sleeves.

"It looks very nice, Mr. Johnson."

I catch my sisters rolling their eyes at Nigel's formal use of my dad's name.

"Dad, this is my friend, Nigel." I'm not quite ready to call him my date.

"Nigel, nice to meet you." My father always jokes that he doesn't want to know a man's name until there's a ring on our finger. So the chances of him remembering Nigel's name is slim.

"So when does Anna Mae show up?" Ben asks.

"She should be here any minute."

"What about my date?" Tessa asks. "Is he going to stand me up?"

"No, he's a wonderful guy." My dad turns to look at Nigel. "This is my friend from the cemetery. His wife's dead too."

I dip a carrot in ranch dressing and bring it to my mouth. "I pictured him as being, like...*old*."

"No, I told you on the phone that Tyler's in his early thirties with a seven-year-old son."

Tyler?

I choke on the carrot that's in my mouth, and it's not just a little cough. It's one of those major, dramatic chokes that causes everybody in the room to stop and stare. Nigel pats my back, and I swear Brooke looks like she's ready to perform the Heimlich if the need arises.

My mind goes back to the phone call when my dad first told me about his friend. I was only half listening and clearly missed some major details.

I finally manage to cough the chunk of carrot out of my esophagus. "Tyler? As in Tyler Dixon?"

"Yeah."

The doorbell rings, and it's either my replacement mom or the man my thoughts keep drifting to when I have nothing else to think about—which seems to be all the time. I'm not sure which one is the lesser evil.

I hear my dad call for Tessa, and I know immediately it's Tyler.

Nigel leans in. "How do you know him?"

I shake my head. "He's just a parent at my school."

Their voices get louder as they approach the kitchen. I turn around to see the last moment of Tessa and Tyler's introduction. Tessa's smile grows, and she lifts her shoulder in a flirtatious way.

She's into him.

Who wouldn't be?

Tyler is way too easy on the eyes, but he's old—too old for Tessa.

He turns to me. "Meg? What are you doing here?"

His smile is so big and so animated that I know this isn't a surprise to him.

"Do you guys know each other?" my dad asks as he places a hand on Tyler's shoulder.

The glint in Tyler's eyes makes me nervous. "It's actually a funny story—"

"Tyler's son, Krew, is in my class," I cut in. "That's how we know each other."

"Krew's in your class?" My dad's face lifts. "He's such a cute little boy."

"You know Krew?"

"Yeah, he hangs out at the cemetery with us."

He sticks his hand out in front of Nigel. "Hey, I'm Tyler."

"Nigel Faartz."

Faartz?

Charlene didn't mention that part. There should be blind date stipulations. The first one: Does your last name sound like a bodily function? If the answer is yes, the date is automatically off.

I can feel Tyler's amusement rolling off him in waves.

"So you hang out at the cemetery?" Nigel asks, and I shrink with embarrassment.

"It's where the party's at," Tyler says.

Nigel nods like he doesn't catch the sarcasm.

"Actually, my wife died almost two years ago."

"How did she pass?"

Why is Nigel asking so many personal questions? He's supposed to be getting to know *me*, not Tyler.

"Car accident. The driver of the other car was texting while driving."

Nigel points to me. "Hands free. That's what I say. I go hands free for everything."

Tyler's brows raise. "Really? *Everything*?"

I cringe. This conversation is sucking the life out of me.

The doorbell rings again, and I don't even have time to recover. There's only one person missing. Anna Mae. I'm not sure how much more I can take.

I hear her sweet voice before I see her face.

Don't cry, Meg. Don't cry.

I look around the room. Everyone else seems to be fine.

And then she walks in.

I know my mom is dead, but for a moment, it's like my heart forgot. Her black hair and the shape of her face are identical to my mother's. Even her makeup and clothes remind me of Mom. If I didn't know better, I would have sworn it was my mother.

A hole in the pit in my stomach opens up, and my heart drops down inside. It's all I can do to smile and make it through introductions. Everyone is a ball of excitement, talking to her, getting to know her.

Everyone but me.

I nod and give thinly veiled smiles. I slink to the corner of the kitchen, letting the conversation fly around me. I glance at Tyler. He's already staring at me with a look so soft, it breaks me.

My dad offers to give Anna Mae and Nigel a tour of his house, and that's when I make my escape. I open the back door and head into the backyard.

My mother loved it out here. Huge southern live oak trees line the perimeter of my parents' lot, keeping the yard shady most of the day. The evening air is muggy, making my throat feel thick with humidity. I take a seat on the rocking bench where my dad and mom used to rock back and forth *together*. It's here that I finally let the tears fall. There's so much emotion behind each drop.

I miss my mom.

I hate the fact that there's a new woman here. She doesn't belong in this house, standing next to my dad. It should be my mom at game night, my mom arranging the veggie tray.

I'm sure Anna Mae is great, but it wouldn't matter who my dad brought home.

No woman compares to my mom.

I've been outside too long, and it will look bad if I don't go back in, so I take three deep breaths and wipe my cheeks. I have to pull myself together. It's game night, for heaven's sake. Not cry-your-eyes-out night.

Then the back door swings open.

It's Tyler.

He hesitates under the porch light, hands in his pockets. His eyes are kind, as if he knows exactly what I've been doing out here. Even if he didn't know, I'm sure my red eyes and dripping nose give it away.

I stand. "I just came out here to—"

"You came out here to cry," he says, walking over to me. He sits down, using his toe to nudge the swing back and forth. The edge of the bench hits the back of my leg a few times before I finally decide to sit too.

"Yes." I look at him from the side. "I came out here to cry."

"How are you holding up? I can tell this is hard for you."

"*Hard* would be my father dating somebody new. But this —*this* is beyond hard. She looks exactly like my mom. I had to do a double take when she walked in, and even though my mind knew it wasn't her, my heart still lifted as if it were."

"What was your mom like?"

I relax a little, glad that he didn't tell me I was overreacting or that it would all be okay.

"She was so beautiful...inside and outside. She always looked classy with makeup and jewelry and an elegant sense of style. But beyond that, she had the kindest heart. She loved hosting parties and decorating our house so that every holiday felt magical. She gave thoughtful gifts, spent hours serving others, and she made everyone who entered her life feel like they were the most important person to her." I shake my head, wiping away the fresh tears that wet my cheeks.

"I remember when Kristen died, everyone told me it would get easier."

"Does it?"

"In a way." He looks at a nearby tree, and I follow his gaze, watching a leaf slowly float to the ground from the evening breeze. "The ache is always there. But the only reason it gets easier is because you've learned to live with it."

"I guess I'm not there yet, because I'm not learning to live with it."

"Your dad dating someone that looks identical to your mom would be difficult for anyone to get used to."

I snort. "You're telling me."

"Tonight is just one moment. You don't have to have what you're feeling all figured out. Just take it one second at a time. One minute. One hour. One night."

How does Tyler know the perfect thing to say to me? I guess because in a way, he's been here too.

"What was Kristen like?"

His expression melts into a smile, and for some reason, that smile stings.

"She was so much fun. She loved people and throwing parties, just like your mom. She was happy all the time, which made her an excellent mother. At bedtime, she would make up the most ridiculous songs and sing them to Krew. It's not like she had an amazing voice, but I would still lean against the wall out in the hall and listen to her sing to him. She was great with children, especially those that were struggling. Her entire life goal was to help kids with terminal illness work through their emotions and how they were feeling when they got diagnosed. When she died, I knew I was losing a lot, but my heart breaks for all those kids she was helping and the ones she could've helped. They're the ones that will really miss all of her special gifts." His eyes fix on me. "Sounds like she was just like your mom. A person who was fiercely loved who died too soon."

I can see how much Tyler loved his wife, and it makes me feel better about hanging onto my mom so desperately—like it's okay that I'm not letting go.

"Thank you," I whisper.

His hand closes over mine, and I slowly lift my eyes to meet his gaze. I should pull back, but there's something about Tyler's touch that's so comforting. A sudden breeze drifts between us, causing leaves to flutter together. The moment feels charged, but I don't know why. Is it the warmth of Tyler's hand? Or is it the wind? A gentle breeze does have a way of turning dramatic moments into something ridiculously romantic. In this very moment, I can picture Tyler leaning in for a kiss as the next current wisps my hair back. The sound of the leaves rustling together would intensify in the swell as our lips picked up—

"There you are." The back door slams shut, and I jump back. Nigel looks between the two of us, and I'm sure my wind-charged thoughts are written across my face.

I scramble to my feet, making a beeline to the house. "I needed some air, and then Tyler wanted to see the backyard, but it's getting too windy. Is everyone ready to play games?" I hope talking fast diverts his attention away from Tyler and me and the very illegal hand-holding that just happened.

Hand-holding? I wouldn't call it that. It was a hand *cover*. So innocent—something an eighty-year-old would offer the cashier at the grocery store while saying "bless your heart."

Nigel looks back one more time before I drag him into the house, leaving Tyler behind, along with whatever that charged feeling was.

⎯⎯

TESSA PLOPS DOWN on the loveseat in the family room and smiles up at Tyler. "Will you be my partner for the games?"

The *love*seat? Really?

"Sure." Tyler sits next to her, and I'm wishing that the two of them were sitting in separate recliners with a good twelve inches between them.

I lean forward, breaking into their conversation. "We usually play boys against girls for the games, so you actually won't be able to be on the same team." My face is full of fake pity.

"That's a shame," Tyler says, and the laughter in his eyes bugs me.

Then Tessa loops her arm through his, and now I'm really irritated. I look away, but that doesn't help, because my dad is currently sitting across from me, holding Anna Mae's hand.

This is a nightmare.

Everyone needs to keep their hands to themselves. Including Tyler, if we're counting the innocent hand cover. It's not that hard. I haven't touched Nigel once.

I jump up from my seat and head to a nearby closet. I know the perfect game for this little group of couples—something where you need your arms and hands to act out. I shuffle through the games on the shelves, tossing them around, looking for Charades.

"Do you need some help?" Tyler asks.

My body stiffens. He's standing behind me. I feel the brush of his chest against my shoulder and the heat of his body on my back.

"Nope, but that's kind of you to unlock yourself from Tessa for a moment," I whisper. "I'm sure you're dying to get back to her side."

"Are you jealous?" His voice is low so only I can hear. "It kind of seems like you're jealous."

My mouth opens wide, and I look over my shoulder at him. "She's my sister."

"You can still be jealous of your sister."

The idea is ridiculous. "I'm not jealous. But since we're talking about her, you realize she's entirely too young for you, right?"

Tyler looks across the room at her. "Is she? I hadn't noticed."

I turn back to the game closet, letting out a rough laugh. "Twenty-three. She's twenty-three years old." I pick up another game and throw it on a new shelf, as if rearranging the boxes will somehow help me find Charades. "That's ten years younger than you—in case you can't do math."

"Oh, I can do math. For example, you've said about thirteen words to Nigel tonight. That's a lot less than what you've said to me."

I turn over my shoulder and glare at him.

"Meg? What are you doing?" Brooke asks.

"I'm looking for Charades," I snap at her.

"We're going to play Pictionary. I've already got it out."

"Oh." Pictionary uses hands. That might work just as well.

I scoot past Tyler, ignoring his manly scent and make my way back to my seat next to Nigel.

"You guys are going to have to bear with me," Anna Mae says, looking sheepish. "I don't know how to play Pictionary."

You've got to be kidding me.

"I've never really played any games before."

How is that even possible? Has she never played Uno? Hide and seek? Has she been living under a rock for the past sixty years?

I grind my teeth together and look over Anna Mae's shoulder at a picture of my mom.

This woman doesn't stand a chance in my life.

___

TYLER

I don't like Nigel.

He's nice and all, but he's the one sitting next to Meg, so by default, I don't like him.

"So, Nigel," I say as Brooke erases the Pictionary whiteboard. "What do you do for a living?"

He sits up straight. "I'm in between jobs right now. I just haven't found something that I like."

"What do you do all day?" Tessa asks.

"Watch anime." He points across the room to Paul and his date. "Not *that* Anna Mae. I'm talking about Japanese animation."

"Yeah, we got it," Meg says, cutting him off right there.

"Tyler, what do you do?" Ben asks from across the table. I like Brooke's friend. Or maybe Ben is her date? They seem like more than friends, but I'm not really sure.

"I own a landscaping and property management business."

Tessa bats her eyes at me. "I love being outdoors. Let me know if you ever need a sidekick."

Meg grabs the marker in front of her. "Tessa hates manual labor, so I think she'd make the worst sidekick ever, but that's enough getting-to-know-you stuff. It's my turn to draw." She stands next to the whiteboard.

I bite back my smile. Meg claims she's not jealous, but I'm getting a very different vibe from her.

"We've got this, girls," Tessa says, flipping over the tiny hourglass timer.

Tessa's cute and all, but I'm not interested. Meg's right. She's way too young for me, and on top of that, it's her jealous older sister that I like.

Meg draws two stick figures with objects in their hands. Next she draws a line in between them and a big circle thing coming at one of the stick figures. It's clearly pickleball, but her sisters are stuck guessing tennis and volleyball. She tries to draw what looks to be either a pickle or part of the male anatomy, and it's all I can do to hold my laugh in.

"Oh, I know." Anna Mae's hand shoots up. "Badminton!"

Meg shakes her head. She's doing her best to hide her annoyance, but I can see it.

"Time's up," Paul says.

She looks at her sisters. "*Pickle*ball!"

"Yeah." Brooke nods. "I can see that now."

"You should have drawn the lines on the court or made your paddles a little smaller. I don't blame your sisters for not getting the answer," Nigel says.

Meg drops into her chair. "Thanks for the tip, Nigel."

I grab another marker from off the coffee table and a card. I read what it says. *New Year's Eve.* That's boring. I have something better I can draw.

I stand by the board, waiting for everyone to be ready, and watch as Nigel's hand slips over Meg's.

Clearly Nigel isn't a threat, but I don't like it.

"Hey!" I slap the top of his hand with the marker—the hand that's currently on top of Meg's. "Focus."

He looks annoyed, but he does move his hand away.

"Ready?"

Tessa flips the timer over, and I begin drawing.

The guesses are all over the place. I don't expect any of them to have a clue what I'm drawing. This is purely for Meg's benefit.

The timer runs out.

"You tell me to focus? You just lost us a point." Nigel gestures to the whiteboard. "What the heck is that?"

Ben tilts his head as he studies it. "It looks like somebody swallowed an apple and it's stuck in his throat and the other person is trying to make out with him."

"I bet Meg knows what it is." I turn toward her.

"Nope." She rolls her lips together like they're sealed shut.

"Are you sure?"

"Just tell us what it is," Nigel grunts.

"It's the game Pass the Apple."

Ben's eyes go wide in understanding. "Oh, is that the one where you pass it only using your necks?"

I point at Ben. "That's the one."

"That's actually one game I *have* played," Anna Mae chimes in.

Tessa folds her arms. "That game's disgusting."

"Last time I played it, I thoroughly enjoyed myself." I look right at Meg.

I'm being a little too obvious.

"Why would Meg know what that is?" Paul asks.

"I just figured being a schoolteacher, she would've had a *personal* experience with a game like that."

"I don't think that's the card you drew." Nigel stands, reaching for the Pictionary card, but I pull my arm away.

"Why would I lie?"

He reaches for it again, but I keep it far enough away that he can't get to it.

"Yeah, why would Tyler lie?" Paul asks. I like that he's on my side.

"He's a cheater." Nigel's getting upset. "Why won't he just show us his card?"

"Because I don't want to."

Nigel's chest puffs out. "Now we're losing the game."

"Well, this has been fun," Brooke says as she starts to gather everything up. "But I think we should switch to a different game. Something not so intense."

Meg grabs her cup and heads toward the kitchen. "I'm going to refill my drink."

Nigel sits back down, folding his arms like he's throwing a tantrum. "Can we play Settlers of Catan now?"

I flip the Pictionary card to Brooke, and it lands face up on the table. She glances at *New Year's Eve* and then looks at me with a smile. "You're not so bad, Tyler."'

I smile back at her. "Neither are you."

As everyone else discusses what game to play next, I slip into the kitchen. Meg stands at the sink with her back to me. Her hands are spread out on either side of her, and she stares blankly ahead out the darkened kitchen window.

"Are you mad?"

She looks over her shoulder, shaking her head. "Why are you here tonight?"

"I'm on a blind date."

She picks up her cup and starts filling it with water. "You must like Tessa. You've stayed longer than ten minutes."

"I didn't stay because of Tessa."

She turns around and faces me. "You need to stop."

"Stop what?"

"Whatever it is that you're doing."

"I'm not doing anything."

She draws in a deep breath and exhales. "I'm on a date with Nigel."

"I can see that."

"Then what's your problem?"

I fold my arms across my chest. "I don't like him."

"It doesn't matter if you like him. You're not the one on a date with him."

"Why are *you* on a date with him?"

"That's none of your business."

"As your friend"—I gesture to her—"and you said we *are* friends—I feel like I should tell you that Nigel is all wrong for you."

Meg rolls her eyes. "Like you know what's right or wrong for me."

I slowly close the space between us. Her body tenses as I place my hands on the counter beside hers, pinning her in. Our bodies are inches apart. I could reach up and easily tuck her hair behind her ear or brush my fingers along the side of her cheek.

"I know a little bit about what's right for you."

She lifts her chin in defiance. "Nigel is a nice guy. An uncomplicated, nice guy. He's not cocky, or flirty, or nosy, or a parent of one of my students. He's exactly what I need."

"But is he exciting?" I lean toward Meg, and her breath catches as I whisper in her ear. "Do you guys have any chemistry?"

Her chest rises against my pounding heart, and all I want to do is kiss her. It's an overwhelming feeling. There's no time to analyze whether a kiss is wrong or right or whether I'm ready for it.

My speeding heart says I am.

My head dips down and my lips brush up against hers in the softest, lightest way. Her breath goes ragged as my mouth faintly skims her lips.

"Well, this is cozy."

We jump, and I step back as Tessa enters the kitchen.

She's wearing a satisfied smile. "It looks like you're on a blind date with the wrong daughter."

I sigh. "Sorry, I—"

"We were just talking," Meg stammers.

"That was a little more than talking." Tessa's eyes move to mine. "You don't have to be sorry. I like this little dynamic," she says, pointing between the two of us.

Crap.

What have I done?

"I better go. It's getting late, and Krew's at my brother's house." I reach my hand out to Tessa. "It was nice to meet you."

"It was nice to meet you too, Tyler. I hope this isn't the last we see of you."

I walk out of the kitchen, certain that if Meg had it her way, it would be the last time she *ever* sees me.

CHAPTER 19
TYLER

"The sky is blue. The grass is green." I slap Wayne and Logan on their backs as I come up behind them. "It's a beautiful day to play baseball."

Maybe everything only looks beautiful because I kissed Meg last night. I mean, I shouldn't have kissed her. I wasn't acting like a mature adult. I was acting like a cocky teenager who let his hormones get in the way of all logical reasoning. She specifically said that we're just friends. I know the rules.

And I obviously know how to break them.

Logan glances down at his watch. "Our baseball game is already a half hour behind."

"It's Sunday afternoon," I say. "Where do you have to be?"

Logan's expression drops. "Hillary wanted to go to her grandma's house after the game. Now we're going to be late, and she's not going to be happy."

"Eh." I shrug. "Hillary's never happy."

"Boys!" Wayne calls to the team. "Stop throwing the ball over here. You're going to hit someone watching the games." He points to the grass behind the home run fence. "Go out there to warm up."

"What's the score here?" I ask, folding my arms across my chest.

"The Blue Sox will walk it off if they get that last run in," Wayne says.

"There you are!" Beverly Ulrich comes to my side, squeezing my arm. Her hand stays on my bicep, and I catch Wayne and Logan's raised eyebrows. "I'm wondering if you know which dugout we're going to be in. I want to set up my canopy and don't know if we're going to be on the first base or third base side."

"When this game is done, we'll put our stuff in the third base dugout."

Beverly squeezes my arm again, then drops her hand. "Great. I love third base." She winks at me before turning to go, but then she pauses. "Tyler, there's something else I wanted to talk to you about." She eyes Wayne and Logan like she wishes they weren't there but continues anyway. "Diane said that you're starting to date again."

My head kicks back. "Did she?"

Beverly raises her shoulder. "She said you went on a blind date."

"I didn't realize you and Diane were such good friends."

"Well, I'm one of the members of the parent-teacher association on the PTA at the school. And Diane and I have gotten to know each other really well whenever she comes to support Krew at these baseball games."

"I see."

"Anyway, I just wanted to let you know that if you're dating again, I'd like to throw my name in the hat." Her smile turns flirty, and her finger trails down my forearm. "Let me know if you're interested."

She glances at Wayne and Logan one last time, then turns to go.

We stand there in silence, looking straight ahead until Logan finally laughs. "'I love third base?'"

"Shut up," I say.

Wayne coughs, trying to hide his amusement.

"Do you want to run after her and set something up for later tonight?" Logan teases. "I'll even offer to watch Krew."

"You're going to Hillary's grandma's house, remember?"

"Oh, I'm sure Hillary won't mind if Krew tags along. Especially once I tell her about how Beverly tickled your arm."

"She did *not* tickle my arm."

Wayne nods. "She did."

"That arm tickle is more action than Tyler's had in years," Logan jokes.

I eye my brother as I lift up my baseball hat and smooth my hair out. "That's not entirely true. I kissed Meg last night," I say coolly.

Wayne takes off his hat and throws it onto the ground. "What?"

Logan shoves me. "You little dog. You've been holding out on us."

"How was it?" Wayne asks.

I keep my eyes straight ahead. "It was all right."

It was definitely more than all right.

Both men laugh and shove me even harder, and I can't help but smile.

"I can't believe this." Logan shakes his head. "I never thought the day would come."

Wayne points at me. "You need to kiss her again."

"Nope. I can't."

Logan's expression drops. "Oh. Did you feel guilty because of Kristen or something?"

I'd assumed I would feel guilty afterward, as if I were somehow cheating on Kristen, but I didn't. If anything, I felt more at peace than I have in a long time, like I'm finally living my life after two years of numbness.

It's nice to feel alive again.

"No, that's not the reason." I shake my head. "I can't kiss

Meg again because she's not supposed to date a parent of a student. It's in her contract, and me kissing her was kind of a jerk thing to do when I already know that nothing can ever happen between us."

"That sucks," Wayne says.

I feel the same way.

Logan slaps me on my shoulder. "At least you did it."

I did it, and now I have to figure out how to apologize for it.

The Blue Sox hit the runner on second base to home, and the game in front of us is over.

"Well, boys, let's go play some baseball."

I'll figure out my apology later.

CHAPTER 20
MEG

The repetitive hum and buzz of the copy machine lulls me into a Monday morning trance. The papers shoot out the side, falling onto the stack one after another. I watch them, wishing men were as dependable as copy machines.

"Where's your class?" Jen asks as she walks into the teachers' lounge.

Her words knock me out of my copy machine coma. "They're doing art with Mrs. Butler. What about yours?"

"They're in the gym for PE." She goes to the cutting board and slices a few papers in half. "So, how was your blind date Saturday night?"

I scratch my forehead, trying to find the right words.

"That bad, huh?"

"Remind me to never let Charlene set me up again."

"Why? What was wrong with him?"

I sigh, thinking back over the night. "He was nice."

"That's code for ugly."

"No! I didn't say that."

"But were you attracted to him? Did you feel butterflies in your stomach when he touched you?"

I felt butterflies—so many fluttering butterflies I'm surprised

I didn't slowly take flight like the cute little house in the movie *Up*. The problem is, those butterflies came from the wrong guy. But I'm not about to tell Jen that Tyler Dixon crashed my family's game night and completely turned my world upside down with his mere presence…and his light kiss. I'm already having a hard enough time convincing my sisters there's nothing going on between Tyler and me. I don't need to add another person to the list.

The copier purrs to a stop, and I grab the papers, shuffling them so they fit together evenly. "No, I didn't feel anything when Nigel touched me. In fact, I was bored and completely uninterested in him. He's a little intense about games and anime."

Jen gathers up her clippings and throws them in the garbage. "Face it, Meg. Maybe the average nice guy just isn't for you."

We walk out of the room together, both making our way back down to the second grade hall.

"No, I'm not giving up that easily. There has to be a man out there who checks all of my boxes."

A loud beeping sound outside pulls both of our eyes to the windows that line the school's hallway. Tyler Dixon is guiding a flatbed truck loaded with an excavator into the playground.

He's at game night.

He's on my lips.

He's at my school.

He's everywhere.

His back is to me, but I can tell by the way he walks that it's him. I don't know what it is about him, but he has a way of making everything he does look good, even directing a truck.

"May I turn your attention to Exhibit A?" Jen gestures to the windows. "Why are you not dating this guy?"

"Shh!" I look over my shoulder, half expecting Diane Carter to be standing there, listening to our conversation. "You know why."

Tyler bends over and we both tilt our heads, following his movement.

Jen sighs. "Jobs come and go, but love is forever."

"This moment would really be complete if we had drinks we could slowly stir while watching him."

"See!" Jen pops up. "I knew you were attracted to him."

"Everyone's attracted to him. But that's where my feelings stop. Things don't work out like they do in the movies. What if I lose my job over Tyler, and he breaks my heart like Zak did? I can't take that chance."

"I guess that's true. Besides, his last wife sounds amazing. It would be intimidating feeling like you have to keep up with her."

Intimidating is definitely the right word.

"So it's settled." Jen starts walking again. "We have to find you someone else that's not Nigel or Tyler."

It doesn't feel settled. Sure, Tyler kissed me when he wasn't supposed to, but he's also had a lot of redeeming moments— moments I'm trying to downplay. He's sensitive, a good communicator with his feelings, friendly, a hard worker, a hands-on dad, and thoughtful.

A new thought pops into my head. What if I knew Tyler *wouldn't* break my heart? Would he be worth losing my job?

The logical part of my brain immediately says no.

But a bigger part of my heart screams *yes*.

CHAPTER 21
TYLER

t's Monday night. Time to apologize. I take my phone out of my pocket and form a text to Meg.

Tyler: I thought you might be looking for some new quotes for your Etsy shop...
Tyler: When you stop and look around, this life is pretty amazing.
Tyler: Your life isn't yours if you always care what others think.
Tyler: The most important work you will ever do is within the walls of your own home.
Tyler: All that I am, or hope to be, I owe to my angel mother.

Meg: I love that last one.

I sigh with relief seeing Meg's name on my screen.

Tyler: I knew you'd like that last one. I can't take all the credit. Abraham Lincoln needs to take some of it, since he's the one that actually said it.

Meg: I didn't know you collected quotes.

Tyler: It's a recent hobby. I have a few more...
Tyler: Live. Laugh. Love.
Tyler: I came. I saw. I made it awkward.
Tyler: I'm sorry I ruined game night and your blind date with Nigel by kissing you.
Tyler: Can we still be friends?

Meg: Are those last two ideas for signs or an actual apology?

Tyler: Both.

Meg: I'm sorry too. (Idea for a sign)
Meg: We can still be friends. (Another sign idea)

Tyler: I like those.

Meg: Me too.

I grin. We're back in business.

━━━

MEG

I'VE TAKEN ALL THE necessary precautions.

I've kept Tyler Dixon an arm's length away.

I've told everyone, including myself, that Tyler and I are just friends. And then he goes and writes a cute apology text and makes me question whether or not I actually need my job.

I can live on my Etsy sales, right? Who needs a car, an apartment, or food?

Tyler: PS…go to your balcony for a surprise.

I glance at the sliding glass doors that lead to the small balcony of my second-story apartment. Is Tyler going to be out there holding a huge boombox over his head or something? For some reason, I wouldn't put it past him.

I step outside and look over the rail. There's no Tyler, but there is a string dangling from the railing to the bushes below. I pull it up, and a pink box emerges out of the bushes. There's a note rolled up like a scroll tied between the string and the box, and I'm like a kid on Christmas morning. I can't get it open fast enough.

Meg,

I'm sorry that I acted like a ~~jackass~~ a word you don't say and kissed you. I wasn't planning on it, it's just something that happened. For the record, I enjoyed the kiss, just not the part where I compromised your job. Please accept my peace offering.

Your friend,
Tyler

I open the pink box. Inside is a chocolate chip cookie. Cookies —they're pretty much the best way to my heart.
I run inside and grab my phone, sending off a text.

Meg: You're forgiven for everything you've ever done in your life.

Tyler: I see you got the cookie.
Tyler: I'm surprised your neighbor didn't confiscate it.

Meg: Why? What neighbor?

Tyler: Some guy out having a smoke break. When I set my ladder up under your balcony to tie the string to the railing, he thought I was trying to break into your apartment. He may have tackled me and elbowed me in the eye.

My building BFF tackled Tyler?

Meg: Are you okay?

Tyler: I don't know. I'll tell you later if it was worth it.

If he saw the smile on my face right now, he'd know it was worth it.

Meg: Here is my peace offering.

I go to my music app and send him the love song playlist he's been asking for.

The one called *Un-frog-ettable Love Songs*.

CHAPTER 22

MEG

t's Friday, and I'm headed to the computer lab to pick up my students. As I round the corner, my body collides with something hard—*something* that smells and looks a lot like Tyler Dixon.

His arms wrap around my waist, keeping me upright, as my hands splay across his chest. I raise my chin. I can feel his minty breath against the tip of my nose and see the patterns of blue in his eyes.

His lips quirk into a smile. "Are you trying to get me to kiss you again?"

One second in Tyler's arms has my stomach swirling—I could mix brownie batter in there if I needed to.

My eyes flit across his face to the blueish-green bruise by his right eye. "You wouldn't dare, because then you'd have to bring me another peace offering and face the neighborhood watch guy in my building again."

Is it just me, or is it ridiculously romantic that Tyler got beat up trying to do something nice for me?

"That's true." His smile deepens, bringing out the trademark dimple—the one I can't resist. "I haven't seen you all week."

"No, you haven't," I whisper.

Is he keeping track of how often we see each other, like I am? I mean, it's not like I have a calendar with tally marks on it for every time that he walks past my classroom window.

That would be weird.

And a little obsessive.

So…forget I mentioned it.

"Thanks again for the cookie."

"Thanks for the playlist."

"You're welcome."

There's no reason for us to be embracing like this. The threat of falling is gone. This isn't a nightclub. We're in the halls of an elementary school, a school where they fire people for getting mixed up with parents.

I clear my throat and push back, releasing myself from his arms. "Uh, I need to get to the computer lab to pick up my class."

"I'm here to check out Krew. He has a dentist appointment."

I point in the direction I was walking. "He's in the computer lab."

"I'll walk with you then."

"Sure." I look around, hoping no one is in the hall, watching our interaction.

"How's the hot man ban going?" he asks. "Do you have another date lined up for this weekend?"

My eyes narrow.

"What? I'm asking as your friend. We're friends, right?"

"I don't have another date lined up. I might take a break from that."

"From banning hot men?"

"No, from dating altogether. I'm probably forcing the issue too much."

"I agree. I don't think you should date anyone else." The look in Tyler's eyes freaks me out, like there's a secret meaning behind what he said—a secret meaning that has to do with the words "anyone else."

"How have you been?" I blurt out, trying to keep myself from analyzing what he said even more than I already am.

"Uh-oh…" He stops midsentence, and his expression twists into confusion. "Is that what I think it is?"

My eyes follow his to the library windows. We have a direct view of a screen with a zoomed-in drawing of the female anatomy, and it dawns on me that today is the Maturation Program for the sixth graders.

"It looks like—"

"Stop!" I say before he can say it out loud. I shield my eyes with my hands like the immature woman that I am. Maybe I should have shielded his?

"Very informative," he says with a thick dose of amusement.

I shake my covered head. "It's the Maturation Program. It's supposed to be informative."

"That makes a lot more sense," he says. "Oh, now there's a drawing of a breast."

"Tyler!" I squeal as I duck down. For some reason the lower position helps ease my mortification. And why are my eyes still shielded? It's not like I've never seen a breast before.

"Hi, Dad!" Krew knocks on the computer lab window right next to us, and it's then that I remove my hands from my face. I stare at my little second grade class inside the computer lab that shares a wall of windows with the library—with a straight view of the screen with pictures. Half of the class is pointing at the drawings, giggling, while the computer teacher has her back to the slideshow as she's helping another child.

"Oh, no!" I rush to the door, hearing Tyler's words behind me.

"Somebody should have thought about the giant windows in the library when choosing a location for the Maturation Program."

"Okay, class." I practically run to the opposite side, the one that *doesn't* face the windows. "Computer time is over."

"Teacher?" One of the boys raises his hand. "My mom says it's bad to look at pictures of boobs."

I catch a glimpse of Tyler in the back, doubled over in laughter. I want to die, or maybe join him laughing.

It's a toss-up.

TYLER

I'M LYING IN BED, trying to finalize purchase orders for the playground project at American Education Academy. Krew's asleep next to me, and in the background, a college football game plays on the TV. I've been staring at the computer screen too long. I lean my head back against the headboard and shut my eyes.

Meg's face is the first thing I see.

One encounter with her today has me wishing for more time to get to know her, but I shouldn't want that. She's the *Titanic* slowly heading toward an iceberg, and the iceberg is me. If we collide, the damage will be done. Her career will sink along with her hopes and dreams.

My phone rings, and I dive forward, trying to get to it before the sound wakes Krew. I don't look at who's calling. There's no time.

"Hello?"

"Mr. Dixon?" a woman says.

My brows furrow. "Yeah."

"I just wanted to apologize for earlier today."

I swing my legs around the side of the mattress and stand, walking to the bathroom so that my voice doesn't wake Krew. "Who is this?"

"Oh...sorry. I thought you had my number." She sounds embarrassed. "This is Meg."

I instantly cringe. "I do have your number. Sorry. I was

rushing to the phone, and you caught me off guard. Plus, you called me *Mr. Dixon*. What's with the formality?"

"I'm formal because Diane thought it would be a good idea if I touched base with all the parents today about the Maturation Program mishap."

I glance at the clock on my bathroom counter. It shows 9:47 p.m. "At this hour on a Friday night?"

"No! I emailed most of them earlier, but since I had your number, I figured I'd give you a call." She stumbles over her words. "Since…you know…you were there."

She called me when she could have easily texted or emailed. A shot of confidence fills me. "Yeah, that makes perfect sense."

"So, I just wanted to apologize and see if Krew's okay."

"He's fine. I mean, he's asking about tampons now, but I'm sure it will pass."

"Oh my gosh! Is he really?"

I laugh. "No, I don't think he saw anything. And if he did, he doesn't seem too worried about it."

"Good." She puffs out an audible breath.

"Have you had a lot of angry parents?"

"A few, but Diane said to refer all the upset parents to her."

I fidget with a tube of toothpaste left out on the bathroom counter. "What else are you up to tonight?" It's a dumb question, but I want to keep the conversation going.

"I've been texting my siblings." She hesitates for a moment. "I guess my dad's been hanging out with stupid Anna Mae every day this week."

I smile. "Stupid Anna Mae?"

"Yeah, that's what I call her in my head. I probably shouldn't have said that out loud."

"I'm glad you did." At least, I'm glad she said it out loud to me. "So, I take it you still aren't warming up to the idea of your dad dating her?"

"It's not that I don't *like* her. I'm sure she's a really nice person. She makes my dad happy, and I'm happy about that."

I close the toilet lid and use it as a chair. "But?"

"But they're moving so fast, and I worry that he's just in love with the *idea* of Anna Mae. The idea that she's my mom. But there's no comparison."

"You don't think he's old enough to decipher whether he likes Anna Mae, or if it's just the fact that she looks like your mom?"

"The early stages of love make people act crazy. They don't think rationally, and they let their heart determine their actions. That's what's happening here. I want to take my dad by the shoulders and shake some sense into him. It's like I'm the parent, and he's the lovesick teenager rushing into a stupid relationship."

"I like that about your dad, how fearless he is when it comes to love. You might say he's rushing it, but I admire how he just jumped right back in after your mom died, like life couldn't get him down."

"You make it sound admirable, but I'm not so sure."

"Your dad is a smart man. He's not going to do anything he's not ready for."

"That's what my sisters say."

"I like your sisters."

"They like you back, but the competition for 'best guest' at game night wasn't tough. It was either you, Nigel, or Anna Mae."

"I think you're underestimating Nigel's likability."

"That's not what you said last week. You said that Nigel is all wrong for me."

"I meant it."

Do I dare say that I think I'm right for her? That she's right for me?

"We always talk about my family," she says. "What about you? Do you have any family nearby?"

She's asking personal questions. That's a good sign, right?

"I only have one sibling. My older brother, Logan, and his

wife, Hillary, live five minutes away. Their son, Boston, is Krew's age. He plays on the baseball team too. And then Logan also has a three-year-old daughter, Madi."

"That's nice that Krew has cousins nearby."

"It really is. Especially since they're his only cousins. Kristen didn't have any siblings. And Logan and Hillary have really helped me out a lot with babysitting the last two years."

"What about your parents? Do they babysit?"

"My mom would if they still lived here, but a couple of years ago, they moved to Georgia for my dad's work. He owns a ladder company."

"I bet you really miss them."

"I miss my mom, but it doesn't matter if my dad lives here or if he lives in Georgia. He doesn't care about me no matter where he's at."

"You guys don't get along?"

"We get along fine. He's just more interested in working than being a father."

"Dad?" Krew pushes the door open. His eyes are droopy, and his hair is askew. "I had a bad dream."

"Oh, I better let you go so you can help him," Meg says.

She must have bat-like hearing.

I close my hand into a fist, frustrated by the interruption. I could talk to Meg all night, but Krew is my number one.

"Yeah, I better go settle him down. It was nice to talk to you."

"Yeah, you too. I liked getting to know you a little better."

The problem is, the more we get to know each other, the harder it's going to be to stay friends.

CHAPTER 23
TYLER

"Tyler, can you pass the salt?" Hillary asks between bites of her food.

It's Saturday night. I invited Logan's family to the local Chili's restaurant with us. Krew came home from school with some coupons so we decided to put them to good use.

"Sure." I reach across the table, handing her the shakers.

"Have you talked to Meg this week?" Logan asks.

"Not since she called me a week ago."

"I don't get it," Logan says as he sips on his Diet Coke. "Aren't you remodeling the grounds at the school?"

"Yeah."

"Then how do you go an entire week without seeing her or talking to her?"

I glance down the table at Krew, making sure he isn't listening, but he's playing tic-tac-toe on his menu with Boston.

"First of all, we're both working when we're at the school, not socializing. And second, with Fall Break, it was a short week. I only had three days when I could've seen her."

Logan picks up his cheeseburger but hesitates before taking a bite. "I forgot about Fall Break. Ours is next week."

"I think you should ask her out," Hillary says.

"It's not that easy. I can't date her because of the whole job thing."

"Is the job thing really *that* big of a deal?" Logan's words are muffled by the food in his mouth. Manners are apparently not his thing. "So what if she gets fired?"

Hillary turns to him. "It would be a big deal to me. I wouldn't want to lose my job over a guy."

"Not even for me?" A piece of lettuce falls out of his mouth, landing on the table.

Hillary grimaces and pushes him away. "I would for you because I know everything worked out between us, but Meg doesn't know that with Tyler."

"Can't you just talk to Diane?" Logan asks. "She's the one responsible for implementing the rule. Maybe if you go to her and explain that you and Meg are the real deal, she'll work with you."

"Yeah," Hillary adds. "They could move Krew to a different class."

"I've thought about talking to Diane. I only hesitate because if she doesn't agree, I don't want to get Meg in trouble. I need to be sure that Meg feels the same way I do before I open that door."

Hillary leans forward. "Show her what's possible between you two. Make her feel confident enough in your relationship to risk her job over you."

"How do I do that without dating?"

"I don't know." She shrugs, taking a bite of her taco.

I don't know either.

I look back at the boys, and my eyes glance out the window to a car that looks a lot like Meg's pulling into a parking stall. I stretch my neck, trying to get a good look at the woman stepping out of the car, walking to the restaurant.

It's definitely Meg.

"Hey! Hey!" I snap in front of Hillary and Logan's faces. "I need you guys to do me a favor." I push my plate away as I watch Meg walk to the *To Go* section of the building.

"What's wrong?" Hillary asks, following my eyes.

"I need you guys to take Krew home with you after dinner."

Logan wipes his mouth with his napkin. "Why? Where are you going?"

I lower my voice like it's a big secret. "Meg's here."

"What do you mean she's here?" Hillary starts, looking around. "I want to see what she looks like."

"You just missed her. She's picking up food, and I'm going to go pretend like I'm picking up an order too." I stand, pushing my chair back.

Logan clearly can't keep up. "But you already have your food."

"I know that, but I'm going to pretend that I just bumped into her picking up my order. You know, what we just talked about—show her what's possible between us. "

"But you don't have an order."

I push my plate in front of Logan. "When the waitress comes, tell her to box this up and bring it to me at the To Go counter."

"Why?"

"Just do it."

Hillary claps. "I love this idea." She spins in her chair, looking for the waitress.

I glance at my reflection in the window, running my fingers through my hair so it doesn't look so flat. "How do I look?"

"You look like a desperate man who's obsessed with a woman that doesn't like him back," Logan says.

"It's undetermined whether or not she likes me back." I give Krew a kiss on the head. "Hey buddy, you're going home with Boston. I'll pick you up later. Okay?"

He pretty much ignores me and continues playing his game. I go out the front door of the restaurant and walk around the building. I can see Hillary and Logan watching me through the windows as I walk.

I should probably be embarrassed, but I'm not.

I swing the door open to the section for takeout. Meg's in front of me in line. She doesn't even glance back.

I clear my throat.

Nothing.

I'm going to have to do one of those weird peek-around things. You know, where you invade someone's space so that you can see their face.

"Meg?" I say in my best surprised voice. "Is that you?"

She turns around, and I can immediately see in her eyes that she is not excited about this encounter. She runs a hand through her hair self-consciously.

"Oh! Hey, Tyler. What are you doing here?"

"Just picking up some takeout. You know, using the coupons the school gave out."

"Same. I'm a sucker for a free entrée." She tugs at the hem of her oversized Whitney Houston t-shirt. "I wasn't planning on seeing anybody. If I had known, I would have gotten dressed."

"I think you look great." And I mean it. It's a whole new side of Meg that I haven't seen before—little to no makeup, hair in a messy bun, oversized sweats. It's literally the best look on a woman, even if no woman ever believes it when a guy says so.

"How's your Fall Break going?" I ask.

"Good. I've just been organizing my apartment, sleeping in, taking it easy. What about you?"

"Krew and I went to the beach yesterday and spent the day there."

"That sounds fun."

"Meg?" A waiter comes out holding a bag.

"That's me." She grabs her food and pays.

Meanwhile, I'm wondering where the heck my food is. I'm going to kill Logan if he doesn't come through for me on this.

"Thank you," she says to the cashier, and then she turns to go.

"Hey." I scratch the back of my head, stepping in front of her.

Why is this so hard? "If you're eating alone and I'm eating alone, we should eat together."

"What about Krew? Is he in the car?"

"No. He's with my brother tonight."

She looks around nervously, and I can see that she's about to tell me no. It's on the tip of her tongue.

"Unless, of course, you were going to eat takeout with someone else," I say. "I don't know if you already had plans."

She shakes her head. "No, it's just me tonight."

"Then there's no sense in us both eating alone."

"Tyler?"

I look up, and Hillary is standing there holding a Styrofoam box with a silly grin on her face.

"That's me."

She wags her eyebrows at me as I grab the food.

Thankfully Meg doesn't notice.

"Are you two together?" Hillary asks, gesturing between us.

She's not my favorite person right now.

"Uh…" Meg looks at me. "We're friends."

Hillary laughs, something way overdone. "You guys would make an adorable couple. You should totally think about dating."

"Thanks," I say, turning to go, but not before I threaten Hillary with my glare.

Meg looks down at the box in my hands. "Don't you need to pay for that?"

"Uh, I already paid online."

"I didn't know they had that option."

"It's new." We walk out the door together into the warm evening air. I shake my box of food out in front of her. "So do you want to eat with me?"

She shifts her weight.

"In a very 'just friends' way," I say, trying to convince her.

"Okay. I guess you can come eat at my apartment. I live right around the corner."

Oh, this is better than I thought. I get to see a peek inside Meg's world. It's like a date, but not. It's the perfect situation.

—

MEG

TYLER DIXON IS in my kitchen, filling up two glasses of water. This is definitely not how I saw the evening going, but it's much better than the night of depression I had planned, watching romance movies and eating ice cream out of the carton.

This dinner is casual.

Accidental.

Incidental.

Coincidental.

Allllll the -*dentals*. It wasn't premeditated at all.

Though it occurs to me that you can still be put in jail for murder, even if it was committed with one of the -*dentals*. I push the silly train of thought from my mind and sit down. No one is going to jail.

I open up my Styrofoam container, and the smell of steak quesadillas drifts up to my nose. "What did you get?" I lean over as Tyler opens up his box. There's a half-eaten baked potato and a half-eaten steak.

I gasp. "Somebody ate yours!"

"What?" He looks down. "No, they didn't. It looks fine to me." He moves the box so I can't see it.

"Tyler." I grab the lid, flipping it back open. "Look at your potato. It totally has a bite taken out of it. We should call the restaurant and complain." I stand up and grab my cell phone. "You should get a refund. That's ridiculous."

"It's fine how it is. I can eat it like this." He holds his hand out to me like he's begging for my phone. "You don't need to call the restaurant."

I search their website and begin dialing the number. "It's ringing."

Tyler reaches for my phone again. "Meg, stop!"

"What? You can't eat it like that."

I watch him as he closes his eyes and takes in a breath.

"I have a confession to make." He rubs his hands over his face. As they come down, his expression twists into something pained. "I was inside the restaurant eating dinner with my family when you pulled up. I saw you get out of your car and come in to pick up your order."

I push the red *end* button and slowly lower my phone.

"I had them package up my food so that I could come talk to you."

"Wait. What?"

He straightens. "What part didn't you understand?"

"I think I understood it all. I'm just processing it." My forehead creases. "So *you* were the one who took a bite out of your food?"

"That's correct."

"And then you had them put it in a to-go container so it looked like we just randomly bumped into each other?"

"Yeah."

I start laughing.

"Are you laughing because you're freaked out or because you think I'm the smartest man ever?"

"I don't know, but I don't think I've ever had anyone go to so much effort to have dinner with me."

"So you're flattered?"

"More like surprised."

"Surprised with a little bit of flattery?"

I shake my head. "No."

Actually, yes.

I'm totally flattered.

"What's worse? Me eating food that you thought somebody else already ate, or me staging this whole thing?"

"I'm not sure."

"Now that you know my secret, can I warm up my food? I ordered it like two hours ago." He stands and goes to the microwave.

I cover my mouth, trying to suppress a giggle. This moment is *so* Tyler. He's charming the heck out of me, and I'm falling for it, dropping *hard*.

"What did your family think when you got up from dinner and left?"

"They pretty much thought I was crazy."

"Who was there? Your brother and his wife?"

"Yeah. Actually, you met Hillary."

"I did?"

"She was the one who brought the food to me at the restaurant. I think she wanted to get a glimpse of you."

"Of me? Why?"

Tyler retrieves his food from the microwave and returns to the chair across from me. "Probably because I talk about you a lot."

Tyler *talks* about me? Why does that knowledge make me want to scream into my pillow like a teenager?

"Anyway, sorry she was hinting about us being a couple. After I leave here, I've already decided I'm going to cut out her tongue."

"She was hinting pretty hard, but cutting out her tongue seems a little harsh."

"Probably. Especially since she's babysitting Krew now. I feel kind of bad that I left him so suddenly."

"Dads need breaks too."

"When it comes to parenting, I don't always get what I need, and if I do, I immediately feel guilty. Like I'm not doing enough."

I lean back into the chair and consider him. If there was ever a dad that didn't deserve to feel guilty about his parenting, it's Tyler.

He pauses, his fork midair, obviously wondering why I'm looking at him. "What?"

"You're a good dad, Tyler."

His brows rise in surprise. "You think I'm a good dad?"

"I've taught a lot of kids in the last four years, but none of them have talked about their dads the way Krew talks about you. I can tell you put the time into parenting, and he adores you for it."

The smallest hint of emotion glosses over his eyes, and I'm stunned. In the three years I dated Zak, I never saw him cry, not even at my darkest moment when my mother died. But I tell Tyler Dixon that he's a good dad, and I've touched the center of his heart.

"I don't feel like a good dad. I'm constantly doing things wrong, giving in when I should hold my ground, holding my ground when I shouldn't be too hard on him. I'm literally doing everything wrong."

"Who says?"

A light laugh escapes him. "I don't know. The dad inside my head."

"I think the dad inside your head is being too hard on *you*."

"Maybe, but it's been a rough eighteen months. I've messed up so many things. Most of the time we're barely surviving. That's not a great way for a kid to grow up."

"Children are really forgiving. Krew will look back on this time and appreciate everything you sacrificed for him."

"I hope so." He swipes at the moisture threatening to spill over the side of his eyelid, then clears his throat. "Sorry. That's embarrassing. Pretend you didn't see that."

The problem is that I *did* see it, and it completely melted my heart.

I smile back at him. "You know, my dad cries."

Tyler scratches the top of his head. "I'm not crying. My food is spicy."

"Your baked potato is spicy?"

"Fine." He slides away his food container. "I cry. I'm a crier."

It's humorous that Tyler thinks his sensitive side is a strike against him, because if anything, it makes me want to push the food off the table in front of us and tackle him like I'm a linebacker for the Tampa Bay Buccaneers.

"There's another embarrassing secret about me you discovered. Anything else you want to ask me? Like whether or not I pee in the shower?"

I suppress my smile, trying to keep a straight face. "I think we should hold off on that question for a little while longer."

"Probably a good idea."

"But I would like to know how you and Kristen met." She's the last piece of family in Tyler's life that I need to know about.

His smile widens, and a sliver of jealousy breaks loose inside me.

How can I be jealous of a woman that's no longer living? I'm a terrible person.

"We met in college. I went with some friends to her apartment after one of my baseball games, and we talked the entire night about sports. Teams we loved, teams we hated. Kristen was big into all of that. Everything came easy with her. After that night we spent every waking moment together, and by the next weekend, we were boyfriend and girlfriend. That was thirteen years ago, and I haven't been with another woman since."

Tyler's eyes glow as he talks, and I decide that I'm not jealous of Kristen. I'm jealous of the look in his eyes when he talks *about* Kristen. What if Tyler, or any man for that matter, never looks like that when he talks about me? I don't know anything about sports. If I did, would he like me more? Or would something like that just make him sad, reminding him of Kristen all the time, like Anna Mae reminds me of my mom?

I don't know.

I can't think about it right now.

It's too complicated to sort through and I don't have to figure it out tonight.

TYLER

I'M GLAD THAT INSERTING myself into Meg's night with a half-eaten baked potato isn't our first official date, but I do like how things are going. We're getting to the deeper stuff. She's opened up to me before about her mom, and I've told her about my dad, but tonight feels different. I mean, I teared up in front of her.

Practically *cried.*

It's like I've unlocked the next level or entered the final round of a game neither of us knows how to play.

I wish we were playing Go Fish. I could destroy her at Go Fish.

At least I've finally gotten my foot in the door—literally. I'm walking around her apartment, peeling back another layer to her.

"I like seeing you in your space," I say, surveying the shelves on the wall near the couch. "You have it decorated cute for Halloween. That comes from your mom, right?"

"Yeah. How did you know?"

"You told me in your backyard when we were on the swing."

Her lips lift. "That right. I like decorating for the holidays, like she did. I know I'm the only one who lives here, but I still like to have it festive." She points to a pumpkin on the top shelf. "A lot of these decorations were my mom's."

"That's really cool. It's a great way to keep her memory alive."

"I think so too."

"How are things going with Anna Mae? Have you seen her again?"

"Nope. It's like my dad has completely forgotten about our family, especially my mom, and replaced us with this new woman. He spends all his time with her."

Not *all* of Paul's time is spent with Anna Mae. I'm thrown in there too, sometimes, when we meet up at the cemetery.

"I feel bad for Anna Mae. I really do," Meg says quietly.

"Why?"

"Because one day she's going to wake up and realize that my dad is just using her to replace my mom so he's not so lonely. It's not fair to either of them. Poor Anna Mae will always be second in comparison to my mother. In my eyes, and eventually in my dad's eyes too."

It's not my place to tell Meg if she's right or wrong. Her feelings are real. It's a tough situation that I hope will get better over time.

I reach for a picture on the top shelf. "Is this you and your mom?"

"That was Mother's Day two years ago. I bought her a plant and tickets to see a play."

I know what Marilyn Johnson looks like—her picture is on her headstone. But seeing Meg standing next to her with her arm around her makes things more real. "You look a lot like her."

"Not really. I have my dad's light coloring."

"But you have your mom's smile."

"You think?" Meg takes the picture from me and studies it, tracing the curves of her mother's face. "It's a good picture of us." She goes on her toes, trying to put the picture on the top shelf, but she's struggling. The frame teeters on the edge, threatening to fall.

"Let me help." I step toward her, reaching up. My arm lightly touches hers, and my fingers skim over the top of her hand. A surge of chills travels from where our hands meet down to my toes. Blue eyes peek up at me, and suddenly we're locked in this position—stopped in time. My heartbeat drums louder inside my ears, and my eyes fix on Meg's gorgeous face.

Then they drop to her lips.

I want to kiss her again. I want to feel the same explosion of feeling when our lips touch.

It's a euphoria that can't be replicated any other way.

Her tongue swipes over the tip of her mouth—*slightly*. She knows a kiss is on the table, and she's not pulling away.

But I can't kiss Meg. I can't kiss her when I know she's worried about losing her job. I've already done that, and I felt awful about it.

I have to leave.

I push the frame the rest of the way onto the shelf and drop my arm. "I better go pick up Krew from my brother's house."

Meg tucks her hair behind her ear. "Yeah, of course."

Is she disappointed? She seems disappointed. Maybe I should scoop her up in my arms, dip her back, and kiss her like she's never been kissed before.

It's tempting.

So very tempting.

I shake my head and turn to the door. "Thank you for letting me crash your take-out dinner."

"I'm just glad you were the only person who had taken a bite out of your food."

"Me too."

I force myself to open the door.

I'm doing what Hillary says. I want her to feel confident about me so she's okay risking her job.

I just hope that confidence builds sooner rather than later.

CHAPTER 24

MEG

'm watching my window from my classroom, waiting for
the moment when it looks like Tyler is loading up, getting
ready to leave the school for the weekend. When that
happens, I'll head to my car so we can leave at the same time. I
know it's stupid, but I don't know what else to do. I haven't
talked to him all week.

I've seen him. He's been at the school, working on the playground remodel. My classroom window has a straight shot of his
work space, and no matter how much I try, I can't seem to look
away. But I haven't talked to him at all; even if he only says
"Have a good weekend, Miss Johnson," my effort will be
worth it.

We went from our almost kiss in my apartment last weekend
to...nothing.

Well, not *nothing*.

Tyler's been *doing* things. He's been bringing me drinks
during school and leaving them on my desk. I know it's him.
I've asked Charlene and Jen, and they aren't doing it, so that
only leaves him. Somehow he managed to figure out what my
favorite drink is—diet Mountain Dew.

Then there's my car. Each day after school there's a treat on the hood of my car. No one else's car has a treat. Just mine. Yesterday, it was another delicious chocolate chip cookie.

It's the little things.

And the little things are starting to add up in a big way.

I can't stop thinking about him. I know it's wrong, but I can't help it or hide it. It's like I have to know if this feeling between us could be something more, something worth risking my job over.

Tyler carries a stack of shovels to the back of his truck. I look at the clock; it's five o'clock. He's calling it a day. I grab my purse and turn out the lights, shutting my classroom door behind me.

TYLER

I THROW SOME TOOLS in the metal box in the back of my truck as I finish cleaning up the construction site for the weekend. I'm moving slowly, trying to time my exit with Meg's. Her car is still in the parking lot, so I know she's at the school.

I have a plan.

When Meg walks to her car, I'll strike up a conversation with her, and then I'll ask her what she's doing this weekend. Hopefully one thing will lead to another, and we'll end up hanging out. The details of the plan are unclear, but I'm sure I can improvise.

"Dad!" Krew points to the side. "There's Mrs. Johnson."

He's sitting on the back of my truck bed, playing with some Legos. I told him to alert me the second he sees her.

It's showtime.

"Hey, Miss Johnson," I say, meeting her at her car. "Are you leaving for the day?"

"I am." She swings her keys around her finger. "What about you?"

"Yeah, I just got done. Do you have any big plans this weekend?"

She shakes her head. "Not really. You?"

"Krew and I have a frozen pizza we're going to cook tonight." I would ask her if she wants to join us, but I can't. I can't break the rules, and inviting Meg over to my house is definitely crossing some line.

"Fun." She stands there for a minute like she's waiting for me to say something else, but I have nothing else to say. I'm terrible at making things up as I go.

She presses the button on the car's remote, causing the lights to blink. "Well, I hope you guys have a fabulous weekend." She opens her car door and throws her stuff inside before sitting down.

I'm running out of time, so I do the only thing I can think of. I place my hands on the top of her door and lean over the side of it casually.

It's now or never.

"Are you—"

"Oh, no!" Her shoulders fall.

My throat closes around the rest of the words I was about to say. A man only has so much confidence.

She looks up at me. "My car battery is dead."

I tilt my head, looking down to where her finger is over the ignition. "Are you sure?"

"Yeah, it won't turn on."

"I can give you a jump if you'd like."

"That would be great, but I don't have any cables. I lent them to Brooke."

"I have some in my truck," I say, already turning to get them.

Randomly coming up with plans isn't working, and if I jump her car right now, she'll just leave. I rummage through my tool box, debating my options. Call it desperation if you want, but I decide to do something drastic. I bury the cables in the bottom of my tool chest and slam the lid shut.

"Oh, man. I forgot," I say, holding up my hands. "I left my jumper cables at home."

Meg looks around the parking lot. There are only two other cars left, and one is Diane's. "I guess I can go back inside and get someone else to help me."

I point behind me to my truck. "Or we could go back to my house and grab them. I live close by."

"I'd hate to inconvenience you," she says, shaking her head.

"It's no problem at all." The plan has changed. This is me improvising. "In fact, you could eat some of the cheap frozen pizza I bought."

"Yeah!" Krew says. "And we have some sugar cookies."

"You guys don't want me ruining your Friday night."

"Please. Please, come to our house." Krew looks at me. "Please, Dad. Can she come?"

"It's fine with me if she's okay with it." I feel like begging just as much as Krew is, but I don't. I play it cool. I play it cool in the most manipulating way possible. "Once dinner is over, we can grab the jumper cables and I can bring you back to your car. Then we don't have to bother Diane or anyone else."

"Okay." Her pink lips press into a smile. "I can have some pizza and cookies."

"Great." She gave in way faster than I expected.

I escort Meg to the passenger side and open the door. Krew climbs in the car first, scrambling over the seat. My eyes meet Meg's as she scoots herself inside. I don't hold her gaze, because I'm afraid she'll change her mind. Instead, I slam her door and walk around the car. I use this time to pump myself up. I could really use some AC/DC right now, but my own pep talk is going to have to do.

You've got this.

A woman hasn't been to my house in over a year.

I...don't got this.

I have to pull myself together.

Make a move tonight.

What move? I don't have any moves. This isn't 1988. Meg isn't going to slide over to the middle of the truck so I can put my arm around her as I drive. Besides, just because she's coming over doesn't mean the whole job issue has gone away.

I suck in a deep breath before climbing in my side of the truck.

"I think we're ready to head out."

"Are you sure this isn't a problem? I can call my dad to come pick me up if it is."

"I'm already out. It's no trouble at all."

"Okay."

"Dad?" Krew asks from the back seat. "Can I keep playing on your iPad?"

"Just for the car ride. When we get home you'll need to take a break from screens." I turn the stereo up as I pull out of the parking lot. Meg's love songs fill the car.

"Is this my playlist?"

"Of course."

She shakes her head. "You don't really listen to it, do you?"

"Yeah, I do."

"No, you don't. You're lying."

I begin singing the song playing. Something about getting lost in your eyes.

"Debbie Gibson? You know the words to *Lost in Your Eyes*, by Debbie Gibson?"

"When you sent me the playlist, did you think I wasn't going to listen to it?"

"I assumed you wouldn't."

I turn my head back to the road. "I know every song."

"No, you don't." I can hear the disbelief in her voice.

"Try me." I smirk.

She switches the song to the next.

"*Almost Paradise*," I say flatly.

She switches it again.

"Madonna, *Crazy for You*." I flip my head to her. "I already knew that song before your playlist."

"That's an easy one." She hits the button, changing the music again.

Instrumental music plays before the words start. "*Take My Breath Away*." My lips curve upward as I eye her. "This song's kind of hot."

Meg's hands cover her face like she's embarrassed.

"What? Haven't you seen *Top Gun*?"

"I can't even talk about this with you." She's bright red now, and it's pretty darn cute.

"You can't talk about how hot this song is, or how I've memorized all the songs on your playlist?"

She shakes her head. "Both."

"He listens to these songs all the time," Krew says from the back seat. "Why don't you believe him?"

I point behind me. "The child never lies."

"Okay, so you listen to my songs. Whatever." She's biting back her smile.

Man, if I could get a hold of those lips, I would.

"Let's change the subject," she says, turning to look out the window.

"Fine. We can change the subject." I laugh, watching as she continues to hide her face from me. Embarrassed Meg is my new favorite. "What were you doing at the school so late?"

"I had a lot to get done, and…" She plays with the bracelets on her wrist. "I was avoiding going home to my empty apartment."

"Well, you're not alone anymore. I've got a very cheap frozen pizza we can bake—"

"And don't forget the sugar cookies," she adds. "That's literally the only reason I agreed to come to your house."

"I hope it's not the *only* reason."

I point to the white two-story in front of us as I pull into the driveway. "This is it." I open the garage and see a pile of Krew's baseball stuff on the ground, and suddenly I'm worried. What did I leave out this morning? Are there dirty dishes on the table? Piles of shoes by the door? Wet towels on the floor of the bathroom? Right about now, I wish I had cleaned up a little last night instead of watching TV.

I'm planning on Meg being here a lot longer than ten minutes.

MEG

WHEN I'M WITH TYLER, I want more. I want to throw caution to the wind and see where this fantasy life takes me. And basically that's what I'm doing right now. Being here is like reading one of those *peek-inside* books. I'm lifting the flap, seeing what life with Tyler would be like. And from what I've seen, this peek inside is pretty great.

We go through the garage door into a laundry room. Stacks of clothes are on the ground, and there are little green rings of laundry detergent on the counter from where Tyler keeps setting the cup.

It's cute, picturing him doing laundry. It's actually more than cute. It's the sexiest thing I can even imagine. I'm seeing Tyler in a whole new way. Most women like men who race motorcycles and pump serious amounts of weights, but not me. I like good, old-fashioned dads. And seeing this dad in his domain might just push me over the edge.

"Sorry," he says, kicking a shoe out of the way. "We're kind of a mess."

I smile as I pass him by, making my way into the kitchen. There are white cabinets and white counters and a big window that looks into the backyard. Dishes are piled up in the sink, but other than that, the space is pretty clean.

"It's not that messy."

"It could be better."

Krew drops his backpack and runs to me, grabbing my hand. "Come on, Mrs. Johnson. I want to show you my room and then the rest of the house."

Tyler gives a nervous laugh. "Krew, I'm sure Miss Johnson doesn't want a tour."

I glance at him over my shoulder. "I absolutely want a tour."

Tyler follows behind us with hands in his pockets. He looks scared, as if at any moment I might see a dirty pair of underwear.

Krew weaves his way through the entire house, dragging me behind him; he saves the family room for the last stop.

"And this is where we watch TV," he says.

I look around and notice one of my signs hanging above a bookshelf—the one that says "Family. A little bit of crazy, a little bit of loud, and a whole lot of love."

I turn to Tyler. "Where did you get this?"

He walks up next to me, brushing his shoulder against mine. "This?" He gives me a playful smile. "I've had this forever."

I shake my head. "No, you haven't. This is a new design."

"Dad, we hung that up before Fall Break. Remember?"

I love how Krew always calls him out.

"What can I say? I'm a little obsessed." He raises his brows as he walks toward the kitchen. "With Etsy, of course. Nothing else."

I stare at my sign in Tyler's house. My shop is for digital downloads, so it's not like I "fulfill" orders. I never read through the names of people who order things, so this is a big surprise to me.

I stand there for another second, looking around. It's cozy here, everything that I've ever wanted. A family, a house that's more like a home with pictures stuck to the refrigerator and fingerprints on the glass doors. For a second, I let myself picture what it would be like if I slipped into the vacant role of mother and wife.

It would be amazing.

I would be happy.

"Mrs. Johnson." Krew smiles up at me. "I'm going to build you a Lego tower in my room."

"That sounds awesome."

I watch him run off as I walk to the kitchen.

"The pizza's in the oven," Tyler says as he pulls out three plates from the cupboard.

"I'm starving." I lean against the kitchen island. "Krew's building me a Lego tower in his room."

"I don't know who's happier you're here, me or him."

"You're happy I'm here?"

He takes a step closer, placing his hand against the counter next to mine. "I'd be lying if I said I wasn't."

"I'm happy I'm here, too."

I shouldn't have said that, but I can't help it. Part of me wants this to be my life.

His arm brushes against mine, and all I see are his tight muscles peeking out of his sleeve.

"Miss Johnson, are you checking out my arm?" There's a flirtatious undercurrent to his voice that has my entire body humming.

"Maybe."

He flexes in a dramatic way, drawing out my laugh.

"You know, your arms are one of the first things I noticed about you." I bump my hip into his.

"Really? I'd tell you the first thing I noticed about you, but I don't want to embarrass you." His smile turns wicked.

"Tyler Dixon," I scold.

"*Kneecaps,*" he says. "You have excellent kneecaps."

I laugh. "That was a stupid night." I shake my head as I think back to how ridiculous I was.

"I'm sorry I pushed you away...you know, when you were trying to make Zak jealous."

"I know why you did."

"I just hadn't been around another woman yet. It was all new." He lifts his hand and slowly runs his fingers down a piece of my hair. It's all I can do not to close my eyes and lean into him.

His voice is low and rough. "If you tried something like that again, I would react differently."

The edge of his pinky brushes the side of my hand, causing a shiver to spread up my arm.

I swallow. "I probably won't try something like that again."

His lips lift as the space between us disappears. His cheek skims against mine. "What if I try it? Would it be okay?"

Oh. My. Goodness.

This flirty Tyler is almost more than I can handle. I should probably put a stop to it, tell him to take me home, but that's the last thing I want him to do. His blue eyes drop to my lips, and suddenly all I want is for him to kiss me. I need to know what it feels like to be kissed by a man like Tyler Dixon. A man who is thoughtful, kind, and incredibly sexy.

Would his kiss be tender?

Or would it be more like the rugged version of him?

"It would be okay," I whisper, lifting my chin.

His fingers go to my cheek. The heat of our breaths mingle together, and my heart hammers against my chest. I close my eyes as his head dips down.

BEEP!

The sound of the oven makes me jump, and the moment is ruined.

Tyler rubs the back of his neck, chuckling to himself. "I've always hated that buzzer."

I laugh, trying to hide my disappointment. "I guess dinner's ready," I say. But my mind immediately wonders how I can recreate that moment and that almost-kiss again.

CHAPTER 25

TYLER

"It's still a little light outside." I peek out the window. "Maybe we should turn on a movie."

I half expect Meg to demand that I take her home, but then she plops down on the couch. "Dinner and a movie? This is the most exciting Friday night I've had in a long time."

Krew runs in the room dressed in his baseball pajamas and steals the seat next to Meg. I love that he loves her, but right now, I wish he were asleep. Maybe if I turn on a really boring movie he'll fall asleep, and then Meg and I can have some alone time.

"Let's watch *The Sandlot*," Krew says.

"I was thinking we should do the Planet Earth documentary."

"No!" he groans. "That's boring."

That's exactly the point.

"I've never seen *The Sandlot*. What's it about?"

Krew jumps on the couch, landing on his knees. "Baseball!"

"Baseball!" She snuggles him in close. "We better watch it, since you love baseball so much." She tickles his side, and Krew squirms in her arms.

My eyes tear up.

We've already established I'm a crying man, but seeing Meg

with Krew fills me with happiness. There's never been anything more attractive than a woman loving on my son. I'm a complete goner now. Even if I wanted to stop my feelings for her from growing stronger, I couldn't.

I should probably warn her, tell her I'm absolutely falling in love with her, and there's nothing I can do about it.

She smiles up at me, completely unaware that I'm crazy for her.

"*Sandlot* it is," I say.

I turn the lights off and take the last seat on the couch—the one next to Krew. He leans against Meg, and there goes another corner of my heart. By the end of the night, she will have filled every hole that was left when Kristen died.

I want to look over at Meg every time she laughs during the movie, or glance and see where her hand is so that maybe I can hold it, but I'm currently being barricaded from her by a seven-year-old.

"Who wants popcorn?" I hop up, needing to work off the tension that's building inside me.

"I do!" Krew says.

"Coming right up." I walk into the kitchen and throw a bag of popcorn into the microwave. I stand there for a few seconds, watching it spin around as my mind skips to Meg and the moment before dinner when we almost kissed.

Does everything have to be so difficult? Couldn't we have just kissed? I push both hands through my hair and then bang my forehead against the microwave several times until the popcorn's done. Then I return back to the couch with one bowl.

One bowl.

All hands will be in that one bowl. I hope Meg's not a germa-phobe, but I'm a man trying desperately to break down the physical barrier between myself and a beautiful woman. One popcorn bowl is currently my best friend.

Krew sits up and holds the bowl between us. I act like I'm watching the movie, but really I'm timing when Meg's fingers reach for the popcorn. It takes me a few tries, but I manage to reach for the popcorn at the same time as her. Our fingers tangle together in the middle, and she glances over at me. I turn my head, meeting her stare. The side of her face is lit up from the light of the television, and her lips slip into a smile.

She's perfect.

"Dad, move your hand. I can't get any popcorn."

Leave it to Krew to ruin the moment.

Meg laughs as she scoops up a handful.

Okay, this is getting ridiculous. I can't hold hands inside a popcorn bowl. So I adjust my position, swinging my arm around Krew so that my fingers end right at Meg's shoulder. I hope I look a little better than every movie where the guy yawns as he puts his arm around a girl. And really, my arm isn't even around her. It's around Krew, but I can make this shoulder thing work.

My fingers move slightly.

Then I wait.

They move again—not a lot, but enough for her to know I'm there.

Meg shifts her position, putting her shoulder closer to me.

That's all the cue I need.

I begin rubbing her shoulder, tracing small circles over the edges. It's not a lot, but it's enough to send my heart beating out of my chest. I don't know how long we sit like that with me rubbing her shoulder, but the attraction between us builds more and more with each second.

At least for me.

I find the edge of her shirt collar and slip my fingers under the fabric, tracing over the side of her collarbone. Her skin is warm against my touch, burning the tips of my fingers with each brush of my hand. We play the game all over again, me drawing a circle pattern over her shoulder, but this time under her shirt.

My fingers run into her bra strap, and I swallow. It's been a long time since I've dealt with a bra strap. I'm not complaining. Just making a mental announcement.

We've touched a bra strap, people. Stay calm.

"Dad, I'm thirsty."

"Of course you are." It's as if an alarm went off in his little brain that I had entered bra strap territory.

"I'll get him a drink," Meg says. She stands and heads toward the kitchen before I can even protest.

I look down at Krew, rubbing the top of his hair. "You don't make things easy for your dad, do you, buddy?"

He laughs and snuggles into my side.

It's a good thing I love him.

MEG

I OPEN THE REFRIGERATOR door and the freezer and lean my body inside as far as it will go. I need something to help me cool down, because right now I'm feeling all sorts of hot.

Tyler stroking my shoulder might just be the biggest turn on I've ever experienced. You'd think I wouldn't feel this way with a seven-year-old sitting next to me, but you'd be surprised. I close my eyes, breathing in three more cool breaths.

A drink. Focus on the drink.

"Meg?"

My eyes open, and I slowly turn around. Tyler is walking toward me. His face is lit from the light of the refrigerator, and his gaze looks as hungry as I feel. Not *hungry* hungry. No, we already ate pizza, cookies, and popcorn.

I'm talking about the type of hunger that comes from burning attraction.

I look into his eyes, wondering if he's going to say something else—something like "I want you" or "Kiss me now."

I don't know, I'm just spitballing here.

Instead of speaking my cheesy thoughts, Tyler closes the gap between us in silence. He stops right in front of me, his eyes searching mine. He's a lit match, and I'm a dry field. I know the second he touches me, my resolve will go up in flames, but I don't even care.

His body presses against mine, and his hands go to the sides of my face. My eyes close as his lips come down on mine, soft and scorching—a mixture of tender *and* rugged. My breath catches for the first few skims, and then finally my lungs fill up again. I breathe against the soft tug of his lips and wrap my arms around his waist. His fingers slip into my hair as his kiss intensifies.

My, oh, my.

I'm here to confirm that *Lord of Darkness* is the correct nickname for Tyler Dixon.

I'm pressed against the open refrigerator, the coolness competing with the heat of his kiss. My hands roam up and down his back as his fingers brush through my hair. We pull each other closer and stumble a bit, banging back into the refrigerator shelf, causing glass bottles to clang together. Our lips part, and we both smile, but then the intensity begins again.

This is my first refrigerator kiss. Everyone should try it. There's something so romantic about the soft, glowing light spilling over you and the coolness of the air. His strong hands press against my neck, tilting me toward him even more. Everything is more passionate and—

"Dad?"

We jump apart, banging against the shelves again.

"What are you doing?" Krew asks.

Luckily, he couldn't see *what* we were doing, because both doors to the refrigerator are open, hiding us from his view.

Tyler pops his head around the freezer door. "I was just helping Miss Johnson find the chocolate milk."

I straighten my shirt and smooth my hair, stepping aside from Tyler. "Oh, there it is." I point to the refrigerator door. "I don't know how I missed it."

"I'm tired," Krew says, rubbing his eyes.

"Let's get you to bed, buddy." Tyler scoops him up in his arms, and Krew rests his head on his shoulder. "Say goodnight to Miss Johnson."

"Night, Mrs. Johnson." Krew gives me a small wave as they walk out.

I shove the doors shut and exhale.

My fingers trace my lips.

How am I ever going to recover from *that*?

TYLER

I CLOSE KREW'S DOOR and pause, listening for a second to make sure he stays in bed. He seems to be asleep, so I make my way back down to Meg, keeping my pace casual, nothing *too* eager, even though my body is screaming at me to *run* down the stairs.

I lean against the banister, studying her. She's sitting on the couch, watching the end of *The Sandlot*.

She's completely stolen my heart. I'll never be the same again.

Meg's eyes glance up to mine. "Is he asleep?"

"I think so."

She smiles at me, and I'm so scared I'm going to lose her.

"Are you freaked out?"

Her brows go up. "That we kissed?"

I nod.

"Should I be freaked out?"

"No."

"Then I'm not."

"Can I kiss you again?" I don't know why I feel the need to ask, especially since we've already broken that rule.

"Now?"

I push off the banister and walk to her.

"You want to kiss me on the couch?" she asks.

"It's better than inside the refrigerator, don't you think?"

She smiles. "That's debatable."

Her eyes watch me as I sink down beside her. I take the bowl of popcorn in her lap and set it on the coffee table in front of us.

"What are you doing?"

"Removing all the obstacles, so I have optimal access." I lean in, kissing the sides of her cheek and jaw. Her arms wrap around my body, and her head dips back. My lips trail down her skin.

"Do you always use words like 'optimal' when you're making out?" she laughs.

"Are we making out?" I ask between my kisses.

"We're not playing Pass the Apple."

"Are you sure? It felt a lot like this."

I hear the soft whispers of her laughter, and suddenly I have to kiss her. My lips move to her mouth, and I don't even bother taking my time with this kiss. I have to have her. I'm like a teenager on prom night. I'm running to first base, planning to round it, but all I can see in my mind is my first base coach throwing up both hands in a dramatic *stop* signal.

It's hard. I was married for ten years. Ten years where I could round whatever base I wanted. Ten years where I never had to stop midpassion.

But stopping is exactly what I have to do.

I pull back, shaking my head. "Meg, I *really* like kissing you, but I'm going to stop."

Her extremely kissable lips twitch. "That's probably a good idea."

"I just thought you should know that I could kiss you all night, and even though I want to, I'm going to stop because…" I groan, raking my hands through my hair. "Because I'm an idiot who apparently has boundaries."

"I feel the same way."

"Great." I release a dramatic breath. "No more kissing?"

"No more kissing."

I raise a brow. "At least for tonight."

She laughs, and I grab her hand, playing with the tips of her fingers.

"I really like you," I say.

"I really like you too. But I also like my job, and I don't want to lose it. Especially when…" Her eyes drop.

"When there's no guarantee that things will work out between us?"

Her blue eyes pull to mine. "Exactly."

My hands lock with hers. "I can't promise anything, but I feel like we have a lot of potential, and it would kill me if we didn't try."

"But if we try, I'll get fired."

"What if we talk to Diane together? We could explain that we'd like to date each other."

Meg straightens and shakes her head. "No. She wouldn't understand. I'd be fired if she knew we kissed or that we want to date. She can't know anything about what's happened between us."

"What if we dated for a while and didn't tell her or anyone about it? See where this leads before we mess everything up with your job."

"So you want to sneak around?"

"That's not how I would word it."

"But that's what you're suggesting."

"I'm suggesting we give *us* a chance."

Meg looks to the side, like she's thinking over my words. I don't want to pressure her, but I really want this.

Her head flips to me. "Nobody would know?"

"I won't tell anyone if you don't."

"What about Krew? Won't he be suspicious?"

"He's seven," I say flatly. "I'm sure we can figure something out to tell him."

"We'd have to be careful."

"I can be careful."

"Okay." She smiles. "Let's date in secret."

This feels big.

"I feel like we should kiss again. You know, to solidify things."

Meg shakes her head. "You said no more kissing tonight."

"Fine." I pull her to me. Her head rests on my chest, and we finish out the last few minutes of the movie, cuddling each other. Until this moment, I haven't realized how much I've missed being close to a woman, feeling the weight of a body against mine.

I was empty, but now I'm filled again.

She's not Kristen—but she's not better or worse than Kristen, either. Just different, new, and exactly what I've been longing for. Meg and I bounce off each other differently. I'm not the same guy I was before Kristen died. I've changed. In a good way—in a way that I hope Kristen would be proud of. I've lost my favorite person in the entire world, dealt with the heartache that comes with that, and built myself back up again. And Meg fits together with this new version of me.

"That was cute," she says as the movie ends. "It makes me want to watch more baseball."

"I'm never going to say no to that." I pick up the remote and turn the TV to ESPN, looking for a baseball game, but there's only football highlights from the last week. There's a clip of the winning team throwing a Gatorade cooler over their coach.

"Why do they do that?" she asks. "Doesn't the coach hate getting wet?"

"Probably, but he's also really happy he won."

They show another clip of the coach raising his hand in the air, celebrating his victory with his team, and then the screen flashes to his family celebrating up in the stands.

"His wife looks happy they won, too."

"There are two kinds of coaches," I say. "The ones that celebrate immediately after their wins, and the ones that find their wives in the stands first."

"That's really cute."

I hug her closer, loving the feel of her in between my arms. "Meg?"

"Hmm?" She tilts her head up so I can see her blue eyes.

"Can we pretend that I don't have any jumper cables? Or pretend that I can't leave Krew all alone to drive you to your car? Can you just stay here tonight with me? On the couch like this? I swear we won't do anything but sleep."

I feel so vulnerable, but I don't want her to leave. I want to stretch this moment out for the rest of my life.

Her head nods against my chest. "Yeah, we can do that."

I move our bodies so that we're laying down. Her head rests on my chest. My arms wrap around her body as our feet tangle together at the bottom of the couch. We drift off to sleep, cuddled up in the soft light of the TV as a couple who dates...*in secret*.

CHAPTER 26

TYLER

've never hated my job as much as I do this morning when I get a text that a rock wall on one of my other job sites collapsed. Leaving the arms of a beautiful woman like Meg to go do damage control on a Saturday morning is frustrating. Normally I would wake Krew up and take him with me to work, but today I leave him in bed sleeping, because Meg is there—a definite reminder that parenting is much easier when there are two people sharing the responsibilities.

I pull my truck into the garage at 8:45am. That has to be some kind of record. I'm hesitant about what I'll find inside. I left a note letting Meg know where I was, but I'm worried she'll be upset. Actually, I'm really worried she regrets everything that passed between us last night.

I don't regret it.

It's been coming for a long time, on my side.

But Meg's different. She's the one putting her job on the line to be with me. I'm risk free in this situation. Except for my heart.

I hear the music from the kitchen even before I open the door.

Baby Shark.

That's a song Krew would be annoyed about if I turned it on, but with Meg, he's apparently more lenient.

They're both *doo-doo*ing at the top of their lungs when I open the door. I set my keys down and kick off my shoes, tiptoeing to the edge of the laundry room.

I'm not prepared for what I find in the kitchen. Krew sits on the counter next to Meg as she flips pancakes. They're both dancing and singing.

It's the sweetest thing I've seen in a long time.

My hand goes to my chest, and my eyes well up.

Part of me is instantly sad that Kristen isn't here, that she'll never have a moment like this with Krew again. But the other part of me is filled with an overwhelming sense of gratitude for Meg, that Krew gets to dance and sing in the kitchen with *someone*.

This feels like it could be the opening scene to the rest of our life.

I stand there watching them as the song plays out until Krew notices me.

"Dad! Mrs. Johnson is spelling my name with the pancakes!"

I push off the doorframe and walk to them as Meg turns the speaker down.

"It smells good in here."

My eyes catch hers, and I wonder if things are going to be awkward. I want to come up behind her as she cooks and wrap my arms around her waist. That's what I *want* to do, but this is new territory. Dating with a seven-year-old is so different than anything I've ever done, especially since we're doing it in secret.

"We thought you might be hungry after work," she says. Her smile is timid, but it's there. I'm going to take that as a good sign.

I mess up Krew's hair and turn to Meg.

Do I give her a kiss on the cheek?

Pat her head?

What's protocol here?

She's at my house in the morning, making pancakes with my son. She stayed over last night. Although everything about the sleepover was completely innocent, it still happened.

My expression must give me away, because she holds her hand up, motioning for a high five.

A high five?

I raise my brows as my hand hits against hers. "Miss Johnson, good morning."

"Good morning."

Krew grins between us. "I can't wait to tell the class that Mrs. Johnson had a sleepover at my house."

We both let out a nervous laugh. "Actually, bud, we probably shouldn't tell anyone."

His brows dip down. "Why?"

Why?

Crap. This is one of those parenting moments where I wish I could poll the audience, see how everyone else thinks I should respond.

"Remember how I told the class about privacy?" Meg says. "And how every teacher has her school life and her outside-of-school life?"

Krew nods.

"Well, this is my outside-of-school life. I don't talk about my outside-of-school life because I like having some privacy."

Good answer.

I don't need to poll the audience after all.

Meg is like Kristen. She's got it all figured out.

"And I only slept over because my car was broken," she adds. "I don't want other kids in the class to think that they can invite me for sleepovers. If they did, I would have to say no, and then they would feel bad."

"Okay. Can I have some chocolate milk?"

I sigh, grateful that Krew's attention span is practically nonexistent. I lift him off the counter and throw him over my shoulder, tickling his side. "You want chocolate milk?"

"Yes," he squeals.

"Say the magic word." I tickle him harder.

"Dad's the best." His body twists in my arms. "Dad's the best!"

MEG

NORMAL MEG would have the worst-case scenario dialed up right now.

1. My car battery will never charge again, and I will be carless forever.
2. I'm going to start getting sleepover invitations from every child in my class.
3. Krew will tell Diane Carter that I slept over at his house, and that I'm dating his dad, and she'll fire me on the spot.

Okay, so I do have the worst-case scenarios dialed up, but right now, at this moment, I don't care what the consequences are. Everything seems so natural with Tyler and Krew. We're cleaning up the dishes, listening to silly music.

It's exactly what a Saturday morning in my dreams looks like.

And if I'm honest with myself, it was nice sleeping in Tyler's arms last night. For so long with Zak, I didn't feel adored or cherished. He didn't care if I was there beside him or not. But with Tyler, I feel like his lifeline—like he depends on me to breathe.

"Krew," he says, whipping him softly with a dish towel. "Go get dressed so that we can take Miss Johnson back to her car."

Krew runs out of the room, and we both listen as he stomps up the stairs.

Tyler's blue eyes pierce into mine, a look that shakes me up inside. "Finally alone."

"It looks like it."

He throws his rag down and walks toward where I'm leaning against the kitchen island. I'm a ball of nerves...or butterflies. They kind of feel the same.

His fingers smooth the top of my hair, trailing down to the ends. I love it when he does that.

"You look beautiful in the morning."

My breath teeters as his hands land on my waist.

"I don't actually look like this. I freshened up before you came home."

"Yeah, you do." He presses a small kiss to my cheek, then to the edge of my jaw. I tilt my neck, hoping his kisses continue their path.

"I watched you sleep for a moment before I left." He quickly pulls back and looks at me. "In a noncreepy way. I watched you sleep in a *noncreepy* way."

"I'm totally freaked out right now," I tease.

"We can't have that." The corner of his mouth creases into a smile, causing his dimple to appear. He continues kissing the side of my neck—softly, sweetly. His lips skim across my skin as they make their way to my mouth. The kisses are slow and intentional, nothing like last night. He's taking his time, exploring my mouth and the explosion of feelings surging between us. My hands travel up to his neck, tickling the base where his hair curls up. The neck tickling is all it takes to deepen the kiss. As things progress, Tyler lifts me up onto the counter, which is unexpected and exciting. I wrap my legs around his waist. We're lost in the moment for a few hot seconds until we hear the stomping sound of Krew coming down the stairs.

Tyler backs off, and I slide off of the counter.

What is it with us and kitchens? We cannot be trusted in this room.

"I'm ready!" Krew announces as he hops around the corner.

I cover my mouth like I need to hide the evidence of our kiss. "I'll just go grab all of my stuff."

Twenty minutes later, we're at the school parking lot with both car engines running.

"Thanks for jumping my battery."

"It was no problem." His fingers reach for mine as he glances back at Krew in his truck. "I want to kiss you, but—"

"I get it."

"I'm not sure I'll see you again this weekend, but can I call you sometime...preferably when he's asleep?"

I smile. "I'd like that."

I sink down into my car, and Tyler pushes the door shut.

For the first time in my life, I'm grateful for car trouble and everything it led to.

Meg: I need to tell you guys something.

I PACE back and forth at the foot of the bed, waiting for one of my siblings to respond.

Matt: Then tell us.

Brooke: I think she's trying to leave us in suspense.

Tessa: Let me guess. You finally kissed Tyler again.

My steps pause. I hate it when Tessa is right.

Meg: Yes, we kissed again, but that isn't what I need to tell you. We're dating...in secret. No one is supposed to know or else I will get fired, so you can't tell anyone.

Brooke: If no one is supposed to know, why are you telling us?

Tessa: Because she feels guilty.

Matt: Look at Meg breaking the rules. I need to meet this guy.

Meg: Am I a terrible person?

Tessa: Yes.

Brooke: No.

Matt: Maybe.

I can always count on my siblings to make me feel better...or worse.

Brooke: So is the whole dead wife thing weird for you?

Meg: No. Why would it be weird for me?

My mind flashes back to the glimpses of Kristen in Tyler's house—her clothes in his closet, a pair of her shoes in the cubby by the laundry room, pictures in frames—but I quickly push those reminders out of my thoughts.

Tessa: I just hope you know what you're doing. This seems like a tricky situation for someone like you.

Someone like me?
Why do I feel like I should be taking offense to that?

Meg: Me dating Tyler is only a tricky situation if my boss finds out.

Tessa: Okay!

I throw my phone on my bed. I don't know what Tessa's trying to prove. This is fine. Everything will be fine.

CHAPTER 27

TYLER

"I think I'm going to tell Anna Mae I love her," Paul says. I was happy to see him here next to Marilyn's grave when I pulled up to the cemetery this afternoon.

"Wow. Telling her you love her. That's big." I open my baseball glove, catching the ball Krew throws at me. "Don't drop your elbow," I correct, then turn to Paul as I throw the ball back.

"It is big, but when you know, you know."

I nod, waiting for Krew to throw the ball back. I'm happy for Paul, but I know this new development in his relationship with Anna Mae is going to kill Meg. "How do your daughters feel about it?"

"Tessa and Brooke seem to be doing okay. They're always asking about her and giving me dating advice."

"And Meg?"

Paul draws in a deep breath. "She's not as enthusiastic. She thinks I'm replacing her mom, and she's not happy about it."

That's the feeling I'm getting from her too.

"She doesn't understand that a man can love two women."

I understand him completely. I love two women. I'm here at Kristen's grave. I miss her all the time. Whenever Krew says something cute or passes off a new milestone, my heart breaks because she isn't here to share it with me. I love Kristen.

But I also love Meg. It's a different kind of love. It's new and fragile, and it's the kind of thing that makes my heart beat out of control while also driving me crazy at the same time. I'm constantly thinking about her, wondering when I'm going to see her next or what she'll say when she texts me.

In a way, both loves are painful.

They both break my heart and make me feel uncomfortable, but I wouldn't trade the feelings for anything.

"I just wish Meg could see that me loving Anna Mae doesn't take away from anything I had with her mom. I'm not replacing Marilyn. I'm adding Anna Mae to my life. There's a big difference."

I wonder what Meg thinks about Kristen. We've never talked about her in that way. So she must be fine about everything.

"Paul, you're a good guy," I say, swiping him on the shoulder with my mitt. "I hope everything works out for you and Anna Mae."

"And what about you?"

"What about me?" I throw the ball back to Krew. It hits the edge of his glove and rolls back behind him.

"What about you and that woman you're interested in? Last we talked, you said you ate takeout at her house."

I nod. "Things have progressed a little bit."

"How?"

I told Meg that I wouldn't tell anyone about us dating, but Paul's her dad. If I'm going to tell anyone, he seems as safe a bet as any—as long as I don't tell him I'm talking about his daughter.

"We kissed Friday night." I eye him. "*Several* times."

"Giddy up!" Paul chuckles.

Giddy up?

That isn't the response I'm expecting, but I guess it works.

"So now what?" he asks.

I catch Krew's ball and throw it back. "Now, I guess we're dating, but we're not telling anyone. So don't say anything to Krew."

"You're not telling anyone?"

"Yeah, it's something with her work. She could get in trouble if people find out."

Paul's expression goes serious. "I hope you know what you're doing."

"What do you mean?"

"Just be careful with her. Situations like this can be dangerous, and I don't want to see either one of you getting hurt."

It's as if Paul is warning me as a father—as *Meg's* father? And suddenly I feel like Tessa must have told him about our kiss in his kitchen at game night.

He knows.

"I really care about her," I say. "And I promise I'll be careful."

Paul places a hand on my shoulder. "I know you will."

CHAPTER 28
MEG

My class quietly works on their writing assignment about Halloween traditions while I sit at my desk uploading grades into my laptop.

There's a commotion outside at the construction site, and I look up. Water is shooting everywhere. They must have hit a pipe. Tyler scrambles to his knees by the sprinkler box, using a tool to turn off the main water line. A steady spray of water drenches him until the spray loses its momentum and peters out. He stands, shaking off his hands, and then, before I know what's happening, he's taking off his wet shirt.

Good grief.

I glance at my students, making sure none of them are watching me watch Tyler and his bare chest. When it looks safe, my eyes dart back. Part of me feels like Chevy Chase in *Christmas Vacation*, pressed against the window and drooling. There's no dad bod here, unless dad bods come with six packs. No, Tyler's been hiding a lot of muscles and manliness under his shirt.

This isn't the first time I've seen an attractive man's chest. One Christmas, Tessa gave me a calendar full of men with their shirts off. There was a good-looking chest for every season. But this is the first time that seeing a man without his shirt on has accelerated my heartbeat just by *looking*.

Tyler wrings out his shirt, causing his biceps to ripple with each twist. Then he shakes it out as he examines the pipe with one of his workers. This is the gift that keeps on giving—a visual that I will likely never get out of my head. Throw that shirtless man inside a backhoe, and the picture would be complete. I watch every second as he puts the t-shirt back on, trying to memorize the way each of his muscles move.

"Teacher?"

I jump in my seat and clear my throat.

"Yes?"

Silvee points up to the clock. "Isn't it time for us to leave for lunch?"

It's 12:02. We usually leave for lunch at noon. "Yes!" I stand. "Yes, it is. I don't know how I got so distracted."

That's a lie.

I know exactly how I got distracted.

"Mrs. Johnson?"

"Yes, Silvee?"

"My mom says you love Krew's dad."

I see Monette Peterson is keeping the rumors from the field trip alive and well.

"Does she?"

I want to say something like "Tell your mom to go wax her gossiping upper lip," but I don't.

"Tell your mother that she's been misinformed."

"What's misinformed?" Silvee asks.

"Never mind."

It's after school, and I'm in the teachers' lounge gathering my mail. Why do they always give the shortest teachers the boxes way up high? I go to my tiptoes, straining to see inside my teacher's box.

"Hello, Meg." Diane Carter drums her perfectly manicured nails on the counter next to me.

My chest instantly constricts. I'm the person with a secret. A *big* secret.

"Hi, Diane."

"I haven't seen you all day."

Oh? That's because I'm avoiding you.

"I've just been in my classroom."

"How was your weekend? Did you do anything fun?"

I kissed Tyler in your daughter's kitchen, cuddled with him on her couch, and made pancakes with your grandson.

"This weekend?" I shake my head. "It was good. Nothing too crazy."

It's official. I'm a liar.

"That's nice."

Part of me wants to break down and tell her the truth about me and Tyler and beg her to let us date in public, but the other part of me is mad. It's stupid that I can't date him. I know I signed the contract, but Tyler and I are nothing like the teacher and parent a few years ago. He isn't trading *favors* for grades. We have real feelings for each other, and I hate that if I told Diane the truth, our relationship would be compared to the other people who ruined it for everyone.

And truthfully, if I tell Diane that I'm dating Tyler, she would compare me to Kristen.

So it's settled. I'm not telling her. I can look Diane Carter in the eye with a clean conscience. I may be sneaking around, but I have a good reason for it. We're talking about the potential happiness of the rest of my life.

I might feel justified in my reasoning, but that doesn't mean I want to hang around and talk to Diane. I reach the stuff in my box and pull out the papers. "I'll see you tomorrow," I say, then I walk out of the room.

When I get to my classroom, I begin wiping the board down, prepping it with tomorrow's bell work.

"Teacher? Can I get some one-on-one time?"

Tyler's leaning against the doorframe. His shirt is dry now, but I can still remember how it looked wet and stretched across his chest.

I glance behind him. "Where's Krew?"

"He's doing a puzzle in Diane's office."

My heart pounds. "And where does Diane think you are?"

"Outside working."

I drag him inside my classroom and shut the door. I'm not taking my chances with anyone on the staff walking by and seeing us together.

"Is this my one-on-one time?" he says with a playful grin as I pull him away from the door. "This is better than I imagined."

"I think Diane suspects something. She cornered me in the teachers' lounge a few minutes ago."

He inches his way closer to me. "She doesn't suspect anything. How could she?"

I take a step back in an effort to keep a respectable distance between us. "I don't know. Maybe Krew told her something."

"This is the first time he's seen her all day."

"Or maybe it was one of the parents in my class. There are a lot of rumors flying around about us."

"Those are just rumors, Meg. No one knows the truth."

There goes another step. Is his stride bigger than mine? It must be, because he seems to be closing the gap faster than I can get away.

"Are you sure?"

"I'm sure." Tyler's right by me now. I can smell the woodsy scent of his cologne and feel the heat from his body. His cheek skims across the side of my face, and his warm breath tickles my ear.

"What are you doing?" I swallow.

"What I've been thinking about doing ever since you drove off on Saturday."

The easy thing to do would be to pull his mouth down to mine.

That's the easy thing.

But we can do hard things, so I keep my hands to myself.

"Tyler, we need rules when we're at school."

My words are stopped by Tyler's finger against my mouth. "No more rules."

His finger slowly brushes over my lips before his hand drops. His blue eyes jump behind me to the window. He's likely putting two and two together, realizing that the angle of my desk provides a perfect view of him working every day. His eyes fill with pleasure, and he grins.

"That's a great view you have out your window."

"Is it? I hadn't noticed."

He steps away from me, walking closer to the glass. "Well, you really missed out. There was one guy that got drenched with water today."

"Really?" I raise a shoulder, doing my best to keep my expression masked.

"Yeah, he was so wet, he took off his shirt for a little bit. Right there." He points outside to the spot in front of my window where the sprinkler box is still open. "If he'd known he had an audience, he might have kept it on." His smile turns smug. "Or maybe left it off all afternoon."

My face is even.

My expression is blank.

But there is nothing I can do about the slow pink blush that's currently creeping up my neck, flaming onto my cheeks.

A blush?

Really?

I might as well be in seventh grade.

I clear my throat. "So back to the rules. At school, I think we need to implement no talking, no touching, and no kissing. Too many people could walk in on us."

He turns around, nodding. "That's a lot of rules."

"Necessary rules."

He walks toward me, bending down, whispering in my ear. "Fine, I'll follow your rules. Because I like you, Meg. I *really* like you."

I close my eyes and raise my shoulder, fighting off the chills covering my neck and ear. I can't even think straight enough to form a sentence.

His lips brush the side of my neck slightly. "I better go before we get caught. See you later, Miss Johnson." His smile is so smug and so handsome as he walks out of my room, I'm going to need to chew on some ice to cool myself down.

Sneaking around with Tyler is like riding on a roller coaster that's missing a giant chunk of track. I'm having fun, but in the back of my mind, I know it's dangerous.

I know there is a big chance that I'll get hurt.

CHAPTER 29
TYLER

"Trick or Treat!" Krew yells when Diane opens the door. He holds out his plastic pumpkin for some candy.

"Krew, weren't you a pirate at school today?" Diane asks as she looks him over. "Why did you change your costume?"

"Pirates are stupid. I wanted to be a ninja." He pushes past Diane and runs into her house.

"I don't know." I shrug. "Someone at school must have made fun of his pirate costume, because he came home demanding that I take him to the store before trick-or-treating so he could be something different."

Diane frowns. "And you gave in?"

Well, obviously. He's a ninja now, not a pirate.

"Was I not supposed to?"

"Tyler, you can't let Krew walk all over you. There have to be boundaries in your parenting, or else he'll grow up thinking he can get whatever he wants. This is not how Kristen would've raised him." She shakes her head as she walks into the house, leaving me on the porch. "You need to do better."

I shut the door behind me. "Kristen *isn't* here, so how she would've raised him doesn't apply."

I immediately regret my words. I don't really mean them, but sometimes I get sick of Diane's comments about my parenting.

She turns over her shoulder, and I can see the tears already starting to form in her eyes. "What Kristen wanted for Krew *always* applies."

My head drops, and my hands go to my hips. "Sorry. I shouldn't have said that. I didn't mean it. It's just...I'm doing the best I can raising him alone."

She turns her head and begins walking again. "Let's forget this conversation ever happened. Krew!" she calls. "Come stand out on the patio so I can get a picture of you in your costume."

I let out a deep breath, following after her.

"Are you still planning on coming for dinner this Sunday?"

It's amazing how Diane can push her hurt aside and pretend like everything is okay.

"Yeah, we'll be here."

Krew poses for the camera in his best fighting positions.

"I got some good ones." Diane looks at her phone then back up at me. "Where are you taking him trick-or-treating?"

"We're going with Logan's kids."

"I don't love where your brother lives. Make sure you go through all of his candy when you get home before he eats anything. And only let him have three pieces tonight."

Three pieces?

It's a little too late for that. Krew already ate an entire bag of candy before we came.

"Dad, can we go to Mrs. Johnson's house to trick-or-treat?"

Diane flips her head to me. Her eyes narrow, and although I'm not scared of her, my heart suddenly starts beating hard.

"Uh...students don't trick-or-treat at their teacher's houses." Her glare still hangs with me. "And we don't even know where Mrs. Johnson lives."

"Yeah, we do."

Crap. Why did I say that?

"Remember, we took her that cookie?"

Diane flashes a stiff smile at Krew. "What cookie?"

His little shoulders rise. "I don't know. My dad did it. He tied a string to the cookie box and hung it from her railing so she'd find it."

I scratch the side of my face. "It was no big deal. Teacher appreciation stuff."

"That seems like a lot of effort to let a teacher know you appreciate them. Next time, why don't you just send an email?"

"Email. That's a great idea. I'll do that next time." I clap. "Krew, it's time to head out trick-or-treating."

Before he says something else he's not supposed to.

As we leave Diane's house, I'm wondering if I need to tell Meg about this interaction. I don't want to scare her, so I decide to keep it to myself.

It's not like Diane has any *proof* that we're dating.

It's all just hearsay from a seven-year-old.

⊂⊃

MEG

"DAD, YOU'RE ALMOST out of candy," Brooke says as she walks back into the family room. "I left the bowl out on the porch because I'm sick of answering the door."

My sisters and I came to my dad's house to eat chili, play games, and get sick off of way too much chocolate. It's our Halloween tradition, and I'm glad it's continuing even though my mom isn't here.

"When we run out, we run out," my dad says.

Tessa hands the dice to Brooke. "It's your turn."

Brooke plops down on the couch. "I really need a Yahtzee here if I'm going to stand a chance at all."

My dad's phone rings, and he fumbles with it before reading the caller ID. "Oh, it's Anna Mae." His entire face brightens as he stands. "Hey, pretty lady," he says, answering the call, and I do my best not to throw up in my mouth. "You were right about the candy. I'm going to run out."

I roll my eyes. "Dad, it's your turn."

He dismisses my words with a wave of his hand. "Play without me." Then he exits the room.

So much for our family tradition. Usually, my dad would never miss a single second of playing games with his daughters, but Anna Mae is changing things. And the more she changes things, the more I lose my mom. If this keeps up, my mom will be completely wiped out of my family, and I can't let that happen. I'm my mother's advocate. I have to keep her memory alive, even if that means standing my ground with Anna Mae.

"He is so smitten," Tessa says.

Brooke nods. "Right, like a teenager in love for the first time."

"You guys, this is what I've been saying for the last two months. His behavior isn't normal or healthy."

"I think it's cute." Tessa leans forward and opens a KitKat bar. "He's so happy."

"Aren't you guys worried that he's moving too fast and that he only likes Anna Mae because she looks like Mom? Or that he's using her to replace Mom?"

Both sisters shake their heads.

Tessa shrugs. "He seems to really love her."

He told Anna Mae as much, earlier this week, but I don't buy it.

I lean back into the recliner, folding my arms over my chest. "Well, I'm not calling her Mom or going out on lunch dates with her. Just because dad loves her doesn't mean I have to."

Brooke tilts her head. "None of us *like* this situation. We all wish Mom were still here, but she's not. Anna Mae makes Dad happy. Don't you think you're being a little hard on him?"

"No."

"So why is it okay for Tyler Dixon to date and move on with his life, but it's not okay for Dad to?"

I should've never told my sisters that Tyler and I are dating.

Big mistake.

But I've never been good at keeping secrets from my family.

"That's a completely different situation," I defend.

"How so?"

"For starters, Tyler's wife has been dead longer."

Tessa raises her brows. "I didn't realize there was a time constraint on when widows can date."

"There isn't, but the person should at least be done grieving their wife."

Brooke looks at me. "Is a person really ever *done* grieving?"

"No, but you know what I mean. Tyler is ready to move on, and I don't look like his wife. I'm not trying to replace her. I know I'll never be as amazing as she was."

"That's true." Tessa nods. "Short of growing a third boob, you're never going to be as impressive as her."

Brooke spits out her drink, laughing. "Three boobs is *not* impressive."

Tessa's mouth lifts into a sly smile. "It could be."

"Oh my gosh. Would you two stop?" I say, rubbing my temples. "I need to get this visual out of my head."

Brooke wipes the spray from her laughter off the coffee table. "All I'm saying is, go easy on Dad. His situation might not be that far off from yours."

I bend my knees, curling my legs under me.

Our situations aren't the same.

There's no comparison.

CHAPTER 30
MEG

The day after Halloween is always a nightmare for teachers. Parents load their kids up with fifty pounds of sugar and then send them to school during their detox. But luckily today is Friday, and I only have to deal with my sugar-hyped students for a few more hours.

Earlier this week my class earned an extra recess for good behavior, and since the kids need to run off some extra energy, I decide to give them their reward. The sun is shining down on me as I walk around the section of the playground that currently isn't torn up for the remodel.

I feel a tap on my arm. "Mrs. Johnson?" Krew, Zander, and Noah are standing beside me with Tyler not far behind them. Ugh! He looks good in his fitted charcoal shirt and jeans, his hair coming out the sides of his backward hat. I know it's pretty much the same look every day, but Tyler never ceases to take my breath away. That song really is telling the truth.

Krew steps forward. "Will you come to our baseball tournament tomorrow?"

All four boys look up at me with classic puppy dog eyes.

I already know about the Turkey Trot tournament Krew's

team is in this weekend. Tyler told me about it on the phone a few days ago.

"Please, can you come?" Zander says. "You went to Jane's piano recital and Ruby's tumbling class. Can't you come to our game?"

It's true. I do try to catch one event from each child during the year. If there are three boys from my class on the Stealers, then I should probably try to go. And it doesn't hurt that Tyler will be there as the coach.

"Sure. I can come to your game."

"Yay!" the boys cheer together.

"My dad will tell you where it's at."

The boys begin a game of basketball, leaving us alone for a minute.

I smile at Tyler. "Did you just get your son and his friends to ask me out on a date?"

"It worked, didn't it?" He smirks. "I'll know in the morning whether or not we're in the championship. I'll pick you up."

"I don't think—"

He holds his hand up. "Before you say no, I think you should know that Diane won't be at the baseball game. She has a nail appointment tomorrow. So that might be another reason why you want to come in my car."

That is good information to have.

"Sounds like a date."

"Dad, come play basketball with us."

Tyler turns to the group of boys. "I'll only play if Miss Johnson plays."

I shake my head. "You don't want me to play. I'm not very good at basketball."

"My dad's really good."

Tyler flashes me a self-assured smile.

"Shouldn't your dad be working?"

"It's my lunch break."

"How convenient."

"Mrs. Johnson, you can be on our team. It's all of us versus my dad."

"Okay, why not?"

The boys pass the ball around the painted square. They throw up a few shots, missing most of them. Tyler does a good job of acting like he's trying to defend them, but that they're too good for him. Then Krew throws the ball to me. Tyler shuffles to guard me and I turn my back to him, bouncing the ball. His body presses against my back, and his arms swipe for the ball. He's all over me, bumping into me with his back, reaching into my space.

I'm not going to lie. I'm enjoying it.

"That's a foul!" I call out playfully.

"What? Can't you handle it?"

"You're not supposed to touch me. Remember the rules?" I pick up the ball and run closer to the basket, trying to get away from him.

"Travel!" he says, following after me.

"What? Can't you handle it?"

"Now look who's cocky."

He reaches for the ball, but I pick it up, holding it away from him. His hand wraps around my arm and the other pulls on my waist, trying to move me closer to him. We're not even playing basketball anymore. We're playing some flirty keep-away game where it seems like the goal is to get your body as close to the other person as you can, and I'm here for it. I break free from Tyler's grasp and run to the basket, but both his hands close around my waist, pulling my back into him.

"Miss Johnson." His words are breathy on my neck. "I don't think you understand the rules of basketball."

I turn my head so my lips are by his cheek. "I think you have a fouling problem."

He smiles, and I can't help it…my eyes drop to his lips.

A voice clears behind us. "Tyler, can I speak with you for a moment? That is, if you're not too busy."

My eyes skip to Diane Carter, and I wiggle out of Tyler's grasp as fast as I can.

One brow raises. "The playground equipment we wanted is on backorder."

"Sure." Tyler says. "I was just playing basketball with Krew and his friends."

"You weren't playing basketball with us," Krew groans. "You were only playing with Mrs. Johnson. You guys ruined the game."

I glance around. All the boys are standing there watching us.

"Yeah, Mrs. Johnson is a ball hog," Noah says.

"Miss Johnson, might I ask who is watching your students right now?"

"I am." I shift my weight.

"We don't want one of the kids to get hurt on the playground because we were being negligent."

"Meg wasn't being negligent," Tyler says.

Oh, but I was.

The basketball game was dumb of me.

So very dumb.

AFTER SCHOOL, I open up an urgent email from Diane addressed to all of the employees.

Dear faculty and staff,

As you may know, the playground is being remodeled, and we have a crew of workers here at all times, trying to meet the pressing deadline. Please don't socialize at recess with any of the workers, as we don't want them to be distracted while they work. Remind your students to follow these same guidelines.

Sincerely,

Principal Carter

Dang.

That email is about me, and everyone at the school probably knows it. I sit back in my chair and purse my lips. Then I shove my laptop away before closing it with a firm thud, pushing Diane's words out of my mind.

CHAPTER 31
MEG

L et me tell you about third base coaches.

They're extremely attractive.

I scrunch my nose as I look at the field next to ours. Okay, maybe not all third base coaches are what dreams are made of. But Tyler Dixon, coaching third base—I'm a fan.

He's got on a pair of black shorts with a Stealers t-shirt, a matching black baseball cap, and sunglasses. He looks athletic and sexy. And every once in a while, a foul ball gets hit over to his side, and he fields it with his *bare* hands.

It's a turn on.

Majorly.

He also has this coaching swag about him that I'm definitely liking. It's a little bit of cockiness mixed with confidence, and it's to die for—like, sign me up to be the team's water girl, because I need to cool myself down.

But let's move on from how good Tyler looks and talk about how sweet he is with the boys on his team. He doesn't take the game too seriously. He's relaxed and has the kids laughing and having fun while they play, which is so endearing.

I assumed I would be sitting on the bleachers, but no. Tyler brought me my own chair. He also came prepared with snacks for me—sunflower seeds, popcorn, and water. He packed a cooler, like an actual cooler full of stuff. It's adorable and just another thing to add to the growing list of things I like about him.

And despite my lack of knowledge about baseball, I'm having a great time. It's the championship between the Stealers and the Hitmen. We're winning six to five, but the Hitmen have last ups.

"Look out!" Tyler says as he throws a baseball at me in between innings.

I flinch as the ball hits the chain link backstop and falls to the dirt. "I thought I was dead," I say, clenching my chest.

"Sorry." He leans against the fence, looping his fingers through the metal. "I just wanted to make sure you're paying attention."

"Are you kidding? I'm sitting on the edge of my seat during every pitch."

He raises his brows. "Look who's invested."

"I'm totally invested."

"I'm totally invested, too." His eyes go serious, making my heart pound. And suddenly, we're no longer talking about baseball. "You look cute over here on the side. So cute it's kind of distracting."

I roll my eyes. "Yeah, right."

"I'm serious. If we lose this game, I'm blaming it all on you."

"You better not lose this game."

"Don't worry, we'll be fine." He kicks the fence in front of me as he walks off.

I lean into my chair, biting back my smile. I like him a lot. I shouldn't be liking him *this* much, but lately I've been spending all my time thinking about a future with him. What if there was a way to be with Tyler openly and keep my job? Like a secret door #3 that I didn't know about?

I'd really like to find that door.

A chair plops down next to mine. "Meg? I'm Hillary, Logan's wife."

"Right. I recognize you from the restaurant."

I suddenly feel nervous. Tyler has very little family, and I'm meeting one of them for the first time. What if Hillary doesn't like me? She was probably best friends with Kristen and hates the fact that I'm here.

She points to the catcher. "My son, Boston, is on the team, and Logan helps coach when he can."

"That's great."

"I saw you came with Tyler."

How much should I say? Does Hillary know the truth about us?

"Yeah, he was nice enough to give me a ride."

Her head turns in the direction of the dugout where the coaches are sitting on buckets. "Tyler's a little broken and rough, but I promise he's a good guy."

My eyes flicker to him.

Broken?

"He just loved Kristen so much. We all did. When she died so suddenly, it tore our whole world apart."

I know how he feels. That's how I felt when I lost my mom.

"Be careful with him," she says. "I don't want to see his heart broken."

Again, I know how he feels.

I also don't want a broken heart.

I glance at Tyler. "I won't hurt him."

TYLER

"Dude," Wayne says. "I'm living vicariously through you. You brought your hot teacher girlfriend to the game today."

I turn to my friend. "I'm starting to feel worried for Nikki over how much you envy me dating again."

"Pfft. Nikki and I are fine. I'm just saying you've got it good. I hope you're enjoying it."

Logan hits Wayne on the shoulder. "He may have it good now, but his wife died. Show some sensitivity."

My head tilts to Wayne. "True. My wife did die."

Wayne kicks the bucket of balls. "I don't know why you guys are trying to make me feel bad when all I was saying is that I'm happy for you, Tyler."

"Thanks, man. I'm happy too."

How could I not be?

Meg brought me back to life.

"Now are we going to win this game, or what?" Wayne claps.

"We're going to win."

MEG

WE'RE DOWN TO the final out of the game. Krew's on the mound pitching, and the bases are loaded. From what I understand, if the Hitmen get a hit—which is literally their name—they'll win the game. I'm so nervous I can't sit still. I don't know how moms do this all the time. At this point, the game probably means more to me than it does to the kids.

Tyler asks for a time-out from the umpire and walks to the pitching mound. He bends down, hands on his knees, and says something to Krew that makes him laugh. They both turn their heads and look at me with huge smiles on their faces. I have the feeling that whatever Tyler said had nothing to do with baseball and everything to do with me. He taps the tip of Krew's hat and walks back to the dugout.

Krew throws the first pitch.

Ball one.

Ball two.

I cup my hands around my mouth. "Let's go, Krew! You've got this."

Strike one.

Strike two.

Ball three.

It's a full count, and I'm dying. Krew lifts his knee. His body lunges forward, and he releases the last pitch. The batter hits the ball, a grounder to the second baseman. I hold my breath in anticipation as Zander scoops up the ball and tosses it to Noah at first base. The umpire calls the runner out…

And the Stealers win.

Everyone is cheering. Heck, I'm standing, jumping up and down with Hillary like a maniac. I don't even recognize myself right now. The entire team rushes to the mound where Krew is, and I'm so happy I actually have tears in my eyes.

Then Tyler looks at me.

Me.

His lips move into a huge smile, and he pumps his fist. I give him a thumbs up. There's probably something cooler than two thumbs up, but I'm new at this.

He said there were two types of coaches, and the fact that he looked at me before celebrating tells me a lot. He joins his team on the field, lifting Krew onto his shoulder.

And that's the moment I become addicted to Little League Baseball.

⊏▭⊐

THE BOYS ARE HUDDLED up after the game, listening to Tyler while all the parents wait patiently to take them home.

"Ms. Johnson," Beverly Ulrich says. She's dressed in black yoga pants, a black sports bra, and a pink athletic jacket. The front zipper of her jacket is zipped to just below her chest, leaving a perfect view of her perky cleavage. "I had no clue you'd be at the game today."

"Noah and the boys asked if I would come and watch," I explain. "I like to go to as many events of my students' as I can."

"That's nice of you."

"I didn't see you during the game," I say. "Were you sitting in the outfield?"

She points to the bleachers. "No. I was actually sitting behind you."

I panic.

My mind races through the entire game, to every moment when Tyler smiled at me, or he came over between innings and talked to me. If Bev is looking for things to gossip about, I gave her plenty to work with.

"And did I see you climb out of Tyler's car?"

Oh, no.

"Krew begged me to ride with them, and it's kind of a hard field to find."

It would be a good excuse if we didn't live in a day and age where there's something called Google Maps, but since we do, I'm sure Bev knows I'm lying.

"I see." Her lips slip into a tight smile. "I've been waiting patiently for Tyler to be ready to date after his wife's passing. I was worried that you jumped in there before me."

Is beautiful Bev jealous of *me*? I get a lot of satisfaction from the possibility.

The possessive side of me wants to tell her that Tyler and I are in a relationship, but I can't. I can't risk it just because *I'm* jealous of her and her assets that always seem to be on display.

"No, there's nothing going on between Tyler and me. We're just friends."

"Good." Her stiff face relaxes. "Well, thank you for supporting the boys."

I nod politely as she walks off.

I was convincing, right?

There's no need to worry about my job security.

CHAPTER 32

MEG

"Dad, can we stop and get ice cream?" Krew asks on our way home from the game.

Tyler glances at him in the rearview mirror. "Are you the champion?"

"Yes."

"Did you get the game ball?"

"Yes." He holds it up.

"Then I think you deserve ice cream."

"Yay!"

Tyler looks at me. "You like ice cream, don't you?"

"Ben and Jerry are basically my best friends."

"Good." His fingers shift, brushing against mine—*barely*—spreading heat through my body.

This is torture.

I want to hold Tyler's hand more than anything, but Krew would see it if we did.

We pull into a mom-and-pop restaurant and park. I try to hang back, letting them walk ahead in case we see someone we know from our school. I'm probably crazy for agreeing to go out in public with Tyler. I deserve to bring up the rear.

He pauses and looks back at me. "What are you doing?"

"Nothing."

He shakes his head then grabs my hand—*my hand!*—and pulls me toward him. He doesn't let go immediately, and I'm distracted by how well our hands fit together. It's dumb. Everyone's hands *fit* together, but for some reason, Tyler's hand feels like it was made for mine.

Four seconds.

He holds my hand for maybe *four* seconds. It doesn't seem like a lot, but you "one Mississippi" that, and you'll be surprised.

"What do you want to order?"

"Oh, I'll pay for myself."

"Meg, stop being stupid. I'm paying for you."

"In that case…" I look at the cashier. "I'll take a large cookie dough shake."

Tyler seems amused. "Do you think you insulted me by ordering the large?"

"Maybe."

"I'll take an *extra* large cookie dough shake."

The cashier's expression falls. "Sir, we don't have *extra* larges."

"Oh. Then I'll have the same as her."

I cover my mouth with my hand, holding in my laugh.

"Here's your number." The cashier hands him a blue stand. "We'll bring it out to you."

I turn to go find Krew in the arcade, and suddenly Tyler's arm is slung over my shoulder, pulling my body closer to his. He leans in next to my cheek, sending hot breath down my skin.

He loves to do that.

My body tenses from his nearness. I'm focusing on breathing.

In and out.

In and out.

"Meg?"

I swallow. "Yes?"

"Do you know how to play pinball?"

"No." I shake my head. Then I realize I'm an idiot and that everyone knows how to play pinball. "I mean, yes."

"I'll make you a deal," he says against my cheek. I'm not sure what he's about to say, but the answer is yes.

Yes to everything.

If it means keeping Tyler Dixon this close to me and feeling his arm around me a little longer, then the answer is YES.

"If I win pinball, I get to walk you to your door...like a date."

I slowly turn my head, putting our faces inches apart. I love this close-up view of Tyler. I love how I can see the different shades of stubble that dot his chin. I love seeing the perfections and imperfections of his face, the pattern of blue in his eyes, the creases of his crow's feet, the way his hair flips out the front of his backward hat, the subtle bounce of his Adam's apple as he waits for my answer.

I raise my brow. "You have a deal."

Now I just have to lose pinball on purpose.

⸻

ANOTHER SILVER BALL goes through the flippers at the bottom of the pinball machine. Tyler hides his gloating smile with a bite of his cookie dough shake.

"If I didn't know any better, I'd think you were losing on purpose so I can walk you to your door, because no one can be *this* bad at pinball."

I place my hand on my hip and face him. "I think you set me up, because nobody is that *good* at pinball."

Tyler gets a million bazillion points on his turn. It's cute that I was *choosing* to lose, because there's no choice here. I lost the moment I made the deal.

His light-blue eyes dance back at me. "Your form is all wrong."

"There's no form in pinball."

"Sounds like I'm going to have to show you what I'm talking

about." He sets his shake down on the table near us; then he looks over his shoulder to where Krew is playing a car-racing game. Once he's satisfied that Krew isn't watching us, Tyler walks to me. "You're a teacher; you know the value of a *hands-on* demonstration."

Hands on?

My body breaks out into a cold sweat just thinking about what that might mean.

I straighten as Tyler steps behind me. His body presses my hips into the pinball machine, and his hands cover over the top of mine. His chin hovers just above my shoulder, and forget about the game—I'm the one pinned here, between Tyler's muscular arms and chest.

He takes my hand, pulling the plunger back on the machine and releasing it, sending the next ball flying into the game. He takes our hands and moves them to the buttons on the side.

"Use the bumpers to get points," he says into my ear, and there go the chills again. "If you can, let the ball slide down the flipper to the very end before you shoot it back out." His fingers continue to tug mine with his. "And, most importantly, when the ball gets to the bottom of the machine, use only one flipper. If you try to use both, the ball will fall, and you'll lose."

I watch the ball bounce around inside the glass.

Lights are going off. Sounds are beeping.

And I feel like the same thing is happening inside my body.

I'm a freaking pinball machine, and Tyler is the ball, making me go wild.

"Got it?" he asks.

"Yep."

Nope. I wasn't even listening.

"Your turn." He lets go of my hands.

The ball is at the top of the machine. I have a few seconds to get my bearings straight. But all that goes out the window when Tyler scoops my hair off my shoulder and brushes it back from my neck. Without the strands as a buffer, I feel his stubbled cheek against my skin, and it's glorious. Then his hands wrap around my torso, and I close my eyes.

My body temperature rises, and my breaths come in short, fast bursts.

Would it be wrong to make out in an arcade? Because I'm seriously thinking about it.

Bom, bom, bom. "You lose!" the machine sings.

"What happened? You didn't even try to shoot the ball out."

What happened is that your arms wrapped around my waist, and I can't focus on anything but how nice it is to be held by you.

"I guess I lost my focus," I say.

"I can't imagine why." I can hear the amusement in his voice. "It looks like I get to walk you to your door."

If a simple game of pinball looks like this, what is our door scene going to be like?

TYLER

I MAY BE PLAYING IT COOL, but I'm nervous. I haven't walked a woman to her door in over eleven years.

I leave Krew in the car out front, but I can still see him—and more importantly, he can still see us. That makes things interesting.

As we walk up to the door of Meg's building, my mind runs through what I should say. I don't want to come with the classic "I had a really great time tonight." I'm better than that.

Think, man.

What's a good thing to say? We're almost there. Time's running out. I'm about to say "I had a really great time tonight." I can feel it coming.

Meg stops at the front door of the building and turns around. "You got yourself here, now what are you going to do with me?"

I smile.

That, folks, is Meg Johnson flirting with *me*.

My nerves melt away, and I slip my hand into hers. I nod toward a large bush that's out of Krew's eyesight and gently tug her behind it, pulling her body to me. I feel her soft curves and her racing heart against mine.

The upside to being single again is that I get to have moments like this. Moments where my heart rate is climbing, my stomach is swirling, and my throat is going dry.

I get to fall in love all over again.

I tuck a lock of her blonde hair behind her ear, letting my fingertips skim down the side of her face. "Meg, I want to kiss you again."

Her pretty smile widens. "You won pinball fair and square. This is your doorstep scene. You can do what you want with it."

I press my mouth to hers, and it's complete bliss. It's been more than a week since we last kissed. I'm a man that's been trapped in a desert, and Meg's the water I crave.

I'd love to keep this going, but I can't. I slow the kiss and pull back...reluctantly.

"I'd better go," I say. "I'll call you later?"

"I hope so."

And then I walk away, like the gentleman Kristen taught me to be.

I hop back into the truck and turn to Krew. "All right, let's go home."

"Why were you and Mrs. Johnson in the bush?"

"Uh..." I have to think quickly. "Miss Johnson fell in the bush, and I had to help her get out."

Krew puckers his brow. "It looked like you pushed her in and held her there."

"Is that what it looked like?"

"Yeah."

I let out a small laugh. "Well, that's silly."

I pull out of the parking lot. Next time, I've got to find something more private than a bush.

CHAPTER 33
MEG

It's like I'm living in a dream world. I'm in Tyler's kitchen, eating pancakes for the second time in a little over a week. I probably shouldn't be here, but when Tyler's text came in at 7:56 this morning, inviting me over for breakfast, I had to come.

I'm completely defenseless when it comes to him.

We make up an elaborate story for Krew about how I left something at their house and just came by to pick it up, and then Tyler invited me to stay and eat breakfast with them.

I know it's bad—all the lying—but if I want to be with Tyler and keep my job, I don't have a choice.

Or at least, I'm *telling* myself I don't have a choice.

"I'm going to go get dressed," Tyler says once the kitchen is cleaned.

I kind of like seeing Sunday morning Tyler in athletic shorts and a t-shirt.

"Krew, can you keep Miss Johnson entertained while I'm upstairs?"

"Yep," he says.

Tyler gives me a high five as he walks past me. And I know it's stupid, but it makes my stomach spin. It's our thing, the way we touch when we *can't* touch.

"Mrs. Johnson?"

"Yeah?" I look over my shoulder to the table where Krew's coloring.

"Do you like my dad?"

"Uh…" I laugh, taken off-guard by his question. "Of course I like your dad. We're friends."

"He likes you."

My brows rise. "He does?"

"Yeah. He always asks me what you talk about at school and if you ever ask about him."

Why does that make me smile?

"And he told me he likes you."

I turn to face him, leaning back against the counter. "When?"

"When I was pitching yesterday. That's what he said when he came to the mound."

"That he likes me?"

"Yeah. He said he likes you a lot." His head is down, still focusing on his drawing.

"Well, we're good friends."

"I think he likes you more than a friend."

My fingers grip the edge of the counter. Involving Krew in our relationship takes things to a whole other level.

"Can you be more than friends?" He finally looks at me. "Can you be my mom?"

My heart drops. "Krew, you have a mom."

"She's dead."

Emotion fills my voice, and suddenly I'm aware of every picture of Kristen in the kitchen. There's one on the fridge. One on the bulletin board. One on the windowsill.

"Even though she's dead, she's still your mom."

"But I want you to be my mom."

Brooke and Tessa are right. What I'm doing with Tyler is no different from what my dad is doing with Anna Mae. I've been making impulsive decisions, losing control, slowly *replacing* Kristen. I pretended earlier that it wasn't the same, but now it's so obvious.

I force a smile. "Krew, you have a mom, and I know it doesn't feel like it, but I'm sure she's always with you."

He shrugs. "Okay."

Suddenly, I have to leave. I walk to the front door and frantically put on my shoes. "Krew, can you tell your dad that I have to go?"

"Is everything okay?" Tyler asks as he comes down the stairs.

"Yeah, I'm just tired."

And scared.

And confused.

And a hypocrite.

"Are you sure?"

"Yeah, I'm fine." I open the front door, stepping outside before Tyler gets too close.

Tyler hesitates by the door. "I'll call you later. We're going to dinner at Diane's, so it will be late."

"Sure." My smile is tense.

I turn and run to my car without a glance back.

CHAPTER 34

MEG

"*W*HAT ARE YOU DOING?*" I yell at myself.

This is what I do.

I yell in my car.

It's much cheaper than paying for therapy.

Krew's words play on repeat in my head. *Can you be my mom? She's dead. I want you to be my mom.*

My phone buzzes inside my purse, and I wait until the next stop light to pull it out. There are seven missed calls from a combination of Matt, Tessa, and Brooke, and I can see the sibling group chat has exploded with texts.

My mind immediately goes to the worst-case scenario.

Something's wrong with my dad.

I call Brooke on my car's speaker.

"Meg, where have you been? We've been trying to get a hold of you."

"Is dad dead?" I blurt.

"What? No! He's *engaged*."

That can't be right.

"He proposed to Anna Mae last night. They're getting married in a couple of weeks."

My heart's shattering to pieces in slow motion.

It feels like the moment the doctor said there was nothing more he could do for my mom, a blow so hard it knocks the wind right out of your chest.

"Meg? Are you okay?"

"No." Tears fall freely down my face, rolling over my lips.

"Did Dad tell you he was going to do this?" Brooke asks.

I shake my head even though she can't see me.

"Do you want to come over?"

"No. I've got to go."

I hang up, and that's when the ugly cry comes out, the cry that's so hard, it's technically not safe for me to be behind the wheel of a car. I'm on autopilot, somehow making it back to my apartment. Once inside, I kick off my shoes and grab an entire roll of toilet paper—it's a necessity for cries like this. I climb into my bed, settling in for the most pathetic and sorrowful cry since my mom died.

CHAPTER 35
MEG

After the cry heard around the world, I pull up to the cemetery. I'm here for advice.

Too bad the person I'm seeking advice from is dead.

I stay in my car with my hands on the steering wheel and my foot on the brake until I finally have the strength to get out.

I follow the pathway of grass to my mother's grave, and I know instantly by the can of Diet Coke leaning against her tombstone that my dad's been here. Did he come with Anna Mae? My heart hurts just thinking about it.

I bend down so I'm eye level with my mom's picture. Her brown eyes stare back at me.

I miss her.

So much has changed since she's been gone.

Zak broke up with me.

I met Tyler.

My dad met Anna Mae.

Now he's getting married.

"Mom," I whisper. "Why is it so hard?" Warm tears trickle down my cheeks. "Do you want this? Do you want Dad to marry her?" I exhale, looking up at the blue sky. "I know you want him to be happy, but surely this isn't the way. It's too soon." More tears fall. "And I don't want a new mom. I want you. Why did you leave me? I need you to tell me what to do with my life. You said to marry Zak, and now I can't even do that. What am I supposed to do?"

I sob into my hands for a few minutes, letting out all my heartache, until I finally catch my breath enough to pull myself together.

A car pulls up next to mine, and I quickly wipe my hands over my tears. I hear a car door slam, then someone is walking my way. I shift to stand so I can leave. Company of any kind isn't what I had in mind for my visit today.

"Meg? Is that you?"

Diane Carter, of all people, is coming toward me. She has a big thing of balloons in her hand.

"I didn't realize your mother's grave and Kristen's were so close together."

"I didn't either." I watch Diane walk to a grave a row ahead and maybe ten feet away from my mother's.

"It's Kristen's birthday today."

I feel like I've been punched in the gut.

Today is Kristen Dixon's birthday? I kissed her husband last night. I was at her house this morning. Her son asked me to be his mother instead of her.

Happy birthday, Kristen!

"She loved birthdays." Diane smiles as she places the balloons next to the grave.

Why didn't Tyler say anything?

She straightens. "How's your weekend going?"

"It's going okay."

That's a lie. My perfect weekend has turned into the worst day imaginable.

"I heard you went to Krew's baseball game yesterday."

I stand there, frozen, next to my mother's grave.

"I was sad I couldn't go," she says. "I had a nail appointment

I couldn't miss. But Beverly Ulrich said it was a very exciting game."

Why is Diane bringing this up? She wouldn't, unless she suspects something.

"It was a good baseball game," I say. "I was happy for the boys that they won."

"Kristen would have loved his games. She would have been the perfect team mom, taking pictures and bringing treats."

"I'm sure that's true."

"In fact, when Tyler was in college, he played baseball, and she was his biggest fan. She went to every game and knew all his stats. It was annoying how proud she was of him."

A weird, jealous feeling tugs at my heart again.

Diane looks up at the sky. "Kristen would have loved the weather today. She would have had something fun planned for her birthday. Maybe a trip to the beach with Tyler and Krew. She said they were a trio, their best selves when all three of them were together."

A trio.

Why does that hurt so much to hear?

"Have you ever seen a picture of her?" Diane asks.

I have. They were all throughout Tyler's house when I was there last weekend and this morning, but I hadn't wanted to truly see them. I had *overlooked* them. I wanted to pretend that there was space in that home—in their lives—for me.

But I'm not part of the trio.

Diane motions for me to come to her. "I love this picture."

I weave through the graves and join her. "She's beautiful," I say reverently.

Kristen has the kind of face that screams charisma, hair that I would kill for, and a smile that probably took Tyler's breath away.

"She was always the life of the party, always happy, always laughing."

I'm nothing like that.

I'm not even *at* the party, let alone the life of it.

Diane lets out a small laugh. "That's what Tyler loved about her the most, her spirited personality and her kind heart."

That's not good news for me.

I don't have a kind heart. I'm jealous of Kristen, and I hate Anna Mae. I'm the farthest thing from kind there ever was.

"She sounds like a lovely person, " I manage to get out.

"She was. It's a good thing Tyler isn't dating anyone, because they would never be able to live up to her. She was *that* great."

My eyes drop.

Surprisingly, it's not losing my job that I'm worried about right now. It's Kristen. I'm not Tyler's first love. I would be his second. It's a lot to think about, and when I do think about it, I'm not sure I can handle everything that comes with being second best.

I don't belong.

Not standing next to Kristen's grave.

Not with Krew.

Not in Tyler's life.

"Well, I have to run," I say. "I have a bunch of errands to do. I'll see you on Monday."

Diane nods with a knowing glint in her eye and lifts a hand in farewell.

I keep my face even until the moment I turn my back, and then the tears fall.

I walk to my car, knowing that I'll never compare to Kristen Dixon—just like Anna Mae will never compare to my mother.

CHAPTER 36

TYLER

Krew and I pull up to Diane's house and park on the street. We walk past a gray Audi in the driveway.

"I wonder who's here. I thought it was just us celebrating Mom's birthday."

Krew glances up. "That's Noah's car."

"How do you know?"

"Because there's a Stealers sticker on the back."

I see the familiar sticker on the back window. What the heck is Beverly Ulrich doing at Diane's house?

I knock on the door, and within a few seconds, Diane opens the door. She's wearing a nice party dress, and I know it's to celebrate Kristen's thirty-second birthday.

She smiles big, kissing the side of my cheek. "The boys are here! Krew, there's a surprise for you in the living room."

Krew kicks off his shoes and runs to see what it is.

"Diane." I tug on her arm, lowering my voice. "Is Beverly Ulrich here?"

"Yes. I invited her and Noah to dinner with us today."

My jaw hardens. "I thought we would celebrate Kristen's birthday alone, as a family."

Diane meets my hard expression with her own. "This is my

house, Tyler. I can invite whoever I want to dinner. Be sure to use your manners." Then she turns on her heels and heads into the kitchen.

My shoulders sink.

This is Diane's way of setting me up on a date so that she can act like she's being supportive of me dating again. But she's smart. She knows that I would never be interested in a woman like Beverly Ulrich. She knows that spending the afternoon with Beverly will likely make me miss Kristen even more. This is a new level of manipulation. Diane's never gone *this* far to get me to do what she wants.

I walk into the kitchen. Beverly is standing by the counter, watching Diane finish up with the meal. She's wearing a tight, fitted red dress with a low-cut front—definitely not what I would deem Sunday appropriate. Her smile is bigger than the entire state of Florida as she leans into me for a hug.

"Tyler, you look nice."

My hand barely wraps around her. "Thanks. You do too."

"It's really nice of you guys to invite me to Kristen's birthday dinner."

"I didn't invite you. Diane gets to take all of the credit for that."

Beverly raises a shoulder. "Either way, Noah and I are thrilled to be here. Since my divorce, Sundays have been such a lonely day."

Diane takes her apron off and folds it neatly on the counter. "I'm sure Tyler feels the same way. Maybe we should make this dinner a monthly tradition."

Beverly beams. "I'd love that."

"Boys!" Diane calls, leaning into the living room. "It's time for dinner."

Beverly loops her arm around mine. "You'll sit by me, won't you, Tyler?"

Diane ushers us into the dining room. "Of course he will."

Krew and Noah pull out chairs across from us, and Diane sits at the head of the table. "I made Kristen's favorite meal. Salmon with lemon noodles and garlic-herbed green beans.

"Gross," Krew mutters to Noah.

"Krew, that's not nice manners. Hasn't your father cooked you salmon before?"

He shifts his focus to me. "No, we eat chicken nuggets, pizza, and Panda Express for dinner."

"Tyler, he can't live off of that kind of food. You need to expand his palate."

"I thought Panda Express *was* expanding his palate."

Diane puts a large helping of salmon on Krew's plate. "When you're at grandma's house, you need to eat grandma's food."

Krew pushes his plate away. "No."

"Krew." Diane's voice turns stern. "You will sit at this table until you eat every bite."

"But I'm not hungry."

"Yes, you are."

"No, I'm not. I had pancakes this morning."

Beverly turns to me, brows raised. "You made pancakes?"

I open my mouth to answer, but Krew cuts me off.

"No, Mrs. Johnson made the pancakes."

Diane's fork freezes midair, and Beverly lets out a strained laugh.

I'm thinking of every swear word in my mind right now, but no way I can say any of them in front of Krew. Or my particularly judgy mother-in-law.

"Um…" I clear my throat. "Miss Johnson left something in my car last night after the game and came by this morning to pick it up. I didn't want to be rude, so I invited her in for breakfast."

Diane's lips press together into a thin slash. "And she agreed?"

"I'm very persuasive."

Beverly straightens out a napkin on her lap. "I'd be careful, Tyler. The entire school is starting to think that you and Miss

Johnson are a couple. You don't want to encourage rumors like that."

I glance between the two women. "Maybe I *do* want to encourage it."

Diane is visibly upset. "I forgot the wine with dinner. If you'll excuse me for a moment."

I sigh. This is not how the afternoon was supposed to go.

"I better go talk to her."

I make my way into the kitchen. Diane's standing next to the counter, pinching the bridge of her nose with her fingers.

"I'm sorry."

Her hand drops, and she looks up at me. "What are you doing, Tyler? Do you know how many rumors are going around about you and Meg Johnson? Several people have seen you together outside of school, and now I find out that she was at your house this morning. Did she sleep over?"

"No. But if she did, that would be none of your business."

"It is my business when she works for me and is breaking the rules."

"They're stupid rules."

Her shoulders square. "Do you want Meg to get fired because of you?"

"If it means that we can be together, then yeah, I'm okay if she gets fired because of me."

"You better make sure she feels the same way before things go too far."

"Can't you just overlook the rule one time?"

She shakes her head. "You remember what happened last time I had a teacher involved with a parent. The school almost lost its accreditation."

"This isn't the same situation as before. What's happening between Meg and me is a *good* thing. It's different."

Her eyes narrow on me. "It's not different in the eyes of the board."

"You're the principal and head of the board. I'm sure you could explain to everyone how this is different."

"I can't. I answer to the board of trustees and to all of the people who fund this private school. If word gets out that I let my son-in-law break the rules, what does that say about me?"

"Then I'll take Krew out of the school and put him in a different one."

"You'd take Krew out of a school that he loves where all of his friends are"—her voice quivers—"where his *grandma* is, and where Kristen wanted him to go to school, just so you can date one of the teachers?" She clears her voice, gaining her strength back. "That sounds awfully selfish of you."

"I don't want to just *date* her. I want more than that."

"No." Her head shakes again. "You don't have room in your life for more than that. You need to focus on Krew—focus on raising him the way Kristen would want."

"If you don't think I should be dating, why did you invite Beverly here today?"

"I didn't say that you couldn't date. I just said that I don't think Meg is a good fit for you, and with the scandal it will cause at the school, I was trying to show you there are other options."

I throw my hands out to my side. "Why isn't Meg a good fit for me?"

"I saw her at the cemetery this morning. She was there visiting her mom."

"So?"

She folds her arms over her chest and leans against the back of the counter. "So I don't think she's ready for everything that comes with being a widower's second wife."

"What makes you say that?"

Diane raises her brows. "She's too weak, too intimidated by everything Kristen was."

"How do you know?"

"I told her how much Kristen meant to you, to all of us, and Meg was clearly upset by that."

My jaw hardens. "What did you say to her?"

"I merely told her how wonderful Kristen was. And she *was* wonderful. I shouldn't have to hide that, and if Meg Johnson can't handle living in Kristen's shadow, then she shouldn't be a part of our lives."

"Not *our* lives. *My* life. This is my life, and whether you like it or not, I can choose who I want to be with."

"And whether you like it or not, I'm Krew's grandmother, and I should have a say in how he's being raised and by whom."

My eyes cast over Diane's face. "Do you have a problem with me liking Meg because you're Principal Carter, or because you're Kristen's mom?"

"Don't be ridiculous," she scoffs. "I told you already. I'm worried about the school, the board of trustees, and about Meg losing her job. That's it."

"If you really wanted me to be happy, you'd talk to the board of trustees."

She brushes away my words with the flip of her hand. "My hands are tied."

"They're tied because you don't like the idea of me dating again."

Her chin lifts. "I didn't say that."

My voice gets stronger, matching my frustration. "Diane, what are you so afraid of?"

Tears fill her eyes. "I'm afraid of losing Kristen again." Her eyes drop, and she fidgets with her hands. "There are rules at the school, but beyond that, it's hard to see you moving on with your life." Her head lifts, and her eyes meet mine. "There's no moving on for me. My daughter is just gone—forever. I can already see things shifting with you, and I'm worried if you keep this thing up with Meg, I'm going to be the only one who remembers Kristen."

"Diane, I'll always remember Kristen. She was—"

"I know what Kristen was. You don't have to tell me. She was incredible, and I don't want her replaced with someone new. *I* don't want to be replaced with someone new. If you marry again, there will be new in-laws, and where does that leave me?" One tear falls down her cheek. "I don't have anyone left."

My shoulders drop. I should be furious with Diane, with the way she's trying to dictate my life, but I feel sorry for her. She lost Kristen too. I see glimpses of her daughter in her eyes and the way she's trying to stay strong, fighting her emotion. My relationship with Diane might be complicated, but I would never replace her. She's a part of me always, just like Kristen is.

I take a step forward and place my hand on her wrist. "There's always a place for you in our lives. You're Kristen's mom."

She shakes her head as if she's trying to regain composure. "None of this matters." She pulls her wrist out of my grasp. "If I were you, I'd focus on remembering Kristen instead of chasing after another woman you can't have. Because you can't have Meg Johnson, and there's nothing you can say that will change that." She raises her chin. "I'm only having this conversation with you to let you know that I can't keep these dating rumors away from the board much longer. Consider this your warning to end things."

Her shoulder bumps mine as she exits the kitchen.

I guess the birthday party is over.

CHAPTER 37

TYLER

That evening, Paul's name appears on the home screen of my phone. I'm glad he's calling. I should probably be honest with him about *who* the woman is I've been referring to these last few months.

I'm sick of hiding my feelings for Meg, and if my conversation with Diane is any indication, our relationship won't be hidden much longer.

"Hey, Paul," I say.

"Tyler, I'm glad I got ahold of you."

"Why? What's up?"

"Have you talked to Meg?"

Is this a trick question?

Paul breaks my silence. "I know she's the woman you've been talking about and that you two are dating."

"You do?"

"Ever since game night when Tessa saw you two in the kitchen, I think my whole family knew."

"I'm sorry I didn't tell you sooner. Are you mad?"

"Don't worry about it. I understand why you didn't tell me, and I'm not upset."

"Good."

"So have you talked to her?" There's an anxiousness in his voice that I don't understand.

"I saw her this morning, but I haven't talked to her since."

"I asked Anna Mae to marry me last night, and she accepted."

"Paul, that's great."

"It is for me, but you know Meg. She's taking it really hard. She won't speak to any of us. I was wondering if you could go over there and talk to her."

I do know Meg, and I know that this news was probably devastating.

"Sure. I'll see what I can do."

I need to talk to her about Diane anyway.

"And, Tyler?"

"Yeah?"

"There isn't a better man than you for my daughter. I'd be honored to have you as part of our family."

Emotion takes over. I try to clear my throat to save myself a little bit of embarrassment. "Thanks, Paul. That means a lot."

We hang up, and I immediately text Logan to see if he can watch Krew so I can go over to Meg's apartment.

I have a feeling that things between us just got a lot more complicated.

MEG

MY FAMILY HAS been calling and texting all day, and I've politely told them to leave me alone.

Actually, if you asked them, they'd say I wasn't so polite.

I'm bitter, and I can't understand why everyone else is okay with *this*—okay with stupid Anna Mae. I'm a sore loser, and I don't want to talk to any of them.

Traitors.

That's what they all are.

Or maybe I'm the traitor—the one betraying my family for selfish reasons.

When a knock sounds at my door, I don't move from my spot on the couch. It's probably my sisters, or worse, my dad and his poser fiancée.

Another loud knock.

I don't budge.

"Meg, I know you're in there."

It's Tyler.

Seeing him sounds not much better than seeing my dad.

"Open up," he says.

I don't even bother smoothing my hair as I make my way to the door. I'll never be as good as his first wife, so our relationship is doomed for failure no matter what.

When I open the door, Tyler's eyes sweep over my less-than-stellar appearance. I'm sure there are bags under my eyes, and I've definitely cried off all my makeup.

"Rough day?"

I hate the kindness in his eyes.

"How did you know?"

"Your dad called me."

"Of course he did."

I walk away from the door and go back to my spot on the couch. Tyler follows me inside, shutting the door for me. He pushes my feet aside, making room for him to sit beside me.

"I know this is hard for you. Are you okay?"

No, I'm not okay. I'm letting my broken heart ruin every relationship that is important to me.

I raise my chin. "It doesn't matter if I'm okay. What's done is done."

Tyler reaches for my hand, but I pull away. Breaking up with someone is like a removing a Band-Aid. You just have to rip it off.

"I can't do me and you," I say.

His eyebrows lift. "You can't do me and you?"

"That's right."

"Meg, what you're feeling about your dad has nothing to do with us."

"It has everything to do with us." I stand, pacing the room. "Can't you see? I'm Krew's Anna Mae."

"I don't even know what that means."

"I can't replace Kristen. I'll never compare to her."

"No one's asking you to."

"Krew did. Do you know what he said to me this morning? He said he wanted me to be his mom instead of her. I can't be the person who tears apart your family."

"I think Kristen's death already tore us apart."

"You don't get it. Kristen will always be your first love, and I'll always be the girl that can't live up to her. I'll be second best the rest of my life."

"Have I ever made you feel second best?"

"No, but you're not seeing this clearly. If I stay with you, I'm just slipping into her shoes. None of it would be real. I would be living the life she was supposed to have, playing the part of Kristen. And in the back of my mind, I'll always wonder if you wished she was still here instead of me."

Tyler stands, coming toward me. "How can you say that? Where are you even getting this?"

"I've heard how you talk about her. How everyone does. Kristen was incredible, and I don't measure up."

"Meg, you're incredible too."

I fold my arms across my chest. "Not like her."

Even as I say the words, I know I'm being petty and ridiculous, but I can't stop myself.

"You know how it is when someone dies. You put them on a pedestal. Kristen was amazing, and I loved her with all my heart, but she wasn't perfect. We had our problems."

"Tyler, it doesn't matter. I don't want to compete with her memory."

"I'm not asking you to."

"But I will be anyway." I shake my head. "I can't be Krew's Anna Mae."

"Is Anna Mae really that bad? There are people out there who don't even have one loving mother. You get two."

"She's not my mother."

He tilts his head. "You know what I mean."

I roll my shoulders back, fighting the tears that I'd hoped were all dried out. "You're just like my dad. So reckless. Full of optimism. Blinded by love so much that you can't see the obvious red flags."

"Being like your dad is the best compliment anyone has ever given me. I want to be just like him. Unafraid of jumping into love as many times as I can. It's not reckless, Meg. It's fearless."

"Then I'm full of fear." I shrug. "Fear that I'll never compare to Kristen, fear that I'm losing control, fear that I'll lose my job, fear that everything in my life is changing, and with each change, I lose my mom more." I shake my head. "I'm sorry, Tyler, but this isn't going to work."

He rubs his forehead in frustration. I hate that I am breaking his heart, but I see no way around this situation.

"You know, I'm not the first person to lose a spouse. People die, and the people they left behind move on with life because they have to. Everyone else in the world seems to understand this. People get married again, after death, after divorce, and nobody compares them."

"I'm not everyone else."

I wish I was like everyone else. I wish I could get over all my insecurities about Kristen and Anna Mae and just let myself be happy. But I can't.

"Listen," he walks to the door, "we don't have to solve any of this tonight. When you're ready to talk, you know where to find me. I'm here for you."

I watch him leave, knowing that a few days won't make even a little bit of difference.

CHAPTER 38

MEG

The next morning, I walk into Diane Carter's office before school.

"Diane, do you have a minute? There's something I need to talk to you about."

She glances up from her computer screen and looks at me. "Sure. Take a seat."

"I prefer to stand."

"Very well." She sits back in her seat. "I'm listening."

I take a deep breath, trying to find my courage. "For the past few weeks, I have been involved in a relationship with Tyler Dixon." Her face is expressionless, so I keep going. "I realize that it is against the contract I signed. I came here this morning to be honest with you and to let you know that from here on out, I will keep my relationship with Tyler purely professional."

"Does he know that?"

"Yes. I told him last night that I didn't see a future between us."

Her eyebrows rise in interest. It's the first reaction she's shown. "Can I ask why you told him that?"

It's none of her business, but I'm here in the name of honesty, so I don't hold back. "Well, there's my job to think about. Hopefully, I still have it. And I think everything with his past is too complicated. If he's looking for someone like your daughter, I'm afraid I don't fit that bill."

"I see." She nods. "I commend you for coming to me about your relationship. Obviously, I wish you hadn't broken the school rules in the first place, but since it only lasted a few weeks and you were honest about your actions, I can probably convince the board to keep you on the staff."

"That would be great. I really do love working here." I turn to go.

"Meg?"

I pause. "Yes?"

"I think you made a good decision by ending things with Tyler."

"It seemed like the best thing to do, given the circumstances."

The satisfaction in Diane's expression tells me she believes what I'm telling her.

If only I had half her confidence.

If only I didn't feel like my heart were breaking in two.

TYLER

I ARRIVE EARLY to school to drop Krew off at Diane's office so I can start working outside.

What I don't expect to find is Meg telling Diane that she broke up with me.

Which I refuse to accept, by the way. But the sound of the words leaving Meg's lips still gut me.

Krew stopped at the prize machine in the front, so that just leaves me, back pressed against the wall outside of Diane's office. I'm shamefully listening in on their conversation.

"Tyler's doing the best he can to parent on his own," Diane says. "But it's been a challenge for him. He's not equipped to handle the responsibility of being a single parent. Half the time, he doesn't know what he's doing. That's why he shouldn't be dating anyone."

My head drops. Diane sure knows how to make a man feel good about himself.

"I think Tyler's doing an excellent job parenting by himself." Meg's voice is strong, and I can picture the defiant look in her eyes as she speaks. "He's managing Krew better on his own than most parents do when there are two of them. Krew feels more love from Tyler on a daily basis than some kids get their entire lives. And I'm not saying that because I like Tyler. I'm saying that as a teacher who has been around a lot of children. If you can't see what a wonderful father Tyler is, then you're not as smart as I thought you were. You can't expect him to stay single forever, Diane. Maybe it isn't supposed to be me. Maybe I'll never measure up, but eventually, it *will* happen. And I hope when it does, you'll think about what's best for Krew."

Meg walks out of the office, and there's no time to react.

She sees me.

Our eyes meet, and I take a deep breath, willing my unshed tears to stay put.

Her steps pause for a moment. Beneath her expression of surprise is compassion, love, and maybe even a bit of *longing.* I'm hoping that the myriad of emotions flitting through Meg's eyes means that she still has feelings for me, even though she told Diane we're over.

But she doesn't say anything. She only nods and walks away.

CHAPTER 39

MEG

I pull into the parking lot of my apartment building after school. The past three days since I broke up with Tyler and my father got engaged have been hard. I'm avoiding my family, only because I know they'll make me confront my insecurities about losing my mom completely, and I'm not ready to do that yet. Everything is still so raw.

Plus, I pushed Tyler away. So basically, I'm the worst human being ever.

And I'm all alone, so that doesn't help things either.

It's your own fault you're alone. You have no one to blame but yourself.

I shake my head, ignoring my pesky inner voice.

I stop at the top of the stairs, completely surprised by who I see standing by my door, waiting for me.

"Hey, babe."

"Zak, what are you doing here?" He looks lean, dressed in a navy suit, and he appears to have gotten a fresh haircut.

"I came to talk."

My chin drops, and I raise my brows. "You came to talk?"

"Is that all right?"

"I don't know."

I walk past him and use my keys to open the door to my apartment. It's been two months since I've heard from or seen Zak. I've licked my wounds—actually, that sounds gross.

I've mended my broken heart, and I hate how one look at Zak takes me right back to where I was when he told me he didn't love me anymore.

"Meg, you have every right to be mad at me," he says, following me into my apartment.

I walk to the counter and set my purse down. "I'm not mad."

I'm sad. He broke my heart and ruined my faith in happily ever after, but worst of all, he took the last words my mother said to me—her dying wish—and made a mockery of them.

"If you're aren't mad, then what are you? You seem distant."

I don't know what I am.

I open the refrigerator and pull out some leftovers.

"Meg, can you just stop what you're doing and talk to me?"

I set the Tupperware down and meet Zak's gaze. "Okay. I'm listening."

Zak draws in a deep breath like he's nervous, and it's nice, for once, to see him lacking confidence. "I made a mistake. I should've never left you. I was scared of marriage and making that kind of commitment, and I thought those fears meant that I didn't love you."

I blink back at him from where I'm standing in the kitchen.

"Are you going to say anything?" he asks.

I don't know what any of this means. Zak thinks he made a mistake. Am I supposed to hand him an award for finally getting in touch with his feelings at twenty-nine years of age?

"I think I'll just keep listening."

"Okay." He sighs. "Then I'll say what I came here to tell you. Meg, I love you. I'll always love you."

"How do you know you love me now when you didn't two months ago?"

"Haven't you heard a word I've said? I was scared."

"What about Genessa?"

"What about her?"

"Last time I saw you, you were with her."

"I'm not going to lie." His eyes drop. "Genessa and I dated a little bit."

I thought hearing him say it out loud would hurt more, but it doesn't. I've been dating Tyler, so I can't really be upset about him and Genessa.

"She was a good thing," Zak says. "She made me realize how great you are and how much I really want to be with you, not somebody else."

"Shouldn't you have *already* realized that?"

"Probably, but for some reason, I didn't see how perfect you are for me until you were gone." He steps forward, taking my hands in his. "I want us to be together again. I want us to finally build the future that you've been talking about for years. I want to marry you. I would get down on one knee right now if you'd let me."

I glance down at our joined hands, trying to figure out what all of this means.

Zak is back.

He's saying everything I've wanted to hear for the last three years. I should be happy, but all I feel is confusion. I can't understand why, at the moment Zak said he wanted to marry me, Tyler's face crossed through my mind.

He squeezes my hand. "What do you say, Meg? Can you forgive me for being such a jerk and take me back?"

There's a part of me that wants to flip him the bird and kick him out of my apartment, but there's also a vulnerable piece of me that wants to curl up in his arms and cry.

I'm sad about my dad.

And I'm sad about Tyler—that things can never work out between us.

Then there's my mom and the final words she said to me. Marrying Zak was what she wanted for me. I can't just send him on his way when I could finally fulfill her dying wish. Can I?

"You don't have to decide anything right now," Zak says softly. "I just want you to give me a chance to make things right. Let me back into your life. Let me show you how much you mean to me."

His offer is tempting, because I'm sad about my dad and Tyler. But even if I know things can't work out with Tyler, I've experienced what a great relationship is like. And it's nothing like what I had with Zak. I can't go back to how things were with him. Tyler changed my standard. He readjusted the bar and raised it. I'd rather be alone than be with someone that doesn't see me.

"I don't want to go back to how things were," I say.

"I know." His eyes light up. "I've changed. Things will be different between us."

"It's too late, Zak. I've changed too."

"You don't have to decide right now. You can think about it."

"I don't need time to think about it. Things between us are over."

"Meg." He squeezes my hand. "You're confused. That's understandable."

"I'm not confused." I pull out of his grasp. "You've spent the last five minutes telling me what *you* want and how *you* feel. It's my turn to tell you how *I* feel. I don't love you anymore."

Zak puffs out an insecure laugh as his eyes drop to the floor. "This isn't how I saw things going."

I shift my weight. "I'm sorry."

There's another knock at the door.

His head jerks up. "Are you expecting someone?"

"No." I walk to the door and open it.

It's Tyler.

The world hates me.

This is my punishment for treating everyone in my life so badly.

He looks miserable. "I tried to give you space to figure everything out. I waited as long as I could, but I miss you."

Zak peaks around the door, and everything about Tyler darkens. He glances between the two of us.

"Zak just showed up unannounced," I explain.

"You're the guy from the pier," Zak says.

Tyler nods, reaching his hand out. "Tyler Dixon."

"Zak Kershaw."

Tyler looks directly at me. "Sorry to interrupt. I didn't think you'd have company over."

"We were just talking, and Zak was getting ready to leave."

I don't know if he was getting ready to leave or not, but I can't have both men here together, and there's nothing more to say between us.

"Okay." Zak nods. He leans in for a hug. "It was good to see you. I've missed you."

"It was good to see you too." My eyes drop. I don't know what this looks like to Tyler.

Zak releases the hug and steps past Tyler, leaving us alone. We stand there for a minute, watching him go down the stairs.

"Can I come in?" Tyler finally asks.

I open the door wider, letting him pass through.

"Are you and Zak getting back together?"

"He wants to."

He turns to face me. "Meg, he strung you along for years, then broke your heart. You can't possibly be thinking about letting him back in your life."

"I thought about it." I fold my arms, trying to keep myself from bursting at the seams with emotion. "My mother said Zak was the one." A rush of moisture fills my eyes. "She wanted me to marry him. She had this whole idea of what my life would be like, and it was with Zak. It was her dying wish that I marry him."

"Meg, I'm sure it wasn't her dying wish."

I hug myself tighter. "Her eyes were closed, but she opened them to slits so she could see me. Her words were whispers. 'I want you to marry Zak and be happy.' It was literally the last thing she said to me."

"She probably said that because she thought that's what *you* wanted. She didn't mean for you to stick to her words even if he's not right for you."

I know that's true. Deep down, I know I'm being ridiculous, holding onto her last words, but I feel like by letting go of Zak, I'm letting go of another piece of my mother, and I can't afford to lose any more of her.

"Meg, I think if your mother were here, she'd tell you to get rid of Zak and be with me."

I let out a soft laugh. "You're a little too confident, don't you think?"

"No. If she knew me, she'd love me."

"That bothers me too." My voice cracks as I speak. "How can I be with someone my mother never met, someone who didn't know her? You don't know how amazing she was, but Zak does."

Tyler's countenance softens, and he pulls me into a hug. "I'll know how amazing she was, because I know you."

Tears are falling pretty heavily now, wetting Tyler's shirt.

"It's just too much," I say into his neck.

"What's too much?"

I pull back so I can look into his eyes. "You and me. There's too much between us to try to figure out. I meant what I said the other day about not being able to compare to Kristen, and I haven't changed my mind."

"Yes, I loved Kristen, but I love you, too."

His words burn inside my heart.

I *know* Tyler loves me, but I'm scared.

"I'm not sure love is enough."

Tyler's hands are on my cheeks, wiping away tears with his thumbs. "This love is different with you than it was with Kristen. When she first died, I couldn't even imagine falling in love again. I literally thought that I would be alone for the rest of my life. And then you came along, and now I can't imagine not being with you." Tyler presses his forehead against mine. "And what you did the other day in Diane's office, the way you stood up for me, no one's ever done that before. Your confidence in my parenting—in *me*—is the most helpful thing anyone's done for me since Kristen died."

"I meant what I said. You're a good dad, Tyler. You don't need me or anyone else to help you see that, or even to help you raise Krew. You're doing a great job."

"You're right. I don't *need* you. I see that now. But Meg, I *want* you. You're the person I want to be with. The person I want to turn to when I've just won the championship. When the entire team runs to the pitcher or to the kid who just hit the home run, I want to run to you. You make everything better. You make the losses bearable and the wins complete."

It's the sweetest thing anyone has ever said to me, and yet, my heart can't convince my head that his words are enough.

—————

TYLER

SHE'S GOING TO TELL ME NO. I can feel it. I can feel my heart breaking again, like it's the first night without Kristen. It's surreal. I know it's going to hurt so badly. I know my chest will feel tight and my breaths will be difficult, but I can't feel the pain yet. I have to hear Meg say the words. I have to hear her reject me one last time before I can believe it.

"I love you." I pull her shoulders into my chest, hugging her tight again. "I love you, Meg."

She doesn't say anything. We stand like that for what seems like forever, crying in each other's arms, until Meg steps back, wiping her face with the sleeve of her shirt. Her eyes are puffy, but she still looks beautiful. I hope I remember her like this forever—fragile, vulnerable, and painfully beautiful.

I glance at her blue eyes, a question lingers in my gaze, an intense desire to know what she's going to do.

"I'm sorry, Tyler," she says as she releases the hug. "The situation is too much."

The space between us crushes a piece of my heart, and I clasp both hands behind my head, my elbows sticking out like triangles. I pace back and forth for a moment, breathing deeply.

"You're making a mistake."

"I'm sorry."

I drop my hands to my side. "You're making a mistake."

Then I walk out of her apartment...alone.

CHAPTER 40
MEG

Breaking up with Tyler was rough.

I stop my car in my dad's driveway, and I turn the ignition off. My hands stay on the steering wheel, and I rest my head against them, looking over at his house. There's a soft light coming through the front window. I can picture my dad sitting in his recliner with the news on. He's probably half-asleep, half listening.

Normally, I wouldn't hesitate to go in, but I've been so awful to my family lately, especially my dad. And now that I need support, I come running back. I hate the hypocrisy of it all, but I need my dad. It's time to swallow my pride and apologize.

The porch lights turn on, and the front door swings open. My dad stands there in his pajamas, waving me inside. I don't know how he knew I was here, that I need him, but he does.

I get out of the car and walk to him. The tears are already coming. He opens his arms out wide, and I fall into them, sobbing.

"I'm sorry," I cry. "I'm *so* sorry."

"I know." He pats my hair, letting me sob into his shoulder. "Meg?" he finally asks.

"Yeah."

"Can we move this inside?"

I laugh and slip out of his hug. He wraps an arm around my shoulder as we walk into the house.

"So what happened?" he asks, handing me a glass of milk. He takes the seat across from me at the kitchen table.

I look down at my fingers, playing with the bottom of the cup. "Zak came back." I peek up at him.

"Is that why you're so upset?"

"A little bit." My voice breaks with emotion. "Maybe him coming back is a sign from Mom."

"You think Mom brought Zak back into your life?"

"Right before she died, she told me to marry him. Maybe this is her way of making that possible."

"Meg, if you don't want Zak, Mom doesn't want him either."

"I know you're right. But her last words are all I have left. They're the things that replay over and over in my mind. I close my eyes and I picture her holding my hand, whispering them to me."

"Her last words are just that. What about every other moment or conversation you ever had with her? Don't those count for something?" His lips slacken into a small smile. "Because I know she told you your entire life to find a good man that loves you like crazy. Do you think that's Zak?"

"No."

"Then what are we even talking about?"

My voice cracks. "I just don't want to lose more of her, you know?"

"You can't lose her, Meg." My dad rests his hand on top of mine. "She's a part of you in everything you do. Her memory can never die."

I wipe at my tears, letting his words sink in.

"Have you ever thought that maybe Mom brought Tyler into your life for a reason?"

I hadn't thought that before.

"Dad, Tyler's a great guy"—*probably the best guy I'll ever meet*—"but things with him are too complicated."

"What's complicated?"

My dad wouldn't understand about living in Kristen's shadow my entire life and how I'd always be comparing myself to her, and if I bring all that up right now, the conversation will inevitably lead to Anna Mae. I'm not sure my heart can handle hashing all of that out. I've been awful and I need to make amends, and I plan to. Just not tonight. My dad knows I'm sorry. Hopefully that is enough for right now.

"Things between Tyler and me aren't going to work, okay?"

"Okay, fine." He sighs. "Do you want to sleep here tonight?"

"I may be depressed, but I'm not that low."

My dad's words circle through the back of my mind.

What if my mom *did* bring me Tyler to help me realize that I can't keep insisting everyone live in the past?

Not my father.

Not Diane.

Not Tyler.

But even that thought doesn't make me feel better.

CHAPTER 41

MEG

The last three weeks have been miserable. Like combine all the worst things and feelings and mash them together, and you get me.

I miss Tyler.

I haven't seen him since the night he told me he loved me, and sometimes I question if that really happened or if I'm making it up in my head.

He said he loved me, right?

I think he did.

Then I broke up with him.

Who the heck am I?

And although I haven't seen him, I can't get Tyler out of my head. I avoid recess duty so that I don't accidentally bump into him. Krew walks into my classroom, and I want to hug him, but I can't. He wears his jersey to class, and I want to ask how the Stealers are doing or if I can come to one of their games.

This is a new level of misery that I never reached when Zak and I broke up.

I'm in the kitchen pulling out a pumpkin pie for Thanksgiving dessert when Anna Mae walks in.

"Meg, thank you for all of your help with dinner," she says as she fills up a pitcher of water.

"I should be thanking you," I say.

"Me?"

I keep my eyes focused on the pie in front of me, because what I'm about to say is going to be difficult to get out.

"Thank you for making my dad so happy." I finally glance up. "And I'm sorry that I haven't been very kind to you. It's not *you*, I just miss my mom, and I don't want her memory or influence over our family to die."

Anna Mae reaches out, placing her hand on top of mine. It's such a simple touch, but I can't deny how good and comforting it feels. It's something my mom would have done.

"I don't fault you. You *should* miss your mom. She sounds like an amazing woman who deserves to be missed."

"She was." My heart pounds with a question I'm dying to ask. "Does it ever scare you when we talk about how great she was? Like you won't live up to her?"

Her expression softens. "I don't look at your mother like she's my competition. I look at her like she's my friend. She loves the same people I love, and therefore, I love her."

Moisture fills my eyes. "Thank you for saying that. You're a good person, and I'm going to try harder to get to know you."

This is a necessary step. If I want to fix things with me and Tyler I need to fix things with Anna Mae. And I'm starting to think that I *want* to fix things with Tyler.

"I'd like that." She gives my hand one last squeeze. "Now, we better get back outside, or everyone will wonder what happened to us."

For the first time since I met Anna Mae, I'm actually glad to have her here. She won't replace my own mom, but maybe now and again, she can fill in for her.

TYLER

KREW PLAYS WITH HIS toys on the floor under the soft glow of the television. I wish he was as tired as me after the long holiday, but he's still going strong.

"Dad?" He looks up at me with his big blue eyes.

"Yeah, bud?"

"Am I ever going to get a new mom?"

My heart breaks a little...okay, a lot. My heart breaks *a lot.*

"You have a mom."

"I know, but am I going to get a mom that isn't dead?"

I keep my voice even and put on a brave face. I should be used to it by now. "Do you want a mom that isn't dead?"

"I don't know." Krew shrugs and goes back to playing with his cars. "It might be kind of nice."

"I think it would be nice too." I pause for a second, trying to understand the feeling expanding inside me. "Krew," I say, pulling his attention back to me. "Even if it doesn't happen, if you never get a new mom, you'd be okay. You'd have me. I know I'm not a mom, but I'm a good dad, and we'll be okay on our own. I love you, bud, and I'll always be here for you."

"Okay." His head drops back to his toys.

I chuckle. So much for my amazing parenting moment. But in the end, I think what I said was more for me than for Krew. I'm finally realizing that I'm enough for him, no matter what anyone else says.

Meg helped me realize that.

My phone in my lap buzzes, and I decide to let this conversation die, especially since it seems like Krew has already moved on. I look down, and it takes me a minute to trust what I see.

Meg: Can I vent?

I sit up straighter, running a hand through my hair. It's been three weeks since I've seen or even talked to Meg, and I can't figure out why she chose Thanksgiving—a pretty important holiday—to text me.

Tyler: Sure.

Meg: Okay, good, because I just need someone to talk to.

Tyler: I'm here for whatever you need.

Meg: It's my first Thanksgiving without my mom. How do you do this? I need someone to tell me how to do this, because I don't know what I'm doing, and I feel like I can't breathe. My dad, my sisters, EVERYONE, seems to be handling it fine. What's wrong with me?

I exhale. There's no way around it. The first *everything* is tough.

Tyler: There's no right or wrong way to grieve. Stop comparing your grief to someone else. Everyone goes through it differently. It's okay if you're struggling. Feeling things deeply is a good thing.

Meg: You're right. I know you're right. It's just so hard.

I debate whether or not I should send my next text, but I do it anyway.

Tyler: I wish I was there to hug you...tell you in person that everything will be okay.

Meg: I wish you were here too.
Meg: Sorry to interrupt your holiday. Thanks for talking.

Tyler: No problem.

I set my phone down, wishing the ache in my heart would go away, but her text tonight just made it worse. As much as I want to keep the communication going between us, I have to protect Krew and my heart.

CHAPTER 42
MEG

I grab another stack of my mother's clothes and carry them across the hall to the guest bedroom in my dad's house. We're moving my mother out, making room for Anna Mae. It's the literal *replacement* that I've been talking about for the last three months since my dad met her. And I have to learn to be okay with it. The wedding is tomorrow—the first weekend in December—and although it's hard for me, I'm trying to work through it.

I'm slowly accepting the change.

"Look at this skirt," Tessa says, holding up a knee length pencil skirt of my mom's. "I think I could wear this as a dress."

"Nope," I say, snatching the skirt from her hands. "We're not taking mom's clothes and turning them into nightclub attire."

"What are we going to do with them, then?" Brooke asks, carrying a box of shirts into the room.

I pick up a striped sweater and bring it to my nose, hoping to smell her perfume. "We could have them made into a quilt. One for each of us four kids and one for dad."

"She certainly has enough stuff for five quilts," Tessa says.

Brooke smiles. "I love that idea."

"What idea?" My dad enters the room with another large

box, but this one is full of books and keepsakes. He sets it on the floor and looks up at us expectantly.

"We're going to make quilts out of mom's clothes."

"That sounds perfect."

"But what about her shoes?" My dad waves us to follow him. "Are you sure none of you guys fit in her shoes?"

"We're different sizes," Brooke says, trailing behind him. "But they might work for Tessa."

Tessa rushes out the door. "I am not wearing Mom's shoes to work. They don't scream corporate dominance."

I sit on the corner of the bed, looking around the guest room. It's odd how an entire life can be boxed up in a matter of an hour or two. My eyes glance to the top of the bin that my dad carried in, to a notebook that says *My Journal*. I sink to my knees, slowly swiping my fingers over the dusty cover.

You should never read someone's journal.

It's the number one rule in life, but does that rule apply to dead people?

I'm going to say no, but just in case I'm wrong, I look behind me to make sure I'm alone. I open up the front cover and see the scribbles of my mom's cursive. I flip through the pages, stopping to read passages.

I think I'm going through a new phase in my life. It seems as though I am "mourning the passing of my youth." Young motherhood is gone with the joys of new babies and little ones. How difficult it is to let go of, even though you know that other new and rich experiences lie ahead. I'm getting so old—but there are a lot of joys. As you get older and nearer to the end of your life, you seem to appreciate it more, and you want to savor each day.

My mother was so wise, so eloquent with her words. No wonder I took everything she said to heart. She's my role model, my rock, my compass. If she were here, would she tell me to push my fears aside with Tyler and be happy with him?

I flip through more pages, reading her thoughts. I like this glimpse inside her mind. I get to the last page and see a single sentence.

The words are nothing new. I've seen them before. But seeing them in my mom's handwriting makes me feel like this sentence was written for me—the answer to all of my questions—as if she knew somehow I would find it when I needed it most.

"Comparison is the thief of joy." —*Theodore Roosevelt*

Joy.

I don't even know what that is anymore.

I had joy when I was with Tyler, and now it's gone.

Teddy knows what he's talking about, because comparing myself to Kristen or comparing Anna Mae to my own mother has robbed me of the relationships that give me the most happiness in my life.

It's not a competition between my mother and Anna Mae, or even me and Kristen.

I pick up my phone, suddenly needing Tyler more than ever. I love him, and the thought of not being with him seems crazy.

Meg: Hey.

I know, it's a terrible text, but I'm testing the waters a bit. I texted him last week on Thanksgiving when I was feeling low, but I haven't talked to him since. I've been trying to work through everything in my mind.

I fidget with my lip, waiting for him to respond. These are agonizing seconds. My heart is ripped out of my chest and is now in my cell phone provider's hands.

Tyler: Hey.

That wasn't the *"I love you. I've missed you desperately"* text I was hoping for that I definitely don't deserve because I've repeatedly pushed him away.

I'm going to have to say a little more than *"Hey."*

Meg: You were right about us. I was making a mistake.

Tyler: What are you doing right now?

Thank goodness. He wants to see me.

Meg: I'm packing up my mom's stuff, getting things ready for my dad's wedding tomorrow.

Tyler: Meg, you only text me when you're sad. Right now you feel like you've made a mistake, but how are you going to feel tomorrow or next week? This is what you do. You get sad and lonely and pull me in, and then when that feeling passes, you push me away.

I don't do that.
Do I?
My mind goes back through the few months since I've known Tyler. The bench on the pier, all the nights I texted him about Anna Mae, Thanksgiving.
It looks bad.
There might be a slight pattern.
But the truth is, I wasn't using Tyler. I really do love him. I'm not texting him right now because I'm sad or lonely. I'm texting him because when you realize that you want to spend the rest of your life with someone, you want that person to be the first to know.

Meg: I'm sorry if it seems that way. I'm not texting you right now because I'm sad.

Tyler: Meg, I can't keep playing this game. It's not just me I have to think about. It's Krew too.

Meg: Can we talk…in person? Please. There's a lot I want to say.

Saying "I love you" through text feels insincere, and for a guy like Tyler, who is so sincere, I don't want that.

Tyler: It's not a good time. I have to leave for Krew's baseball game.

Meg: Are you coming to my dad's wedding tomorrow? Maybe we can talk then.

Tyler: Yeah, I'll be there.
Tyler: Goodbye, Meg.

That felt really *final*. Not like, *"Goodbye, I've got to run for now,"* but more like, *"Goodbye, I hope to never see you again."*
Have I taken too long to get my crap together?

CHAPTER 43
MEG

'm sandwiched between Tessa and Brooke, holding each of their hands as we watch my dad marry Anna Mae. Matt sits next to Tessa. He seems completely calm considering the fact that he just met Anna Mae two hours ago.

This isn't a funeral, it's a wedding. I can't be the lunatic lady bawling on the front row, so I keep it together.

I have on my waterproof mascara just in case.

The wedding is in my parents' backyard, next to my mother's pink impatiens bush. The clouds part, the sun shining down on my dad and Anna Mae, and I have an overwhelming feeling that my mom is here, and she's happy. She's so happy that my dad has found someone to spend the rest of his life with and that he doesn't have to be alone. It's like she's whispering to me, *"Stop comparing Anna Mae to me. And stop comparing yourself to Kristen. There's room for all of us."*

Okay, that seems oddly specific and a little too on the nose.

Maybe that's what *I'm* whispering to myself.

I look behind me and catch a glimpse of Tyler and Krew in the back row. Tyler's wearing a navy suit with a pink tie. His hair is styled back, and his face is freshly shaven. I've never seen him dressed up like this before. He looks so good. I now understand the phrase *a sight for sore eyes*. It's like I'm looking at a J. Crew model. He could go from his fancy suit to his t-shirt and baseball cap in a matter of minutes and still look equally as good.

I'm so stupid.

A J. Crew model said he loved me, and I didn't say anything back.

Actually, I broke up with him, so technically I *did* say something back.

I need to fix this.

—————

I SEE Tyler congratulating my dad and Anna Mae, but between the luncheon and the guests, I haven't had a chance to talk to him yet.

"Why are you undressing that guy with your eyes?" Matt asks. He flew in for my dad's wedding...or maybe just for this moment right now when he gets to torture me.

I hit him on the shoulder. "I'm not! I was just waiting for a chance to talk to him."

"Is he *the* guy?"

I eye him. "Yes."

"He seems nice. Why did you screw it all up with him?"

"I didn't screw it *all* up. I can still fix it."

"By the way he's been ignoring you all day, I'm not sure you can fix it."

I glare at him. "I don't like taking relationship advice from someone who's had it easy with love. Everything always works out for you."

He smiles like he finds my assessment of him amusing. "You think everything works out for me when it comes to love?"

"Doesn't it?"

Matt lifts his drink to his mouth. "Sure."

For some reason it feels like I hurt Matt's feelings. I want to ask him about it, but there's no time.

"It looks to me like Tyler is leaving." Matt nods to where he is across the yard. "You better get over there if you stand a chance."

Tyler motions for Krew to come to him.

I think Matt might be right. I think Tyler's planning on leaving without even talking to me. I ditch my brother and make my way over to where Tyler's standing.

"Krew, it's time to go," he says.

"I don't want to leave yet. I want some cake."

"Are you leaving so soon?" I brush Tyler's arm and notice how he steps back from me.

His eyes stay fixed on Krew. "Yeah, we've got to go."

"Not until we have cake," Krew says, running off.

"You know, he's right. The cake is the best part. You should really stay."

Tyler finally meets my gaze. "Why? Why should I stay?"

"Because I want you to."

"For how long, Meg? Until you're not sad anymore?"

"I meant what I said in my text. I made a mistake. I shouldn't have pushed you away. I've never been in a situation like this before. I was scared, and I didn't respond the right way."

"What kind of situation have you never been in?"

I take a breath, drawing in some courage. "I've never been in love with a widower before."

His eyes are hard on mine. "Are you in love with a widower?"

I look around at the backyard full of people. "This isn't how I wanted to announce it to you, but yes. I'm in love with you."

Tyler rubs his forehead, like he's thinking.

I was hoping more for a big smile or an exuberant laugh.

I guess we can't have it all.

"I think you're right." His hand drops. "Maybe love isn't enough."

"No, I'm never right." I place my hand on his arm, trying to make him understand. "Don't listen to anything I've ever said. I'm *never* right!"

He sighs. "I'm just not sure if you've really thought this through."

"I've thought it through." I step closer. "I love you."

"Do you even know what loving me means?" His jaw hardens. "You'll lose your job, you'll become a huge part of Krew's life, you'll have Kristen's memory to deal with. She'll always be a part of me, whether you like it or not."

"I know. I *have* thought about all of that, and—"

"Great!" Tyler's eyes flicker behind me. "Your boyfriend is here."

"What?" I turn and follow his eyes and see Zak coming at us. I have no clue why he's here. I haven't talked to him since he came to my apartment almost a month ago, and I certainly didn't invite him to my dad's wedding.

"Tyler," Zak says, extending his hand out to him. "Meg didn't tell me you'd be here today."

"Zak, what are you doing here?" I ask, but it's like I no longer exist. Both men are only looking at each other.

"I came for Paul," Tyler says. "We're friends."

"I see." Zak nods. "I'm glad you're here. I'd love a chance to get to know you better. Any *friend* of Meg's is a friend of mine."

Tyler laughs, meeting Zak's stare-down. "I bet."

I tug on Zak's arm. "Zak? Can I talk to you for a moment in private?"

He ignores me, keeping his focus on Tyler. "So what do you do for a living? I mean, besides being a dad?"

I can tell by Zak's tone that his comment about being a dad was meant as an insult. And how did he even know Tyler is a dad? I'm so confused right now.

"I own a landscaping and property management business."

Zak laughs, looking at me. "What he means to say is that he mows the lawn. He's a lawn boy."

This is terrible. "Zak—" I go to say, but Tyler cuts me off.

"I do mow lawns. What do you do for a living?"

Zak straightens. "I'm in sales."

I hate it when Zak says that, as if the product he sells is too complicated for the rest of us to understand, so he doesn't tell us what it is.

"Oh, like retail?" Tyler asks.

I give Zak a *stop-this-right-now* look, but he's too busy laughing in his patronizing way to notice.

"No, Tyler." His voice drops an octave or two as he gives him his pitch. "I'm the lead sales manager at Renegade Medical Supplies. I'm sure that means nothing to you, so let me just say it's a pretty big company. I have thirty sales associates that I manage on my team alone."

"Sounds like you do well."

He heaves out a laugh. "I do *extremely* well."

"Actually, I'm glad I saw you," Tyler says, looking at Zak. "There's something I've been wanting to tell you."

"Tell *me*?" Zak kicks his head back in surprise.

"Yeah."

"What?"

"You're an idiot."

Oh, boy.

My panic is at an all-time high.

Zak puffs his chest out. "Excuse me?"

"You're an idiot. You had the most perfect woman right in front of you for three years, and you couldn't even see it."

This time I tug on Tyler's arm, trying to get him to come with me. "Tyler, can we talk?"

"I don't know what you're talking about," Zak says.

"Even now, you don't appreciate her. She'll be lucky if you stick around a year."

Zak pushes Tyler's chest and gets right in his face. "I'll be sure to remember that when I'm married to her." Zak's expression turns to mock pity. "Oh, didn't you know I proposed to Meg?"

"Zak!" My voice is stern, but the two of them don't even hear me.

The fake pity in Zak's eyes is still there. "I feel sorry for you, Tyler. You can't keep Meg happy, and you obviously couldn't keep your first wife happy. I bet she couldn't wait to leave you."

And that's the moment Tyler punches Zak in the face, knocking him off his feet to the ground.

I freeze.

Actually, I don't freeze. I cover my mouth with my hand. Then I freeze.

The wedding guests around us gasp.

I feel like I'm in the middle of a movie.

"You're such a prick," Tyler says, leaning over him. "You don't deserve Meg."

I'm in *Dirty Dancing*. Tyler is Patrick Swayze. This is his "Nobody puts Baby in the corner" moment, and as I watch it play out in real life, it's not as romantic as the movie makes it seem. It's stressful.

I grab Tyler by the arm and pull him away from Zak.

"What are you doing?" I ask through clenched teeth.

"What am *I* doing?" Tyler huffs. "You just told me you loved me when you're back together with Zak."

"I'm not back together with Zak. I have no idea why he said that or why he's even here."

Tyler turns his head from me, and I step to the side so I can still look into his blue eyes.

"I didn't invite him today."

Tyler doesn't say anything, just shakes his head.

I pull on his arm. "You have to believe me."

Finally his gaze shifts to mine. "I don't know what to believe anymore."

There's another commotion, and the crowd of guests gasps —*again.*

Tyler and I turn to see the small, round cake table tip over, sending the three-tiered chocolate cake to the ground.

Krew stands there, looking guilty.

His index finger shows the traces of chocolate where he went for a lick of the frosting when no one was looking.

Tyler rushes to him, but Krew bolts.

"I didn't do it!" He runs away from the table, stepping in the cake as he goes, smashing it into the grass. A huge piece of it sticks to the bottom of his shoes, leaving a trail of thick chocolate frosting behind him.

Tyler catches up to Krew and grabs him around his waist, swinging his frosting-filled shoes out in front of him.

"Krew, look what you've done."

"It was an accident."

"I know it was an accident, but you still ruined their wedding cake. Now nobody can have any."

"Tyler, it's not a big deal," my dad says. "We don't mind."

He looks at the smashed cake. "I should help you clean up."

"We've got it," Brooke says, coming to the rescue with a dustpan and a shovel.

"I think I'm just going to leave, then." Tyler's eyes are sad as he looks at my dad. "I'm sorry we ruined your wedding."

I take a few steps after him. "I'll come with you."

Tyler turns to me. He still has Krew's wiggling body in between his arms. "Not now, Meg." He turns to go. "I just can't right now."

And I'm left standing there, wondering if I really can still fix Tyler and me.

CHAPTER 44

MEG

didn't sleep last night. My conversation with Tyler kept me awake. Now, I'm pacing back and forth in Jen's classroom. Kids are trickling in, and school's about to start.

"What am I going to do about Tyler?"

"It will all work out. You just need to talk to him."

"I tried! He won't listen."

"You tried once." Jen tilts her head toward me. "Try again."

"I'm worried he won't answer my calls."

"You don't need to call him. He'll be at the school today."

"No, he won't. They finished the playground last week."

"I know, but he'll be here for the assembly about the playground."

My steps pause. "Tyler will be at the assembly?"

"Yeah, he's accepting an award or something for all the work his company did on the landscaping."

"That's it. I'll corner him." I start shaking my hands. "Wait, how do I corner him and confess my undying love with all of my students watching?"

"I could cover your class, bring them in here with me for a little bit."

"What if he won't listen to me?"

"You've got to make him listen."

I point to myself as her words sink in. *"I've* got to make him listen."

Ding!

"That's the five-minute bell. I better get to my class." I move to the door. "Jen, we're doing this. Before he leaves today, Tyler will know how much I love him."

———

THIS IS the longest morning of my life, waiting for the assembly to start. I bring my class into the auditorium. Since we're a younger grade, we get to sit near the front. There's a row of people lined up on the stage with a microphone up front. My eyes scan the faces until I see Tyler's. I try to get him to notice me, but he's talking with the guy next to him.

I sit down and wait for the rest of the room to get settled. My knees are bouncing up and down as nerves spin together inside my stomach. I feel like today is my only chance to reach Tyler. He needs to know how much I love him and that I'm willing to do anything to make our relationship work, and he needs to know it *now*. It's as if there's a timer on a bomb, clicking down each second. I have to say what I need to say before we all blow up.

That's the level of intensity I'm feeling right now—James Bond intensity.

Diane Carter stands at the microphone and welcomes everyone inside. She begins by recognizing all the families that donated money to the school so that we could remodel the grounds. She tells us they've put together a movie that shows the construction of the new playground. A white screen lowers from the ceiling, and the lights dim.

I can't sit still as the movie plays. Nothing seems to matter in my life if I don't have Tyler and Krew.

The crowd claps at the end of the movie, and the lights shine back onto the stage.

Diane goes to the microphone. "There's a few more people I'd like to recognize. Mr. Swenson, our custodian, did an excellent job keeping the grounds surrounding the construction site clean and safe for our students." Everyone claps again as Diane reaches to a table behind her and picks up an award for the custodian.

She continues going down the row of people who helped with the project, thanking them and handing them their prize. She's almost to Tyler. After him, it will all be over, and I will have lost my chance.

My knees go from a slight bounce to a full-on shake. I'm working up the nerve until finally I stand. I'm walking toward the stage, and I don't even know why. It's dark in the auditorium, and with the lights on the stage, shining in their eyes, nobody sees me coming.

I go up the stairs to the side where the curtains are pulled open.

Diane calls Tyler to the microphone. She's saying a lot of great things about him and his team of men and the work they did on the playground, but honestly I don't hear any of it. My heart's so loud, each beat telling me I'm crazy, questioning what I'm doing. Tyler's eyes shift to me in the shadows of the curtains. His eyebrows raise like he's also questioning what I'm doing, but his lips twitch.

That small movement is enough.

As Diane turns around to grab his award from off of the table behind her, I walk out to the middle of the stage.

The lights blind me, but I can feel the weight of eight hundred pairs of eyes. I grab the microphone stand with my hands and take a deep breath.

"I also have something I'd like to say."

I faintly hear Diane behind me. "Miss Johnson, what are you doing?"

She must've taken a step toward me, because Tyler holds his hand out to the side like he's stopping her from intervening.

Whispers ripple through the room, and I feel like I'm going to faint.

What am I thinking?

I can't do this.

At least not in front of everyone.

My eyes skip to Tyler. He's in light-blue golf shorts and a fitted, blue-and-pink-striped shirt. He doesn't have a hat on, and his brown hair is styled like he put in a little extra effort for the assembly. He's everything I want in a man. He's thoughtful, caring, strong, capable, optimistic, and full of so much love.

He's not the man I thought I would marry, but he's the man I *want* to marry, and I'd do anything for him to know that—even if it means losing my job. Which is exactly what will happen after I get done with my speech, but somehow, I'm okay with that outcome. He's worth it.

I look back at the shadowed heads in the crowd. "There have been some rumors going around that Tyler Dixon and I have been dating, and I think it's about time that we address them, because every week I have a couple of parents and students come up to me and ask me about it." I pause for a moment to swallow back my nerves. "The answer is yes, we are dating."

Child screams and claps erupt throughout the room.

I glance at Tyler. His entire face is blank. This might be a mistake, but I'm in too deep now. I've already jeopardized my job. I have to see this thing through and win Tyler back.

My eyes shift to the crowd. I motion for the students to calm down, then I begin again. "At least, we *were* dating, until I messed everything up. I was afraid of losing my job. And I was afraid of other things too." I don't need to elaborate on *all* the reasons. Nobody here cares that I was comparing myself to Kristen. Actually, by the way the room has hushed, I get the feeling they care *a lot*, but that's beside the point. I'm here to apologize and set things straight.

"There are two things in my life that I love." Technically, I love more than two things. I love my family, chocolate chip cookies, romance movies, etc., but I'm not here to list *every single thing*. So I ignore the technicality and keep going. "The first one is my students." I smile down to where I know my little class is watching me, then I peek over at Tyler. "And the second thing I love is Tyler Dixon." The excitement in the room picks up again, but I plow forward. "So I guess you could say we were a little bit more than dating, because I fell completely in love with him."

The auditorium gets even louder than before, but I focus on Tyler. A smile fills his entire face, and it's as if there's a spotlight on his cute dimple. He's doing this surprised laughter thing that's adorable, while he shakes his head like he can't believe what I've done.

I can't even believe it.

"Quiet, please," I say into the microphone, trying to get the room silent enough so I can continue. "So," I say, turning to Tyler. "I just want to say that I'm sorry for pushing you away and for being scared of all the little things that don't matter." My eyes fill up with tears, and my voice cracks. "I know now that the only thing that matters is that we're together. I love you." I shrug. "And love *is* enough. Or can be, if you're willing to put in the work to overcome your weaknesses."

I don't have anything else to say, and I don't even know if what I said was what he needed to hear. When you plan it out in your head, it sounds so great, but in real life, I think I looked more like a deer in headlights than anything.

The room is louder than an amusement park. Kids are standing, jumping up and down and clapping, but I can only see Tyler.

He pulls me into a hug. I'm glad he didn't go for the kiss. I'm not sure I could've handled that much public display of affection. I think confessing my love in front of everyone was plenty good.

"There's something I need to tell you," Tyler whispers in my ear, above the noise. "With the way the light shines onto the stage, everyone can see right through your skirt."

I was expecting an "I love you too."

I immediately close my legs together.

Of all the days not to remember to wear a slip, it had to be today.

His lips drift into a smirk. "Don't be embarrassed. I thoroughly enjoyed the show."

CHAPTER 45

MEG

've never been in the principal's office before. I mean, I've been in here as an employee, but never as a person in trouble.

Tyler reaches across the arm of the leather chair to hold my hand. I grasp his fingers for a second, but somehow it doesn't feel right. Maybe it's the fact that Diane Carter is glaring at me.

At our hands.

At *us*.

I wiggle my fingers away and place them in my lap.

We can hold hands later.

"You've put me in a very difficult position," Diane says as she looks over at the both of us. Then her eyes land on me. "Especially you, Meg. What did you think would happen when you got up on that stage? Did you really think that you'd be able to keep your job after something like that?"

I knew losing my job was a possibility, and that was a risk I was willing to take if it meant I could be with Tyler. I *hoped* things wouldn't come to that, but I also had the worst-case scenario tattooed inside my brain when I walked up on that stage.

"I—"

"Diane, this really isn't that big of a deal." Tyler smiles at me. "Meg loves me. I love her back. So what? I don't see why we all can't move on with our lives."

"You know why we can't move on. You both broke the rules." Diane opens up the folder in front of her and flips my contract open to the last page. "That's your signature, Meg. No one forced you to sign our contract. You *agreed* to it."

"I know that, and I fully intended to follow the rules, but then—"

"But then she met me, and she couldn't resist," Tyler says with so much smugness I want to strangle him.

Humility—that's what we need right now if I have any chance of keeping my job.

Diane lets out a heavy breath. "I've noticed some changes in Krew. Good changes. He seemed happier, more motivated, better behaved. I couldn't figure out what the cause was." Her eyes skip to me. "And then you broke up with Tyler, and things with Krew changed again. He seemed sad and more difficult to deal with." She looks down. "This is hard for me to say, but I think that Meg's influence in his life is a *good* thing. Krew benefitted a lot from your relationship."

My jaw drops a little at the same time Tyler squeezes my hand.

"Tyler, I can't stop you from moving on, and maybe now, I *don't* want to stop you. I truly want what's best for Krew."

"I know that," Tyler says.

"I'm willing to try to be happy for you both."

"Thank you." Tyler's voice cracks. "That means a lot to us —to *me*."

Diane looks right at me. "Meg, despite what I just said, I still have to follow the rules. I'm sorry, but I'm afraid I'm going to have to terminate your contract. As of today, you are no longer a teacher at American Education Academy."

Ouch.

I've never been fired before.

Terminated, as Diane put it.

Tyler sits up. "Diane, are you sure—"

"It's fine," I say. "I can handle the consequences."

It's not really fine. I'm about to sob, but I can at least put on a brave face for the last thirty seconds in Diane's office.

I stand, reaching my hand out to her. "Thank you for the opportunity to work here."

We shake hands, and then I leave and head straight for the women's faculty bathroom. Tyler follows after me, and before I know what's happening, he scoops me into his arms, letting me cry on his shoulder.

So there we are, standing in the middle of a bathroom, me crying into his shirt and him running his fingers through my hair.

I'm so sad about my job, but at the same time, I feel peace.

Jobs will come and go, but Tyler will be forever.

"Look at the bright side," Tyler says. "We don't have to kiss behind bushes anymore."

I laugh into his shoulder. "That's true."

"But maybe I still want to make out behind a bush every once in a while. You know, just to spice things up."

I pull back and look up at him. "Or maybe we could kiss in the women's faculty bathroom to spice things up."

He smiles. "I'm all for that."

Then he leans in and kisses me.

EPILOGUE
MEG

I t's here.

I've been dreaming of this day my entire life.

Every Nicholas Sparks book that I've read, every romance movie that I've watched, has led me to this day—my wedding day.

It's not exactly how I imagined it. I didn't imagine that I would marry a widower with a son, or that my mom wouldn't be here to share this day with me.

It's bittersweet, but the sweetness outweighs the bitterness, and that's because of Tyler.

He's so amazing.

And I am *so* in love with him.

"Congratulations," Diane Carter says to me.

I turn around and greet her with a hug. "Thank you for coming today. I'm sure this is hard for you."

Diane smiles, but it doesn't reach her eyes. "It is hard, but in a lot of ways, I'm glad it's you, Meg. I know you'll take care of Krew."

"I will take care of him."

"Good." She nods. "Now, I know it's your wedding day, but is it okay if we also talk a little bit of business?"

"Who's talking business?" Tyler asks, coming to my side.

"I am," Diane says. "Since two months ago, when I terminated your contract, I have received nonstop phone calls and emails from parents demanding that I reinstate you. And this last week, a group of parents from your class signed a petition to hire you back."

I look at Tyler. "That's really nice of them."

"It's more than nice of them," Diane says. "Their petition worked. I talked to the board this morning, and they want you to have your job back."

"Are you serious?" I jump up a little—as much as you can in a wedding dress.

"Your class will be waiting for you when you get back from your honeymoon."

I leap into Diane's arms. "Thank you so much!"

I've missed my students. Now I can teach at American Education *and* have Tyler.

I finally found door #3.

━━

"HEY! THERE'S THE HAPPY COUPLE." My siblings cheer as Tyler and I finally make our way to their table and take a seat.

"Did you guys hear? I got my job back."

Brooke nods. "Krew came and told us a few minutes ago. He's really excited to have his new mom as his teacher."

"Yeah, he's trying to decide if he should call you 'Mom' or 'Mrs. Dixon' at school," Tessa says.

"Either one works for me."

I pick up the drink in front of me and take a sip. "Is this party almost over?"

"We can leave whenever you want," Tyler nudges me. "In fact, let's leave right now. I'm ready to get our honeymoon started."

Matt laughs. "Easy, buddy. You guys haven't even cut the cake yet."

"Maybe I should tell Krew to knock it over so we don't have to do it and we can leave now."

"We can't leave until I see what happens between Ben and Jen." I crane my neck, looking behind me to the dance floor.

Brooke looks up. "My Ben?"

Tessa smiles. "I didn't know he was *your* Ben."

Brooke rolls her eyes. "You know what I mean."

"Yeah, I introduced him to one of my friends that teaches second grade at American Education Academy. She just broke up with her boyfriend."

Brooke's brows dip. "Why would you do that?"

"Why not? Ben's cute, and Jen is great. I thought they would make a good match."

Brooke sits back into her chair, looking a little miffed. "Ben's not really looking to date anyone right now, so I wouldn't get your hopes up."

"Sorry, Brooke," I say. "For years you've said that you and Ben are just friends."

She smiles, something fake. "We are."

Tessa laughs. "Then why are you so upset?"

Brooke looks around the table. "I'm not."

"Leave her alone," Matt chimes in. "If Brooke is stupid enough to fall for her best friend and not tell him, then she deserves to feel a little jealous right now."

Brooke glares across the table at Matt. "And what about you? Where's Remi? You guys have been together so long. I find it hard to believe that she wouldn't come to your sister's wedding."

Matt shifts in his chair. "I told you already. She had to work. That's why she couldn't come to the wedding."

"Well, I don't know why all of your love lives are so complicated," Tessa says, flipping her hair back behind her shoulder.

"Wait a second," I say. "It's my wedding day, so I would hardly classify my love life as complicated."

Tessa gives me a flat stare. "You guys were a mess in the months leading up to this day."

"So Tessa, are you saying that your life is better because you're not in a relationship?" Tyler asks.

"Not better, just less complicated."

"Tessa's in a relationship with her job," Brooke laughs, but I catch her eyes as they follow Ben and Jen on the dance floor.

"I'll tell you who has the most *adult* relationship out of all of us," Matt says. He turns his head to my dad and Anna Mae on the dance floor. "Good ole' Dad has it all figured out."

I smile as I watch him. "Yeah, I think you're right. We all could take a page from his book."

Tyler stands and holds his hand out to me. "Do you want to dance?"

"Now?" I lift my brows. "We just barely sat down."

"Yes, I'm taking a page out of your dad's book. And besides, aren't they playing our song?"

"*Take My Breath Away* is your song?" Tessa laughs, rolling her eyes. "You two were made for each other."

"I think we were." I smile as I let Tyler help me stand. "Let's dance."

Tyler Dixon is the happy ending that I've been dreaming of, but the coolest part is that it's not the end.

It's the beginning.

The End

I hope you enjoyed Meg and Tyler's story. I love hearing what readers liked most about my books, so don't forget to leave a review and tell me.

If you'd like to learn about future books and get bonus chapters, sign up for my newsletter at www.kortneykeisel.com. Stay connected with me at www.kortneykeisel.com, or follow me on Instagram, Facebook, or Pinterest

MEG'S PLAYLISTS

Un-frog-ettable Love Songs

1. I Wanna Take Forever Tonight - Crystal Bernard & Peter Cetera
2. After All (Love Theme from Chances Are) - Cher & Peter Cetera
3. Lost in Your Eyes - Debbie Gibson
4. Crazy for You - Madonna
5. Take My Breath Away (Love Theme from Top Gun) - Berlin
6. Making Love out of Nothing at All - Air Supply
7. Almost Paradise (Love Theme from Footloose) - Mike Reno & Anne Wilson
8. (I've Had) The Time of My Life - Bill Medley & Jennifer Warnes
9. I'll Tumble 4 Ya - Culture Club
10. Suddenly - Olivia Newton-John & Cliff Richard
11. I Can Wait Forever - Air Supply
12. Up Where We Belong - Joe Cocker & Jennifer Warnes
13. It Might Be You (Love Theme from Tootsie) - Dave Grusin
14. Eternal Flame - The Bangles
15. The Promise - When in Rome

Geriatric Breakup Songs

1. I Will Always Love You - Whitney Houston
2. Can't Smile Without You - Barry Manilow
3. The Winner Takes it All - ABBA
4. Nothing Compares to You - Sinead O'Conner
5. Almost Over You - Sheena Easton
6. Insensitive - Jann Arden
7. Look Away. - Chicago
8. Hopelessly Devoted to You - Olivia Newton-John
9. You Don't Bring Me Flowers - Barbara Streisand & Neil Diamond
10. Against All Odds - Phil Collins
11. Total Eclipse of the Heart - Bonnie Tyler
12. You've Lost that Lovin' Feeling - Erasure
13. If You Leave (From Pretty in Pink) - OMD
14. With or Without You - U2
15. Always on My Mind - Pet Shop Boys

ALSO BY KORTNEY KEISEL

ROMCOMS

The Sweet Rom "Com" Series

Commit

Compared

Complex

DYSTOPIAN ROMANCE

The Desolation Series

The Rejected King

The Promised Prince

The Stolen Princess

The Forgotten Queen

ACKNOWLEDGMENTS

I wrote this book one month before my father suddenly passed away. I believe it is no coincidence that right before he died, I was in the process of loosely basing a character off of him. He was excited to read "his story," and I only wish he had the chance to read it before he died. I think he would have liked his character, Paul. So a big thank you goes to my dad for being the kind of man worthy of being in a book. I loved the strength he showed after my mom died. I especially loved his fearless heart and the way he jumped back into life with optimism. I'm so glad my parents are together again. I hate that they aren't here with us, but I know I will see them again. This book will always hold a special place in my heart and will forever remind me of my dad.

I want to thank all of my amazing beta readers. To my family: Sidney, Kaylen, Shelly, Stacy, and McKenna. I feel bad whenever I send you a link to one of my books because I know you are all busy. Thank you for taking the time to read, comment, and talk about this book around the dinner table at family parties when you could have been socializing with other people. You guys are all part of my team.

Thank you to my friends that beta read. Michelle, I always know I can count on you. Meredith, I completely blindsided you with this book, but you pushed through, and I appreciate that. You added so much. Madi, I love your honesty and bluntness, and I loved all of our Marco Polos back and forth talking about all the things I needed to fix. You are SO helpful, and I don't want to write a book without you in my corner.

A big thanks goes to Jenny and Laura, my editors. They both pointed out plot holes and characterization problems and I am so grateful to have them in my corner.

Thank you to my readers who have stuck with me through a temporary genre change and are still reading my books. I love you guys and am grateful for all the support! And thanks to my new readers. I am so happy you are here.

Kurt, you are the best, and I love all the times you say something funny, then turn to me and say, "That's funny. You should put that in a book." Sometimes I do. Thanks to my kids for writing Krew's 'All About Me' assignment, helping me make decisions about my cover, and for coming up with COM title options. I love how involved you guys are in the process. I'm so blessed to have such an amazing family.

I would be ungrateful if I didn't thank my Heavenly Father and his Son, Jesus Christ, for the strength to finish this book and get it ready to be published while my dad was in the hospital, while we were planning his funeral, and right after his passing. It's hard to write, edit, or even care about a rom-com when you are so sad. I wanted to lay in bed all day, but somehow I found the mental capacity to work during my grief, and I know that strength came from a source bigger than me.

ABOUT THE AUTHOR

Kortney loves all things romance. Her devotion to romance was first apparent at three years old when her family caught her kissing the walls (she attributes this embarrassing part of her life to her mother's affinity for watching soap operas like Days of Our Lives). Luckily, Kortney has outgrown that phase and now only kisses her husband. Most days, Kortney is your typical stay-at-home mom. She has five kids that keep her busy cleaning, carpooling, and cooking.

Writing books was never part of Kortney's plan. She graduated from the University of Utah with an English degree and spent a few years before motherhood teaching 7th and 8th graders how to write a book report, among other things. But after a reading slump, where no plots seemed to satisfy, Kortney pulled out her laptop and started writing the "perfect" love story...or at least she tried. Her debut novel, The Promised Prince, took four years to write, mostly because she never worked on it and didn't plan on doing anything with it.

Kortney loves warm chocolate chip cookies, clever song lyrics, the perfect romance movie, analyzing and talking about the perfect romance movie, playing card games, traveling with her family, and laughing with her husband.

Made in the USA
Middletown, DE
06 November 2022